THE GIFT FROM FORTUNY

TERRY STANFILL

STORY MERCHANT BOOKS
LOS ANGELES
2020

STORY MERCHANT BOOKS

ISBN 978-1-970157-22-2

CREDITS
Cover: *El Jaleo*, John Singer Sargent, 1882. Courtesy of the Isabella Stewart Museum, Boston, Massachusetts

Story Merchant Books
400 S. Burnside Avenue, 11-B
Los Angeles, Ca 90036
www.storymerchantbooks.com

By the same author

The Blood Remembers
Il Richiamo del sangue
Realms of Gold: Ritual to Romance
Les Royaumes dorés
The Power of Myth in My Home: A Memoir

For my husband, Dennis,
with loving memories of our happy times in Spain

"Like the intricacy of a Fortuny gown, with its thousands of pleats—each one its own story—this novel takes the reader to the streets and canals of Venice in the late 1940s, affluent Los Angeles in the 1980s and the ancient cities of Granada and Seville. Weaving its way through family sagas, flamenco dance, the sub-culture of Spanish gypsies and lyricism of Italian opera, it brings together a fascinating and disparate collection of characters whose lives are surprisingly and disarmingly intertwined."

—Pamela Fiori, former editor of *Town & Country* Magazine

Although I have a great love for Italy,
I have always felt that I am a Spaniard,
a Spaniard from Granada.
　　　　　　　—Mariano Fortuny y Madrazo

BOOK I

VENICE, 1946

A ragged flower girl watches as the gondolier moors the long black boat to the *pontile* of the Hotel Danieli.

As the Diva approaches the entrance, the child moves closer, her eyes seeking the woman's kohl-lined eyes, half hidden by a black net veil. The girl plucks a rose from her bouquet and offers it. "*Una rosa, bellissima signora?*"

The Diva averts her eyes from the child's. "Out of my way, I don't need your roses."

The *Direttore* bows, clicks his heels, and kisses the Diva's suede-gloved hand. "We are honored that Madame has chosen to stay with us again. All of Venice awaits her *Turandot.*" She holds the silver fox stole closer to her body and sweeps into the lobby.

He leads the Diva to the royal suite and draws open the crimson damask portieres woven in a baroque pattern of pomegranates. "Behold the lagoon of Venice." he says. Bowing low, he leaves the Diva to admire the celebrated view. Tonight, a full moon is pasted high in the slate-grey sky, like the moon in the painted backdrop of the Druid ritual scene from Norma, her favorite opera.

She opens her purse for the black Sobrani, taps one into the long ebony holder, and touches it to the flame of the solid gold lighter. She takes a long, satisfying pull down into her lungs as her eyes scan the salon. Bouquets everywhere, all tributes from countless admirers. She reads every enclosure then tosses them all in the wastebasket. There are neither flowers nor letters from him. The maid plucks the silver foxes from the Diva's shoulders and helps her to undress. The Diva, still wearing her pale grey suede gloves, kicks off her pumps, unbuttons the black *tailleur:* she unpins the platinum and diamond A. and V. from the lapel and loops the pearl *sautoir* over her head. Each precious American nylon stocking she rolls down carefully, precisely. Finally, she peels the gloves from her fingers and tosses them into the wastebasket. Since she became *prima donna assoluta*, she has never worn a pair of gloves twice.

When the maid leaves the room, the Diva falls naked on the rose satin *letto matrimoniale,* her long black hair fanning over the bolster cushion. Above her head, silk gauze ripples from a carved and gilded crown.

Nine years have passed since her return in triumph to the city of her debut. In a few days she will sing one of the most demanding roles in opera, and an adoring public will hurl more roses at her feet.

As dusk falls, she slides between the lace-edged sheets and tries to sleep, but the lyrics from Princess Turandot's aria, *In Questa Reggia*, keep echoing in her head.

Trascinata da un uomo come te,
come te, straniero là nella notte atroce
dove si spense la sua fresca voce!
io vendico su via, su voi
nessun, nessun, m'avro

Dragged away by a man like you,
a stranger, in that frightful night
When a young voice was stifled!
take revenge on you,
No man shall ever possess me!
No man shall ever possess me!

The Diva is distressed by the vibrato she has been hearing in the high register, afraid that this role might destroy the voice for other roles. Her one consolation is *Tosca*. She could always stand on her head and sing *Tosca*. Perhaps she should heed the advice of that old *strega* in Matera.

The telephone jangles.

Her admirer is on the line.

The Diva's chiseled features soften, her voice becomes girlish. "Oh, yes—I have been looking forward to seeing you, as well. Eight o'clock? I shall be here. Waiting," she murmurs in a throaty voice, octaves lower than she is capable of singing.

She hops out of bed and rummages through her Vuitton steamer trunk until she finds the olive-green satin bag, a gift from her visitor; she opens it. Inside is the twisted, knotted white gown she will wear to sing the role of *Norma* in London. She unties the knots, shakes out the pleats and lays the dress across the bed. After she has bathed, made up her face, sprayed herself with *L'Heure Bleue*, she slips the gown over her head and admires herself in the mirror. Only on stage has she ever worn a white dress.

At nine o'clock the Diva opens the door for her admirer. He stands before her and, although no longer young, he is still handsome, vigorous, in his long robes. On his bare feet he wears leather sandals.

He takes her hands in his and kisses them. "*Mi querida—mi corazon.* How beautiful you are in the white delphos."

CHAPTER I

Los Angeles 1984
The Year of the Olympiad

It was Saturday. The Bel Air estate was almost ready for the reception to be held on Sunday afternoon. Greenhill House, the Killingsworth's pseudo-Palladian palace, stood on a knoll of perfect grass. Marathon grass. Hybrid, sharpbladed grass that never harbored weeds nor blackened under the glaze of January frost. The essence of green, richer than the cliché-color of money, deeper than the green of envy.

Thousands of red, white, and pink cyclamen languished in the shade of live oaks bordering the five acre property. When the cyclamen finished blooming, the gardeners would uproot their corms, toss them away and replace them with pink, red, and purple hothouse cineraria. Seasonal splashes of color. Decoration. Those bedding plants did not reveal a love of gardening; they shouted money as they sprouted. It took sacks of Marshall Killingsworth's greenbacks to plant thousands of cyclamen grown in his on-site commercial glass houses in Ventura.

Marshall Killingsworth discovered the iron gates guarding the entrance of a deserted chateau in the south of France. He had them set between massive limestone pillars that gave access to the long circular drive banded with precisely sliced boxwood. Around the corner, security guards manned the solid steel gate for deliveries and trade.

An engraved card had invited members of the charity Never Too Late to its annual reception. In Los Angeles, membership in this group is emblematic of social success. Demetra Killingsworth was only too aware that society leaders June Cooper and Diana Victor, founders of Never Too Late, were determined to keep it that way. They had asked the Killingsworths for the use of Greenhill House, not as a venue for a benefit fund-raiser, but for one of those coveted "free bonus events" offered as social bait to make belonging to Never Too Late (short for Never Too Late to Learn) worth the high dues. Although some of the women were professionals who could afford to pay their own way, most of the ladies like Demetra, had husbands rich enough to provide the $5,000 annual membership fee.

June and Diana had founded the organization to raise money for the education of young women from various ethnic backgrounds in Los Angeles: gifted women who had been deprived of further education by poverty, sexual abuse, or physical illness would be sponsored to finish high school or pursue college degrees. Women from various ethnic backgrounds (now and then a token Wasp) were screened, tested, interviewed, then voted upon yearly by board members of Never Too Late, with a few academics to add a note of *gravitas*. Worthy women were awarded generous scholarships. A brilliant conception, a worthy charity, but not as altruistic as it might seem, because June and Diana had turned Never Too Late into a social power base for themselves.

In ten years, the group had become much larger than the membership limit of three hundred originally set in its charter. Now smaller mansions and villas could no longer contain the members and guests; those on the social rise bought or built immense palaces like Greenhill House with hopes that one day they might qualify as hosts for Never Too Late.

On Sunday, the ladies, their husbands, or escorts would swarm over the house and grounds. They would be allowed to enter all the public rooms including the master bedroom in the east wing, but stanchions looped with twisted blue velvet rope would keep them from entering the west wing. The family wing.

Now, less than twenty-four hours before the big event, the butler was burnishing silver tea services, polishing tabletops with lavender beeswax polish. From the greenhouse, a team of gardeners hauled in Versailles boxes planted with tall flowering pear trees to place in the corners of the vast living room. For two days cooks had been busy in the kitchen, baking miniature scones and madeleines; a French pastry chef piped the Killingsworth logo on petits fours.

As Demetra arranged flowers in the entrance gallery, the high-ceilinged rooms of Greenhill House were flooded with the pleadings of *Tosca* being broadcast by the Metropolitan Opera. She stood back to admire the antique Chinese celadon pot filled with her favorite "gentle" flowers. Flowers frzom plants she had started from seed; tall stalks of fuzzy greyleaved verbascum, Queen Anne's lace, umbrels of yellow yarrow, foxglove, nodding purple Canterbury bells. The soft, herbaceous meadow flowers contrasted with the strict formality of the mirror-polished, ormolumounted Louis XV commode.

Clipping a stalk of indigo blue delphinium, she placed it behind a spray of white Iceberg roses. Never had she thought of herself as being particularly artistic, yet today while listening to *Tosca* she was pleased to have created something beautiful. It helped her forget last week's meeting in Hollywood with Madame Apollonia, the Greek psychic, a meeting that had disturbed the even tenor of her life.

During the past year Demetra had become fixed on issues of character traits and temperament. Was it nature or nurture, genes or an orphanage upbringing and hard work that accounted for her talents? Or, as her husband constantly insinuated, her lack of them? So, she had arranged a session under the assumed name of Jane Constable to ask the clairvoyant if her parents might still be alive.

She had arrived fifteen minutes early for the appointment. In the padded leather confines of a Rolls Royce she had waited, playing yet again a tape of *Don Giovanni*. Kiri Te Kanawa was singing *Ah, chi mi dice mai,* an aria of Donna Elvira's. Although the lyrics were of betrayal, anger, and outrage, the voice consoled her, as if it sang in counterpoint to her own private furies. Zipping a dazzling diamond solitaire and platinum wedding band into her handbag, emboldened by the soprano's voice still echoing in her ears, she had walked around the corner to the bungalow. She steeled herself to press the buzzer.

The room she entered was pungent with the scent of sandalwood mingled with burnt garlic. After a cursory greeting and a request for cash payment, the caftan-swathed psychic turned on a tape recorder. Eyes fixed on Demetra, she asked her client to pose her questions.

Demetra's usually hesitant voice rang out staccato-clear. "I've come here to ask you about my parents. I want to know if they're still alive before I begin to make a search for them."

But Madame Apollonia, her sloe eyes piercing Demetra's, would only reveal that as soon as her client walked into the room, she'd heard a voice, a soprano voice singing in Italian: that she envisioned an opera house in London, where a woman in a long white dress was singing as flames consumed the stage.

"You have another name, not Jane, you have Greek name."

Demetra was startled by the frisson that shot through her body when the seer intuited that her name was not Jane, that her real name was Greek.

"Fight! Be strong. Stay until the *kataclysmos.* The *kataclysmos* will be your sign. Then you must leave your husband. Do not wait! Leave!" When the session was over, the psychic offered the cassette to Demetra, whispering, "*Pios isthe?* Who are you?"

"I don't know. And I will never know until I find out where I came from," was all that Demetra could reply. Instead of driving off in the Rolls, she'd leaned her head against the steering wheel and sobbed as the voice of Kiri Te Kanawa once again embraced her.

As soon as she arrived at Greenhill House, she hid Madame Apollonia's cassette in a safe place. A place where Marshall would never find it, for if he did, he would surely punish her.

Now, touching the sore black-and-blue mark on her cheek, she assured herself that she would somehow get through tomorrow's reception. She knew in her heart that it was for a worthy cause.

Time and time again she had gone over her husband's lists trying to focus on all the details, making sure that no fine point was overlooked, so that the reception would be perfect for him. But what difference would all her plans make anyway? She was becoming aware that however hard she tried, however many times she checked and rechecked the details, something would go wrong and Marshall would be angry with her. And then, at the Monday morning post-mortem "critiques" she would be at the mercy of June and Diana. How unfairly they had mocked the rusty garden furniture and the pleasantly chaotic garden of a member's home in Pasadena.

A total disaster they had called that reception. She was angry with herself for not disagreeing with June and Diana. And even angrier that she had committed herself to chair Never Too Late's Olympic Year fund-raiser to be held in June. After that event she would resign from the Board of Directors. She had made up her mind.

Now, as she listened to *Vissi d'arte*, she fussed with the bouquet, clipping, pruning leaves and unruly stems with the small shears that hung from a long, narrow red ribbon around her neck. Suddenly, abrupt silence; someone had turned off the stereo.

She heard Marshall's assertive footsteps tapping the limestone floor of the Long Gallery. He was home earlier than she had expected. She turned to face him.

"Mars! I hadn't expected you home so early."

He kissed her cheek. She smelled his distinctive shaving lotion— vetiver, petitgrain, ambergris—a Jermyn Street mixture blended to his order. Marshall Killingsworth had the kind of looks that improved with age and money. With his year-round tan, his prematurely grey hair and penetrating grey eyes, his flawlessly tailored Saville Row suits, he was often mistaken for Gianni Agnelli. He was pleased with the association. It was a look he cultivated.

"You look quite pretty standing there, under the skylight."

His compliment surprised her. She thanked him with a smile. "Mrs. Galway told me you'd be coming in late tonight."

"I decided to fly back early to check out everything for the reception. I want to make sure there are no hitches anywhere."

"Don't worry. Everything's under control. I've gone over all the details again and again. How was Oslo?"

"Cold weather—gorgeous blondes." He looked at her slyly and smiled. "Two weeks was too long, but at least I bought the factory. I closed the deal at my price." He swept some flower petals from the glossy commode into his open palm. "You've got to be careful here. Moisture might damage the patina of this piece." He brushed the petals into the pocket of her garden apron. "Why aren't you using the French tulips and lilies my secretary ordered from Holland?"

"The florist arranged them in the other rooms. I wanted to use flowers from my own cutting garden here in the gallery."

"These flowers look cheap—they remind me of weeds that grew along the roadside in Minnesota."

She blinked back the tears. "I thought a massed English country bouquet would be more effective on this formal commode. It helps to make it less..." She sought the right word... "Formidable".

"And I noticed that you left the Phalaenopsis orchids in those dirty pots," he said.

"I think they look best of all straight from the greenhouse—with that velvety green moss wrapping."

"You call it moss. I call it slime. Uncovered clay pots don't belong in an elegant house. You should have learned that by now, Demetra."

"Please give me credit for what I *have* learned, Marshall," she said under her breath, not wanting to antagonize him so soon after he arrived home.

He picked up the phone to call the kitchen, stroking and stroking his hair with his ringless left hand as he gave orders to the English butler. "Kevin—go to the consoles in the rotunda. Put all the orchids in the Meissen cachepots, the ones I bought on my last trip to London. And if you don't have enough, open the silver safe for the George the Third wine coolers."

She clenched her hands so tight they hurt.

He opened his briefcase. "Here's a sample of the full-color brochure Mrs. Galway had printed for the house tour, hot off the press."

She read the description from the slick catalogue.

The Catherine the Great Room. The walls are upholstered in fabric, a design of baskets tied with ribbons and bows and overflowing with flowers. This textile was woven for Catherine the Great of Russia and was used in her palace at Tsarkoe Selo until the Revolution, when it was stripped from the palace walls. The fabric was discovered in Buenos Aires. Thirty-six yards were recently woven in Lyons (France) to complete the room.

"Are you sure you want to hand these out? Don't you think it's a bit pretentious to…"

"Of course, I'm handing them out. Why the hell do you think I'm spending all this money? People should know what they're looking at. This house is too unique to keep private. It will impress the hell out of them. They'll all be talking about this room. There's nothing like it in Los Angeles."

He was right. The furniture had been chosen from Maurice Segoura in Paris, from Behrendt and Partridge and Mallet's in London. He had bought the Savonnerie rug from Christie's, Monte Carlo, the *objets de vertu* from Kugel, Paris. It was as much rare luxury as could be seen in this city of attempted *grand luxe*, of selfconscious grandeur and intimidating scale.

"And make sure that Kevin places these throughout the house."

She read the card from Smythson's of London —engraved in Spencerian script with the Killingsworth cipher.

The Killingsworths request that you kindly refrain from smoking in their home.

She bit her lip, shaking her head

"Where's Corey?"

"I don't know."

"What do you mean you don't *know*?"

"I did have one message from her today—very early—around sixthirty. I wasn't in my room when she called."

He raised his voice. "Where the hell were you at that hour of the morning?"

"In my cutting garden picking these flowers," she replied in a measured voice.

Before leaving the gallery, Marshall took a long, admiring look at himself in the Louis XVI gilt wood *trumeau* mirror topped with a Roman trophy of cuirass, cutlass, and crossed spears.

Demetra began to fidget with the arrangement. She no longer felt the same about the soft, unstudied bouquet. The flowers looked faded, spent. Maybe they weren't right for the important Riesener commode, she thought.

The phone rang, one of at least eleven separate telephone lines. Two for Demetra, three for Marshall, one for Corinna, their daughter, one for the staff, two in the guest wing, the gardeners' line, the security guard's line in the gate house.

"The count for tomorrow is four hundred and ninety-six," said the secretary from Never Too Late's office. "We're supplying police to assist your security guards. Please put away all your small objects, Mrs. Killingsworth, just in case. It's unfortunate, but sometimes they do go off with the smalls, you know."

She turned on the stereo and listened until the curtain fell on Act II of La Tosca. Then she lowered the sound of the opera quiz until the curtain fell in the final act.

Kevin, tall, lean, aristocratic looking, was a retired movie extra handpicked and hired by Marshall. Kevin played his role as stock English butler so well his feigned hauteur terrified the more insecure members who arrived at Greenhill House's massive front doors. But Demetra knew Kevin was only doing his job. They often joked about this when Marshall was not around.

This evening Kevin had already lit the artificial gas fire in the sitting room of the master suite. Wood no longer burned in the house because Marshall worried about soot and smoke soiling antique upholstery fabric and the precious silk stretched on the bedroom walls. Demetra agreed that the silk had to be protected, yet she missed the aroma of burning wood, the comforting hiss and sputter of a real fire. She detested the mock ashes heaped around the grate. Longing for less formal surroundings, she often daydreamed about owning an antique shop, a cozy place where she could serve tea and biscuits and stock the shelves with charming, witty treasures unlike the blatantly imposing objects bought by Marshall.

In her bathroom a closet housed another stereo system. She inserted Alicia de Larrocha's tape of Granados' *Goyescas,* letting the melodies wash over her, reveling in each of the pianist's sustained single notes, the fluid arabesques of *The Maja and the Nightingale.* What was there about this music, Spanish music that seemed to stroke her soul and lift her spirits? Sometimes it pinched her heart until it hurt; sometimes it made her wistful, full of yearning, or pitched her imagination into boundless, almost uncontrollable motion. She closed her eyes and tried to imagine her mother's face. Her father's face. What was it she had been fearing? Parents with whom she might have nothing in common, parents who might be dead? Or her husband's anger? Marshall had forbidden her to make the search, threatening that he would not be responsible for helping her find a hooker mother, or a pimp father.

When Demetra had changed into her nightgown, she lay down on her damask-swagged and draped lit *à la polonaise,* a lace bolster tucked behind her neck, an Indian shatoosh ring shawl spread over her shoulders. She seemed always to be cold in California, yet she had grown up in Minnesota where cold had never bothered her.

When Marshall had asked her about Corey, she had tried not to let him know that she was worried about their teenage daughter. Although Demetra had been trying to reach Corey for two weeks, she had not had a response from her.

Reflected in the mirror of her dressing room, Demetra could see the ivory *crepe de Chine* Chanel dress that she would wear for tomorrow's reception. Marshall had ordered it especially for this occasion on a recent trip to Paris. The haute couture *vendeuse* had convinced him that the dress would be perfect for a tea reception even though he would have preferred an outfit more showboat than chic. (Marshall knew, as well as Demetra, that Members planned their outfits weeks in advance of these gatherings). Not too long ago she'd heard a woman urging a friend to become a member.

"No, thanks, I just don't have the wardrobe or the jewelry to belong to Never Too Late," was the woman's reply. That statement disturbed Demetra because she was aware that she too, had been swept up into this world of appearances and luxury. She too was guilty of falling into the velvet-cushioned trap after having been initiated into the organization's rites. Tomorrow she would festoon herself with masses of gem-studded Bulgari chains, screw fourteen-millimeter pearl earrings into her lobes. With her short dark hair clipped into a strict, sleek cap, she would seem the arbiter of taste, of graciousness, of *savoirfaire*, a mannequin for the clothes Marshall chose for her, for the important jewels he collected and insured in his name only. She knew that her membership in the exclusive group gave him the social status he craved. How else could he feel at the top? It seemed as if a billion dollars piled up in the bank was not enough: his goal was the social power that money, along with the right wife, could so easily buy in Los Angeles.

***

Demetra sat at her writing table reviewing the guest list while waiting for Marshall to join her for dinner. They usually dined in their bedroom, and this Saturday was no exception even though the room would be on view tomorrow afternoon. On Sunday morning, after breakfast, the staff would put the room back in Architecturally Digested order, spraying it with deodorant, and lighting a perfumed candle lest it betray the scent of human habitation. After a Never Too Late member's house tour in Palm Springs, some board members had complained of the distinct smell of sleep in the master bedroom.

Kevin draped the round table with a square white linen cloth embroidered with daisies. Its corners grazed the antique Savonnerie rug. He set a gold-encrusted, magenta-bordered porcelain service plate at both places, each plate adorned with the Killingsworth intricate cipher, MDK twined and intertwined. Nymphenburg in Munich had made the service to Marshall's order.

Demetra thought how charming the setting would be without those overly opulent service chargers. She believed that a simple salt glaze or Leeds creamware plate would be more suitable for such a setting, but she couldn't convince Marshall that a humble object tended to relieve the monotony, the boredom, the surfeit of so much luxury.

Marshall appeared after his workout and massage wearing a royal blue velour sweatpants outfit, his usual dinner attire. Settling down in his English Regency klismos chair, he tasted the champagne Kevin poured into a crystal flute and nodded.

"Why aren't we using the Buccellati silver tonight? You know I prefer it to the Cartier." He shuffled the cutlery around on the tablecloth. "Are we having salad to start, or soup? It's hard to tell."

"Your favorite, lobster bisque made from scratch. One of the pilots flew in the lobsters from Maine."

He shook his head. "You really have to train your staff to set the table right, Demi."

His nickname rankled her. She did not like its implication. He'd called her Demi from the beginning of their marriage and she had always regarded the diminutive as a term of endearment, until the day when she overheard him tell a business friend, "I call her Demi because it cuts her down to size." She had cried a long time over that remark. But she never told him that she had overheard it.

Demetra did not respond. Avoid conflict and confrontation at all costs, she thought. Instead she scraped away at the gardening callous on her index finger.

They ate their soup in silence.

When Kevin left the room, Marshall spoke again. "Who's on the guest list for tomorrow?"

"It's a good group."

"Where's the list? I hope the right people are coming."

Demetra found the list on her writing table and put it on his service plate. "Have a look. It's only our members and their husbands or escorts."

"You know what I'm talking about. Even within the group there are the A people."

"Marina and Harcourt McFarland, for instance?" She knew at once that she should not have brought up their name. Marshall had a fascination bordering on obsession with the McFarlands. She tried to read his honed-steel eyes, wondering if he'd taken the McFarlands' previous regrets as a personal rejection. Marshall didn't like it when certain people refused his invitations.

"The McFarlands haven't accepted one of our invitations yet," he said, tossing the list across the room.

She got up from her chair to pick it up.

"His secretary phoned to say they will be coming," she replied quietly, "but they'll be late because they'll be driving in from Santa Barbara."

He nodded, a pleased look on his face. "I see the Claibornes have accepted. At least their name appears on your list. But you know how movie people are. They say yes and then they never show up."

"I think the Claibornes are different. Gail wrote me a lovely note to tell me how much she was looking forward to the reception."

"I forgot to tell you that when I had lunch at Willowood Studios a few weeks ago, her husband was there shooting a movie. Claiborne and his wife were having lunch in the commissary. She's something else."

"I think she's original."

He laughed. "Is that what you'd call it? She looks more like a friggin' gypsy to me."

Demetra considered Gail Claiborne to be one of the most interesting women in Never Too Late. She didn't dress like everyone else; she didn't act like anyone else. She lived far from the West Side, in Sierra Madre, in the foothills of the San Gabriel Mountains. Her house had never been on Never Too Late's venue list because it was too far away, too small, and far too rustic. Marshall pushed away his dessert plate, then gulped down the remaining champagne as if to brace himself for what was to follow.

He stood behind his wife's chair and put his arms around her, stroking her breasts underneath the fine white albatross wool peignoir. She sat there, unmoved by his caresses, her spine straight against the back of her klismos chair.

"I missed you last week. Every time I looked at those cool Norwegian beauties, I thought of you. You used to remind me of a dark-haired Catherine Deneuve. I always told you that," he said with a hint of derision in his voice.

She nodded. Marshall's way of complimenting was to compare her favorably to another woman, usually a famous woman.

"You don't like my compliments, Demi?"

She felt the tide of rage mounting within. "Never call me that again!" The force and command in her voice surprised her.

"What do you mean? I've always called you Demi."

She winced as he twisted her arm. "You know exactly what I mean. Don't you remember what you once told Andy Martin?"

"So you overheard that?" He laughed. I was only joking. Besides, that was a long time ago. Why the hell didn't you confront me at the time?"

"That's my problem, not yours." Tears filled her eyes. "Mars, what's happened to us? And why have we let it happen?"

"Don't start that crap again. I'm not going to listen to your complaints."

"Please let us find a marriage counselor. I've heard about a woman doctor in Westwood…"

"Forget it. You know damn well I'd never let some goddamned manipulating shrink know what's going on in my head."

The flowing tears, the distress in her voice made her even more desirable. He peeled the peignoir from her shoulders and tugged at her nightgown.

She pushed away. "Please—not tonight. I'm too tired."

"Too tired? You are always complaining about being tired. For Chrissake, all you do is lay around all day and read art books and auction catalogues."

For a man with a degree from a good Midwestern university, why didn't he use the verb "to lie" correctly and it grated on her ear. The nuns had been fanatic about grammar. "I have more than enough to keep me busy. And I do not *lie* around the house all day," she snapped back, at once sorry that she had stooped to his level.

"Suddenly you're an authority on grammar! I lay-I lie I laid! Just what I'm going to do now- right here in front of the fire." He dragged her off the chair and down to the floor. Yanking the nightgown up, he crushed his pelvis against her.

She was not strong enough to resist. As soon as he let go, she leaped up and raced to her bathroom, bolting the door. Her body trembled as she stared at the doorknob, engraved with the mask of Apollo, twisting back and forth as he tried to enter.

He banged the door. "Come out of there, for Chrissakes." When she did not answer he kicked. The glass around the doorknob shattered into an irregular sunburst.

"Leave me alone. Please! I only want some peace," she sobbed. Was all this luxury worth the emotional wasteland she lived in? She could tell no one about her problem. How could anyone possibly understand? She knew that she stirred up envy in other women. And that, after all, was Marshall's intention.

"Look at that house! Those clothes, the jewels," they would say. "What more could she possibly want? Happiness?"

He pounded on the door. "I'll let you get away with this tonight. Only because of tomorrow. But if you ever pull that again, I swear I'll kick the crap out of you! You whimpering little bitch!"

Then there was silence.

Locked in the sanctuary of her vast bathroom, she lined the tub with towels embroidered with still another tortuous Killingsworth cipher, then rolled two smaller towels as a pillow for her head. She unfolded a fresh towel robe and slipped it on over her nightgown. Then she stepped into the tub. And in that cold, hard space she cried herself to sleep.

The next morning, she woke up early. She had spent a restless night against the unyielding marble, her jaw was sore from grinding teeth, her body ached, her legs were blotched with hives—a persistent problem this past year. Emotional stress, the doctors told her.

Milly knocked, then entered the bedroom without Demetra's usual breakfast tray. "Mr. Killingsworth expects you in the Winter Garden, Madam. I hope you do not mind. I didn't want to put up a fuss."

"You did the right thing, Milly dear," Demetra said.

Although Milly was now Demetra's personal maid, she had begun as Corey's nanny. As Greenhill House's tenants rose to the top and servants were hired and fired, Milly remained the only constant, Demetra's only confidante. Having long ago set stringent privacy rules for herself, Demetra trusted only Milly. They would often sit together at the kitchen table for a mid- morning coffee, or during the late afternoon, for a cup of Milly's strong Irish tea.

Marshall resented Milly because his wife confided in her, and he had made it obvious that he did not like having people around who were just over five feet tall and wore a size sixteen uniform. Demetra knew that Milly gorged on Winchell's doughnuts and See's chocolates on her days off, but that was her business.

Breakfast was usually served in the glass-walled winter garden Marshall preferred to call his *jardin d'hiver* built soon after he attended an elegant dinner in the Parisian *jardin d'hiver* of a famous *comtesse*.

"Good morning, Marshall," Demetra said. The nuns had insisted that civilized people always said "good morning" to one other.

He did not look up from the newspaper. He did not speak.

Neither of them referred to the evening before as they ate their spartan breakfasts among lush palms, rare orchids, bromeliads, and Marshall's favorite staghorn ferns.

"You look terrible this morning," he said finally. "Why don't you give yourself a facial? Or do *something*. You look worn out. You always look tired lately."

"Do I? That's strange. I should look rested since you told me yesterday that I lie around the house all day and read."

"Maybe it's just that you're getting older. You really ought to do something about yourself, Demi."

"What do you mean?"

"You need a face lift."

She felt the stab but would not give him the satisfaction of letting him know how much he had hurt her. "I'm only thirty-seven years old. Besides, I'd always thought that a woman had to be motivated to do that sort of thing on her own."

"Well, you ought to start thinking about it. I've heard of a good doctor in New York."

She got up from her chair. "Let's not talk about this anymore. I must get ready. Please excuse me."

She fled to her bathroom and looked at herself, turning her face from side to side to catch every angle in the ruthless spot lit mirrors. This morning those lines on either side of her nose seemed to have thickened and formed deep channels, the dark circles under her eyes reminded her of Madame Apollonia's eyes. Her face seemed to have suddenly gone limp on its bones; her skin was still blotchy from those recurrent hives. She hoped they would disappear by afternoon. At least the bruise on her cheek where Marshall had struck her was completely faded.

In the past she had never thought too much about her looks. The sisters had always made a fuss about her dark hair, fair skin, and blue eyes so that she'd grown up thinking she was reasonably pretty. But lately she had become insecure about her face, her body, but most of all about her intelligence. Her husband's eyes were always assessing other women, comparing her to them. "Demi," he'd said more than once, "the road to success is to be critical of yourself. Remember that. *Never* be satisfied." He often reminded her that his high school senior valedictorian topic was, "Dissatisfaction, the Road to Progress." Marshall had taken dissatisfaction as his life's obsession. "Dissatisfaction energizes," he said. "It's the force that propels me."

But these past few years he had begun to evaluate his enormous success in the world of high finance and real estate. He had come to believe in the lore of his public relations agent, in a public persona that was tailormade for him. Now Marshall was no longer dissatisfied with himself, but with Demetra, his wife of nineteen years. And she knew it.

Marshall had always sought his late mother's praise and approval, but he had alienated her by marrying Demetra Duval, an orphan. Even now Demetra felt a jab of pain whenever she recalled the late Mrs. Killingsworth's exclamation, "Why, Demetra isn't even sure of her real birth date—not to mention a mother or father!" Demetra was convinced that his mother's feelings were haunting him, that he was instinctively punishing her for who she was and wherever she had come from. After all, he bore the name Killingsworth with great pride. His ancestor was the one of the founders of this small town in Connecticut, and he often boasted that his great- great grandfather had been taught by Henry Wadsworth Longfellow in Killingsworth's little schoolhouse.

After splashing her face alternately with hot and cold water, she slathered on a thick grey clay masque that would harden and remain for two hours. She hoped she could endure the discomfort of her face being concrete-encased for that long. *"Il faut souffrir pour tre belle,"* one of the girls used to chant as they dried their long hair, beating it over and over against the bathtub rim to make it thick and fluffy. There were no electric dryers in the orphanage in St. Paul. In an instinctive gesture she put her hand behind her head to touch her braid, gone long ago.

CHAPTER II

Sunday afternoon. Three o'clock. Within the hour, members would arrive in their Rolls Royces and Bentleys and Mercedes and Jaguars. The valet service would recognize most of them, and, as they entered Greenhill House, paparazzi would snap their pictures. Publicity hungry ladies would position themselves by the door, not wanting to leave the pop and flash action. Although it was Sunday, society page writers did not have the day off: Greenhill House and the Killingsworths always made good copy.

In an hour guests would throng the house. They would amble from room to room scrutinizing the paintings, the furniture, the objects, the family photographs. They would be overwhelmed. Greenhill House was meant to inspire awe. Marshall had ordered the windows, pediments, and ceilings of the house over-scaled for effect, except for the living room, where the architect had convinced him to abide by the classical proportions of the double cube. It was an imposing house, surpassing in scale and luxury West Wycombe in England, the Palladian villa after which it was modeled. Its Regence and Louis XV furniture, its *bois de placage*, its Vernis Martin and *pietre dure*, Kang Hsi Coromandel and *lacque bergauté*, the gilt wood

Thomas Hope and Thomas Locke consoles, and tall pier glasses were all perfectly in keeping with its scale.

The Killingsworths extended their welcomes at the far end of the Long Gallery. Guests passing through the Rotunda stopped to gaze respectfully at the bronze ballet dancer in her wispy tutu, a genuine Degas.

"Better than some other casts I've seen," said one self-styled connoisseur, his dismissive tone undercutting the compliment.

In the Gallery the guests merged to admire the important Chinese armorial export porcelains crammed in the wall to wall waxed pine cabinets. Subtle beams illuminated each family crest. Another cabinet displayed continental porcelains, mostly Sevres and Meissen, Lomonosov and Gardner, all collected by Marshall on his frequent business trips to the Continent. He had insisted upon museum lighting and labeling each group as to origin and date.

By four-thirty the house was filled with members, along with their husbands or escorts. Many of the younger members were psychologically dwarfed by the scale of the house, intimidated, diminished by its palatial splendor. Some of the less secure guests would look for things that were not quite right, openly criticizing the house to one another, even as they moved through the rooms.

"How many square feet would you guess this home is?" one member inquired of another.

"At least 20,000."

"These days that's not so big. Haven't you seen that 30,000 square foot home filling up that double lot on Bellagio? Now that's *really* something!"

***

Marshall kept glancing at his watch. He pinched her elbow. "Go check out the other rooms—but make sure you come right back here," he mumbled beneath his breath.

Demetra left to follow her husband's orders.

June Cooper, president of Never Too Late, and Diana Victor, her handmaiden, had stationed themselves in separate rooms to enact their self-appointed roles as *grandes dames* of Los Angeles. June Cooper was tall, heavy-waisted, with thick-ankles and pole legs. Her ash blonde hair was so perfect that most people presumed it must be a wig; and they were right. If you stood close by her in the sunlight you could see shiny synthetic filaments. Her nose tended to become pink whenever she ate her favorite hot and spicy foods, so she had developed the nervous habit of pulling out a compact to whiten it whenever there was a lull in dinner conversation.

June's eyes swept over every *bibelot* on each fabric-draped or waxed tabletop, scrutinizing every painting, each identified by a conspicuous, engraved metal plate. She stooped to study photographs framed in elaborate silver *repoussé* or in Marshall's favorite Fabergé *guillochet* enamel.

June had assigned Diana to "library duty." The library was Demetra's favorite room. Her art books filled the shelves of an entire wall: the other shelves held the gilt-tooled volumes Marshall had insisted on ordering by the yard from a leather bindery on the Faubourg Saint Honoré. He would not wait for Demetra to fill them with books she loved. He had insisted that she wrap all her art books in ivory parchment paper so that their bright jackets and varied typefaces would not mar the "seriousness" of the room. They had argued about this two weeks ago: she won the argument but paid for the triumph by the bruise on her cheek.

Today, too-thin, almost too-tall Diana was dressed in couture Balenciaga, black, blackest black, her favorite color. She described herself as either a scrawny flat-chested old crow or a tall glass of water. Now Diana and Frederick Marchand, her "walker," nibbled on watercress sandwiches and sipped sherry from Georgian crystal glasses as their eyes swept over the shelves of art books. She was leafing through a book on Vaux-le-Vicomte and shoved it back hastily when she saw Demetra enter. "Darling, those flowers on the commode in the gallery are divine. *Quelle merveille!* Freddie and I were just admiring them."

Demetra, who grew up speaking French in the convent, had a feeling that Diana resorted to French whenever she was lying.

"Who arranged them?"

Demetra, reverting to her first language under stress, responded defiantly that she had grown the flowers from seed and had also arranged them,

Diana stammered out, "Your French accent is …*parfait.*"

"Thanks. But do you think my flowers look as if they've been arranged by loving hands at home?" She was surprised by the defensiveness, the impatient hostility in her voice, as though she suddenly had no control of the words that came from her mouth.

Diana did not seem to notice her annoyance. "The bouquet is so...so sensitive, with all those wispy garden flowers." She waved her diamond-domed hand toward towards the foyer. "But those Russian porphyry urns in the entrance massed with French tulips and lilies. *Quel luxe!* They must certainly have been flown in from Holland. Ravishing!

Demetra disliked the word *ravishing* used that way. It seemed affected. And she didn't like its implication.

"One of Marshall's executives brought them back on the company plane."

"We've all been dying to see what you'd do with this house. It is utterly amazing. *Amazing!*" Another of Diana's favorite words used far too often. "Those porcelains in the hall are so impressive. It is as though we're in a decorative arts museum. *Wherever* did you find them?"

"They've all been collected by Marshall."

"What do *you* collect?" asked Marchand.

"I collect books. Art books. Feel free to have a good browse," she said sharply, turned on her Chanel heel and left the library.

Grim-faced maids passed trays of watercress and cucumber sandwiches. They were dressed alike in primrose yellow ankle length uniforms ordered by Marshall from the White House, the specialty linen store in London. Each apron was branded with the Killingsworth cipher.

Demetra overheard one-member confiding in another, "I'll *never ever* be able to invite the Killingsworths to my home, not even for one of those let's-get-to-know -each-other luncheons. I'd have to do a major re-haul job first."

As she assessed the crowd, it occurred to her that among all these women, there was not one she could call a friend. Yet two fascinated her: Gail Claiborne, whose off- beat, flower child individuality and style she warmed to, and Marina McFarland who had just arrived with her husband. Demetra was intimidated by her. Not only was Marina womanly and beautiful but she was also well-born, well-educated, refined, and gracious. Demetra worried that Marina might see through to her own invented self. Even though she felt insecure about her lack of formal education, she was grateful for her gifted visual memory. And she knew that she grasped concepts quickly. Marshall had given her the task of researching each piece of furniture, every painting and sculpture purchased for Greenhill House, and she had taken her job seriously. In no time she had become the "in house" expert, The Curator of Greenhill House Treasures. She had been so eager to please Marshall, to gain his approval; and she had educated herself in the process.

When she returned to Marshall's side, he seemed elated. "You'll never guess who showed up with Josie Baylor," he said with a jubilant grin. "Since Josie's husband wasn't in town, she brought her house guest, Larke Brewster, here from New York."

Demetra had not seen him so exuberant in a long time. He was obviously overjoyed by the thought of Larke Brewster, New York's grand dame extraordinaire, entering the portals of Greenhill House.

"I had no idea that Josie was a friend of Larke's," he said. "I promised to fly her back to New York... Somehow I can't imagine her flying commercially."

She heard the childlike awe beneath Marshall's French-polished veneer. He obviously saw this as his big chance for social acceptance in New York. "I'm sure that if she wanted to fly in her own plane she would. She can certainly afford to," Demetra said under her breath. She turned to greet the next guest.

"What an event! What a home!" The latest arrival spoke up wearing still another brass-buttoned, chain-belted, parrot-green wool suit, exactly like four other parrot- green Adolfo suits in the room, ranging from size four to fourteen.

Gail Claiborne was standing in the receiving line. She was without her actor husband.

Marshall nudged Demetra. "At least one of them made it," he said in a cheerful voice.

Demetra wondered if Gail dressed for the curious effect she knew she had on people. Today she looked as if she had raced to get ready. Something about her was invariably awry: a zipper placket twisted around to the side, a necklace clasp turned to the front, a shoulder weighed down by an overstuffed bag. Today a folkloric fringed suede bag flapped open because it was so crammed. Large melon-carved crystal beads hung around her neck. Her embroidered challis skirt reached her ankles.

Gail extended her hand to Demetra, whose slight distance stemming from uncertainty was read by others as aloofness. Marshall often reminded her that this bit of uncalculated restraint gave her a sense of mystery and glamour. When Gail smiled her wide, generous smile, her hazel eyes looked straight into Demetra's. "My husband sends his regrets. He's in England on location for *Morris Dance,* his new movie. He'd planned to be with me today."

"Thank you for coming on your own, Gail," Demetra said.

Marshall's eyes swept over Gail as if to ask, don't you know any better than to dress that way when you visit Greenhill House? He turned away impatiently and began to speak to some gushing women who were praising the architecture, the decor, his collections. For Marshall, everything at Greenhill House was perfect because *he* had marshalled everything. Bigger than anyone else had in Los Angeles and better quality as well. He did not worry about the guests criticizing his home and his reception because it never occurred to him that anything could be wrong with Greenhill House, outside or in. And it had never occurred to him that, except for the library, Greenhill House looked like a hotel. A luxurious, well-appointed, well-run hotel.

When the reception reached its peak, and the house was swarming with chattering guests, Marshall nudged Demetra, "Just like I told you! The McFarlands never showed up. Let's call it quits."

"We should stay here a while longer. I think it's important to greet every single person who walks through the door."

Before he had a chance to respond, Marina McFarland appeared in a simple shell-pink silk dress with a matching cashmere jacket thrown over her shoulders, the pastel shade a perfect complement to her fair, shoulder length silver blonde hair.

Harcourt, her husband, a metals industrialist, had been crippled from a fox-hunting accident. He stood by, distinguished in his navy-blue blazer, leaning on his ivory-handled cane. His thinning hair was combed from side to side to hide his bald spot. One eye was covered with a black patch. Harcourt McFarland was known to be not in the least bit interested in his wife's social activities. He had his own interests and leaving his comfortable home on Sunday afternoon was something he was loath to do. "Unfortunately, I can't stay as long as I'd like," he said, as he shook hands with Demetra and Marshall. "I have to make a flight to Chicago in two hours, but there's certainly no reason why Marina can't stay on to enjoy your beautiful party."

Demetra read the lustful expression on Marshall's face.

"You're so generous to open your magnificent house to all of us." Marina said in her silky, cooing voice. "Such colorful flowers under the live oaks!"

Demetra was annoyed by what she felt was a condescending tone. She extended her hand to the McFarlands, and said, looking past Marina, "How nice to see you again." Marina always had such a numbing effect on her that she could never respond with a witty retort.

The McFarlands moved on.

"I'll go work the other reception rooms," Marshall said. "You check out the tea table."

In the dining room the chosen priestesses of Never Too Late were pouring Fortnum & Mason's Queen Anne blend from Queen Anne silver teapots. The Sheraton table fairly groaned under the weight of Georgian silver bowls filled with giant, long stemmed strawberries, silver trays laden with tea sandwiches, madeleines and *friandises*. Four very grand, very tall silver epergnes, each dangling crystal baskets heaped with chocolate truffles or mints, punctuated the table.

The maids passed scones no bigger than quarters, each dolloped with raspberry jam and a speck of Devonshire cream, like the miniature scones at Cherwell Castle where she was invited to stay while Marshall was negotiating for a newspaper chain in the north of England. Those few weeks had been an education for Demetra. She had admired the efficient, yet casual way Claudia, Countess of

Cherwell, ran her household. She absorbed all the refinements, described in detail the menus, the flowers, the table settings in her travel diary, so that she could please Marshall, earn his approval by emulating Claudia's taste when they returned to Greenhill House. But she soon learned that something was lost in translation from Cherwell to Greenhill. She was becoming aware that she had to develop her own style and today's reception was Marshall's style—his taste, not hers.

The guests flocked around the tea table, many of them feasting with only their eyes, discussing, and then denying themselves the sandwiches and sweets. A Twiggy-looking board member hovered over a tray of madeleines and sugar powdered pecan puffs, her grey-gaunt pallor the not-quite-yet-dead giveaway of too many laxatives and too much throwing up.

Demetra heard Twiggy say to her husband. "Here—try this hazelnut cookie, I like it. I have tried them all. I don't like any of the others," she said pointing to a heap of half-eaten confections on a lace-edged linen napkin placed unappetizingly close to the silver serving tray.

Demetra caught a glimpse of a member's husband as he hailed a waiter and heard him snarl, "Haven't you got anything else besides tea and coffee?"

"We are offering sherry as well, sir. Or would you prefer a soft drink?"

"Goddamn it! Give me scotch and soda. There's gotta be a bar somewhere in this friggin' palace."

"Very well, sir."

Disgusted, Demetra made her way back to the library. Diana Victor and June Cooper huddled over a vitrine, evaluating Marshall's collection of enameled and jeweled eggs and bibelots, amassed in just three years. Neither of them noticed Demetra.

"Do you think these are real Fabergé or those fakes coming out of Russia?" She heard Diana ask. "The enamel doesn't seem quite translucent enough to me, but then I'm not the expert on Fabergé that you are, June."

Demetra fled to the powder room and fell into a chair.

Milly was in attendance, quite happy to work on Sunday so that she might have a glimpse of the famous guests, most of whom she knew from reading the society columns.

"Mrs. Killingsworth! Are you feeling all right? You look a bit pale."

"I'm your first casualty, Milly dear. I've got a wicked headache."

"I have some aspirin in my first aid kit."

"The last time I took aspirin it tore my stomach apart."

Milly soaked a tissue with eau de cologne and blotted Demetra's forehead.

"What a lovely floral scent. What is it?"

"'Rose of the World'—from my sister in Dublin. What's wrong, Madam? I see tears in your eyes."

"Some days tears come more easily. Oh, Milly how did I ever let myself get caught up in all this? I'll be glad when it's all over."

Milly put her arm around her. "Not to worry, Madam. Now—tell me what's really bothering you."

"I'm still agonizing about starting the search for my parents."

"You mustn't be so afraid. Remember that you are what you are, Mrs. Killingsworth. No one can take away your beauty, your intelligence, or your kindness, no matter what you find."

She kissed Milly's cheek. "Oh Milly, you always make me feel better." She drew a deep breath and sighed. "I'd better get back to the reception line or else he'll be looking for me."

Demetra left the room, heading instead to the west wing for a few more moments of quiet. She unhooked the blue velvet rope and hurried down the corridor to the family sitting room. There, in a far corner, standing close together, were Marshall and Marina McFarland. Harcourt McFarland was nowhere in sight.

Demetra, sensing that their conversation was intimate, hurried away quietly, relieved that Marshall had not seen her.

By seven o'clock the guests had said their good-byes to the Killingsworths and to one another. Some drove off to Chasen's or Trader Vic's. Movie industry couples raced home for a Sunday evening of "running" movies. Others were off to the Hilton for a dinner honoring Basil Hadesson. Demetra was relieved that Marshall turned down the invitation. Hadesson was a controversial figure in Los Angeles, although most people closed their eyes to his notoriety, mostly out of fear of his power. Demetra loathed him. She had once heard Basil boast that, before he'd started his painting collection, he thought painting "was something you did to a room." And that "a Pissarro was Italian for a place where you pissed."

Demetra had no urge to confront Marshall about his tête a tête with Marina. He was probably still angry about last night, and she did not want to risk yet another explosion like the one two weeks ago. It had taken two weeks for those bruises on her cheek to fade. She was beginning to suspect that Marshall thought he had outgrown her, that he was anxious for someone to be his equal, someone who could grasp the reins of social power.

Yet she was so afraid of his rejection she was aware that she would put up with almost anything to please him. She had even taken on the chairmanship of Never Too Late's Olympics gala to win his approval.

She flopped in a chair and kicked off her shoes. Her feet were sore from standing so long, her bones ached from sleeping in the tub. Marshall walked into the room, then opened the French doors of their bedroom balcony and gazed out over his cyclamen, a blur of pink under the spotlights. "Everyone raved about my cyclamen!" he said at last.

"Yes, Marshall," Demetra said, but to herself she added, "They may have said 'how colorful, but not 'how beautiful.'" Instinctively she sensed that the gardens of this neo-Palladian house should have more axis, more vistas, fewer serpentine paths.

"You know, Demi, the more I think about it—all I do for you, all the money I spend on you—the more I feel your resistance, as though you're fighting me all the way with everything. The decoration of my house, my garden, my furnishings..."

"Are you telling me you're not satisfied with the job I've done on *your* house?"

He did not respond.

She left him leafing through his stack of papers, while she went straight to bed and cried herself to sleep.

Just past midnight a buzzer rang on the security panel. It was the guard station.

Marshall ran into the bedroom. "Who the hell could it be? Corey? Where is she coming from?" He punched out the new code. Corinna had been unable to get in the gate because the guard had changed the code, not unusual after a big party when outside help had been called in. Or when someone from the staff had been dismissed.

He ran downstairs to open the door for her.

From the bedroom window Demetra could see their daughter

driving up the circular drive in her old Mustang. She put on a robe and hurried downstairs.

The moment her daughter entered the kitchen, her mother sensed that she was depressed. She had put on weight. Her jeans were frayed, her tan leather jacket was spotted with grease, her long, reddish-blonde hair was lank. When they embraced, Demetra thought it smelled like rancid machine oil.

"Corey—why didn't you at least let us know you were coming home? You haven't returned any of my calls. And with all the messages I left for you last week."

"It took me six days to drive here and I'm never going back to Philadelphia."

"What do you mean you're not going back? I just sent the college your tuition check for next term," Marshall said.

Her green eyes flashed. "I'll never go back. I hate the place."

Marshall hit his palm with his fist. "What the hell do you think you're gonna do, then?"

"I want to get a job as an extra. And I'm moving in with Harley Hadesson. You know his parents, Ethel and Basil."

Marshall raised his voice "Goddamnit. After all I've done for you—sent you to the best school and college in the East and you wind up with that spoiled brat ne'er- do-well son of Basil Hadesson—a man with underworld connections. Or didn't you know that?"

"I don't give a fuck what his family is all about."

"Don't you dare use that kind of language in my home!"

Corey snickered and turned away. "Don't worry, Dad, it won't be *my* home for much longer."

Corey was embarrassed by her father's wealth. She had insisted on a secondhand car, and so Marshall had bought her an old Mustang from one of his secretaries. Although she did not care about the car's slovenly disarray, she guarded its contents: books, theater playbills,

Indian blankets, jogging clothes, shopping bags filled with recyclable soft drink cans. And she made sure that the engine was properly cared for.

When Corey was in residence at Greenhill House, Demetra often closed the door to her daughter's messy room because Corey would not allow anyone to straighten or clean it. Demetra tried not to nag her, but sometimes the frustration was so great she could not help complaining. She was dismayed that Corey seemed to have no respect for her personal property, or that of her parents. Perhaps it was her way of claiming a separate identity, trying to be as far away as possible from Marshall's standards, disclaiming the materialism of her parents' lives. Yet while Corey adored her father, Demetra sensed that her daughter was trying to love her less.

"I'm going back to bed. Mark my words we'll talk about this tomorrow," Marshall said, as he left them standing in the kitchen.

Demetra, always unnerved by confrontation, said quietly, "Corey, your father and I can't understand why you'd want to take a job as a movie extra when you can have a good education at a fine college."

"Because I don't want to study what I don't want to know. It's as simple as that—can't I make you two understand?"

"I only wish that I could have had the education that you can have at..."

"For a woman who never went to college you seem to do just fine, Mom. You know so much about history and art more than someone with two degrees. I admire you for being self-taught."

"But I have enormous gaps in my education."

"At least you married the man you loved when you were seventeen."

Demetra sighed. "I suppose I was lucky to have met your father when I did." When Corey was at home, she pretended happiness for her daughter's sake, and, since Corey had spent her pre-college years at boarding school and summer camp she hadn't been around her parents to feel their deteriorating relationship except on holidays. But they always called a truce during her visits.

"You should be glad that I want to be an actress. You won't have to spend all that tuition money for nothing. Then you can donate it all to your Never Too Late pals. Got anything to eat? I haven't eaten anything since breakfast."

"There are leftover sandwiches and cakes."

"Left over from what?"

"The Never Too Late reception we hosted here today."

She snickered. "Ironic isn't it? You out there raising money to send underprivileged women back to school...."

"*Et ma chère fille a tourné le dos à l'éducation que j'ai toujours voulue,*" Demetra responded quietly.

Corey, who never liked it when her mother spoke French, responded, "Whoa...this conversation is getting way too heavy. I'll go fix something for myself."

"I'll come keep you company."

"I can do it myself."

Demetra followed her into the vast kitchen which looked more like a laboratory. When they had built Greenhill House, Demetra had plans for a country kitchen with scrubbed butcher blocks, copper pots hanging from a ceiling rack and old baskets filled with herbs, but Marshall could not abide traces of cooking utensils in the kitchen. So there were no wooden spoons, spatulas or ladles, no canisters marked "tea, coffee, sugar, flour." There were no blenders or Cuisinarts or Mixmasters on view. Not a trace of food to be seen anywhere. Only bare, shiny black granite counters.

Corinna opened one of the two huge stainless-steel refrigerators and took out a plastic box of leftover cucumber and watercress sandwiches. She tasted one, grimaced, and put the box back. "One of my Greek actor friends told me that in America the richer the people, the lousier the food in the home." She rustled around until she found a container of roast turkey slices. She stacked up mounds of turkey, defiantly smearing globs of mayonnaise on thick slices of sourdough bread while her mother sat on a stool watching and worrying about her daughter's weight even as she knew better than to mention it.

"So you really won't go back?" Demetra asked.

"No, I'm through with school. Forever. And so is Harley."

Demetra wondered why she had such difficulty accepting these admissions from her daughter. After all, she had married Marshall when she was younger than Corey. She'd been only eighteen when Corey was born. She put her arm around Corey. "Why don't you take a hot shower and get into bed. I have a feeling you've been sleeping in your car this week."

Corey stiffened and pulled away. "As always you're right."

When they left the kitchen, Demetra passed the security panel and noticed the red light on the business phone line. She knew without listening that her husband was having a conversation with Marina.

The next evening, as Demetra was dressing for the party. Corey came by to pick up cartons of Demetra's favorite old clothes, some china, silverware, household effects that Marshall decided were not good enough for Greenhill House and that Corey wanted for her new apartment near UCLA. The cartons had been stored after the move from Seattle to Los Angeles.

Demetra did not have the heart to donate these relics of happier times, so she was pleased when Cory asked for them; her daughter had always been sentimental about family possessions.

Since Corey and Harley moved in together, mother and daughter had spoken to each other only a few times, usually whenever Corey wanted something.

"How pretty you look," Demetra said. "I like your hair the way you're wearing it."

"Thanks, Mom." She bent to kiss her mother's cheek.

Demetra was happy that Corey's depression seemed to have lifted. She had lost some weight; her hair was clean. Maybe Harley was a good influence on her, after all.

"Where are you two off to tonight?"

"A party in Hancock Park, but I'm sorry I accepted the invitation. The ladies were asked to wear something ethnic, or an exotic outfit bought on a trip, one that had never been worn. What a silly idea!"

"I don't agree with you. I think it's very original. What are you wearing?"

"A long black skirt and a white silk blouse, I guess. I've been so busy working on the Olympics Gala benefit that I haven't really given it much thought."

"Can't you wear something a little more creative than a white blouse and a black skirt? You'll look very uptight compared to the all the other women."

Demetra stiffened. "I'm not trying to compete with anyone."

Corey bent to inhale the narcissus in the blue and white Kang Hsi bowl.

"Harley told me that at one of his mother's masquerade parties a guest arrived as Eliza Doolittle. Then, just before dinner, she transformed herself into Eliza wearing a *My Fair Lady* court presentation outfit, complete with tiara and ostrich feather fan! Now why don't *you* try using your imagination? Be creative with yourself, Mom. Dream up something interesting. Don't be so conservative,"

Demetra bristled. "Why don't *you* make up your mind about how you want me to look! Remember the time I wore a red dress when I visited you at Westover and you asked me to go back to the hotel to change?"

"Yeah—I didn't like your makeup either. Or that hairdo. I thought you were trying to look like Sophia Loren."

"That was the style in the seventies."

"I wanted you to look like the other mothers."

"After that I tried to, even though your father is always after me to be more flamboyant, more show-biz." She sighed. "Oh Corey, these last few weeks I've had so much on my mind."

"Planning another benefit?" Corey asked, her voice betraying her hostility.

"Okay Mom—I'll get right to the point. Dad told me all about the search. He doesn't want you to."

"How do *you* feel about it?"

"I always wondered how come you've never tried to find them before."

"Because it never mattered to me as much as it does now."

"But now it's too late. Think about it, Mom. Suppose you found out that you had a whole other family? Sisters, brothers." She frowned. "I'm not sure I could handle an extended family. Could you?"

"I've not given it much thought. I've only focused on finding my parents."

"Isn't *our* family enough for you? Besides, if and when I ever get married to Harley you'll have all his relatives." She laughed. "Now that might really infuriate Dad!"

Demetra grinned and shook her head. Corey was so lucky to be able to let Marshall's disapproval roll off.

Corey kissed her mother's cheek. "I'd better get going. Give Dad my love. And have a good time at the party."

"Kevin can help load the boxes in your car. Do you need any help with your decorating?"

"Harley and I can manage."

"Would it be all right if I dropped by someday to visit?"

"No. I'll give you a ring when we're ready for you to see what we've done to the place, if anything."

Demetra did not persist. She knew that her daughter was still trying to distance herself.

The Secret Garden was the place to be seen for lunch, especially on Fridays. The most sought-after seating was indoors, on the banquette facing the French doors opening to the patio. Having a seat on the banquette ensured a good view of all who entered and exited the restaurant as well as patio diners. Eavesdropping on other banquette sitters was easy since patrons were squeezed so close to one another; secrets were hard to keep in The Secret Garden.

The ladies of the club, Never Too Late Lunch enjoyed pursuing their culture in groups. Marina and Demetra were the exception. The Club reserved tickets *en bloc* for the symphony, theater, ballet, and opera. Attending these events together helped some of the members feel more secure. Today, at the Secret Garden, they had played it safe by reserving a private room so they could also vent their feelings about what was going on within their organization before they moved on to today's subject. Books.

Demetra had chosen a simple navy-blue suit, a lace edged white blouse and hardly any makeup. Although her outfit was couture, she had lost weight and now the suit seemed too loose on her body.

She had sent her acceptance a month ago, and once committed, she rarely ever backed out of an invitation without good reason. But she would never have come today had she known that Marina had decided to attend. At the opposite end of the table Marina was holding court, her long blonde hair flowing below her shoulders (a hairdo Demetra had recently admired on the cover of *Vogue*).

Around her, Marina had the usual devoted subjects, a cross section of members from the San Fernando Valley, Hancock Park, Beverly Hills, West Hollywood, Santa Monica, and Brentwood.

Today Marina was the sole member from Pasadena. The topic of conversation before books—was naturally—Never Too Late.

Demetra spoke to the women who sat on either side, avoiding eye contact with Marina. Yes, she had heard those rumors about Marina and Marshall. They were probably true

"By the way, Demetra, that was a wonderful reception you gave all of us. Your home is simply gorgeous. Who was your decorator?" chirped Tina Marlowe, a director and handmaiden-drone, who catered to every whim of June and Diana's.

Demetra's usually pale face reddened. She shrugged her shoulders. "I guess I was the decorator."

"You did a *fantastic* job," Tina said. "Our organization certainly owes a lot to you and Marshall for hosting all of us. Too bad you weren't at the board meeting last Monday." As she spoke, she squeezed half a lemon into her Perrier, muttering an obscenity when the juice sprayed the front of her mauve silk blouse.

"Your ears must have been burning when June and Diana discussed your elegant reception," another member chortled.

Demetra's hand trembled slightly as she smiled sweetly and took a sip of peach-flavored iced tea. She had heard those comments Diana had made about the fake Fabergé.

"You are a marvelous *maîtresse de maison*. Greenhill House looked so festive," Marina said. "The auratum lilies in the rotunda were incredibly fragrant. And Diana told me that you arranged that lovely bouquet in the gallery; so beautiful, like a Dutch Old Master still-life. We are all looking forward to your Olympics party with its tributes to classical Greece. I think your Feast of the Gods theme is a brilliant theme for an Olympics event."

Demetra murmured a thank you, eyes focused on her service plate, her hand pressing out invisible wrinkles on her skirt.

Tina beckoned the headwaiter so that Diana could place her order. Then she gave him a stern look. "Carlos, never *ever* serve me a 'naked' lemon again! From now on always put cheesecloth panties on them." As she spoke, she squeezed the "naked" lemon in the air in front of the waiter, pips and juice spattering over his pleated tuxedo shirtfront. She laughed outright.

Marina, mortified by Tina's insensitivity and rudeness, felt her face turn as crimson as the Dior suit she was wearing. She quickly attempted to change the subject. "By the way, I stopped by the office yesterday and read Gail Claiborne's letter of resignation."

"Why did she become a drop-out? She can certainly afford to belong," another member spoke out.

"In her letter she wrote that she'd agonized about resigning," Marina said. "She strongly believes the Never Too Late's cause is a fine one—but..."

"But what?" asked Marla Stevens.

"She wrote that she was changing her life. Simplifying it to give more time to home, hearth, and garden. And to her own creative projects." Barbara piped up.

"Someone told me that she stays home most of the time making Christmas ornaments out of lint." Howls from the ladies.

"I heard she's become very New Age—whatever that means," Vicky Bartlett added.

Marina, always up on the newest trends, spoke confidently. "New Age has to do with spiritual values and the emergence of feminine consciousness in this patriarchal society we live in."

"Well, Gail's always talking about goddesses and rituals and arka..."

"'Archetypes." Marina supplied the word.

Marla continued on the subject of Gail, "The last time I saw Gail was at your home, Demetra. Wasn't that some get-up she was wearing?"

Demetra, who usually guarded her words, sat up straight, her eyes sweeping the tables. "I thought she looked striking. Gail's resignation is a real loss for us."

"I wonder how Clem puts up with her looking the way she does. With all those gorgeous actresses he gets to make love to, he must come home to her. She'd better be careful or someday she's going to find herself out in left field," Marlene Stevens declared. Speculation among the organization was that Marlene was to be their next president. She always took on the gigantic task of seating at all the galas and other benefits, ingratiating herself with certain key ladies, reassuring them, guaranteeing that they would get good *placement*. "Don't worry, you know I'll always take care of you," she was famous for alleging.

Barbara Ryan spoke up. "Gail is a loss, but she's one less. You know how the Old Guard board members worry about the size of the membership. They say we can't get any larger than we are." Her tone became serious. "At the last board meeting June proposed an increase, so I guess we'll have to raise the dues."

"Dues raised?" groaned one of the more affluent board members." We've got to band together and make sure that doesn't happen."

Other well-off members protested. "We've got to keep things from changing —even the dues."

"Well, you just can't have it both ways. Either we increase the dues, or we increase the membership," Marina said shaking her head in disbelief.

Since these were some of the richest women in town, why should they be so adamant about not raising dues? After all, some of their get-ups from Galanos and Chanel cost nearly as much as the annual dues.

"We've not heard much from you, Demetra. You seem to have a lot on your mind today," Marlene remarked, fixing her eyes on Demetra.

The women put down their forks; chatter ceased as they waited for Demetra's response.

Breaking the privacy rules she'd been living by, Demetra blurted out, "As a matter of fact, I do have a lot on my mind. I've been thinking about making a search for my parents." No sooner had she spoken; she knew she'd made a mistake. A terrible mistake. Why, why had she suddenly bared her soul to these women? What on earth had she been thinking, letting down her guard this way!

Feeling the tension, Marina changed the subject to books. "Have any of you read Dominick Dunne's new *roman à clef* novel? It's already made the bestseller list."

"Yes," was the response from of at least half of the group.

"Can you guess who's in it? People we all know." When the identity contest had run its course, Marina announced. "Now it's time to go around the table and tell what book each of us has been reading."

Marlene Stevens was the first to speak. "I just finished the new Judith Kranz novel. It's terrific. I understand CBS is talking about a miniseries."

Demetra seemed distracted and fidgeted with her watch. It was her turn next. She blushed when she spoke. "I'm reading *Pride and Prejudice*. I saw the film on television recently—and decided to re-read it."

"Who wrote it? Vicky asked Demetra.

"Jane Austen."

"Never heard of her."

"Oh, come on! You've *got* to be kidding." Marla tried to stifle her incredulity. "She was an early nineteenth century English novelist who wrote about life in provincial England. My husband just brought home the script for a re-make by one of the major studios. Jane Austen is becoming very hot."

"Hold on while I get my pen. Austin—like in Texas?" Vicky asked.

"No. AUSTEN," Marla spelled. "You'll find it in any bookstore where they sell the classics."

The waiter arrived with artfully "designed" plates of *homard Parisien* and *poulet en geleé*. Some women put down their forks at every mouthful, the way the current "in" Beverly Hills nutritionist advised them to do.

Demetra watched in fascination and disgust as a bony member spit food from her mouth into her napkin, burying the wad in its folds, all the while proclaiming the lunch to be "positively yummy."

Appetites were soon appeased, half-eaten luxury lunches whisked away. There was not a spare ounce of fat on any of these women, so controlled were they in their eating habits. Demetra noticed that Marina, however, savored every bite of her lobster followed by the miniature chocolate soufflé piled with whipped cream.

After decaffeinated espresso, some ladies left for fittings and facials or browsing along Rodeo Drive. But Vicky Bartlett said she would walk over to Brentano's to buy a copy of *Pride and Prejudice*. As they were leaving The Secret Garden she told Demetra that she was intrigued with the title of the book, especially the *Prejudice*.

CHAPTER III

A month had gone by since the final committee meeting for the Feast of the Gods. Turquoise, orange and fuchsia pennants and banners unfurled along avenues and boulevards. The 1984 Olympic Games would take place in the summer, and Los Angeles was jubilant with new-found enthusiasm and self- respect. At last, culture had come to the City of the Angels this year, the City of Olympians. Los Angeles was set, not unlike Olympia, between the mountains and the sea. In January helicopters had scattered wildflower seeds of the Peloponnesus over the Santa Monica and San Gabriel Mountains. The Feast of the Gods—the Never Too Late to Learn benefit chaired by Mrs. Marshall Killingsworth would be the first social event to herald the Olympic games.

On the eve of the Feast of the Gods gala, Demetra woke up in the middle of the night. She lay in bed for a long time, eyes wide open, staring at the underside of the canopy. She had not slept these past few nights, wondering if—and when—she would ever be brave enough to face searching for her parents. And brave enough to defy Marshall.

But now she forced herself to push away her obsessions and pin her anxieties on the reality at hand, the success, or failure, of the gala. Marshall had been after her to chair the major fund-raiser, and in a weak moment, trying always to please him, she had agreed. In the past if something went wrong with the party arrangements, she had been criticized (and blamed) not only by the board of Never Too Late, but also by Marshall. Sometimes, years after the fact, he reminded her of mistakes she had made, or parties that had not been successful.

All the worries about things that could go wrong loomed up. The food might be mediocre, or maybe there would not be enough contributed wine to go around. Would the decorations be effective, the lighting adequate, the music not too loud, the seating acceptable? Seating of the local pantheon was the most difficult. Vicky was notorious for changing the place cards trying to please either herself or a board member with whom she was currying favor.

Lying in bed, staring into the dark, Demetra realized how foolish it was to project what could go wrong. She asked herself what the worst scenario might be. In a few years what difference would it make in the grand scheme of things? Who would remember if the wine ran out, some flowers wilted, guests were displeased with their tables? Or if the printer misspelled a French word on the menu.

She had set the alarm for 5:30 a.m., planning to be at the ballroom by 7:30 to check out the decorations. She was intent on having the place cards on the tables by noon so that she and the members of the committee could go home to rest. She wanted to avoid all that frantic, last minute, up-to-the-wire panic that usually attended these events, and she vowed to herself that this would be the last benefit she would ever chair. Marshall expected her to be at the beck and call of June and Diana. From now on she would say no— even to them.

Towards morning, she awoke from a gruesome nightmare.

She looked on as parts of her body were dismembered and jammed into the plumbing pipes at Greenhill House. When Marshall turned on the tap, her blood flowed out. She could see her face reflected in the dark pool of shiny blood forming on the floor. She tossed some grains of wheat upon the surface.

She woke up grateful, that she was still in her own bed, alive. After that dream, the anxieties about the party were somehow diminished, and she forced herself to get up before the alarm rang.

Demetra's wardrobe closet, a sky-lit room nearly four hundred square feet was designed by Marshall and the architect and was not unusual for houses in Bel Air. Behind tall mirrored doors clothes hung white cotton bags in order of category: sports, tailored suits, cocktail dresses, long gowns. Each hanger was looped with a cardboard disc on which was written a description, the designer, the date, the season of the garment, the occasion when it was worn. Only the price was not part of the data.

The closet had become a battleground for Demetra these past few years, The Valley of Decision, she thought, whenever she stood before the soft, glimmering bags trying to decide what to pull from them. Sometimes the clothes she chose would not fit. Sometimes she simply imagined that they might not fit because she felt bloated and heavy and was unwilling to confront herself. So many dresses and suits hung there, unworn. Some were eventually given to the exclusive, or better yet, excluding, ModeElles, the ladies who, all in the guise of charity, gathered up hardly worn clothes for tax deductions.

Demetra knew there was too much to choose from. With less, she could have been more creative as she used to be when she and Marshall were first married. All this money spent on clothing, and yet she found herself reaching for the same old comfortable favorites over and over, only rarely wearing the newest outfit chosen by Marshall from a couture collection. Chosen by him only because of her lack of interest in her wardrobe, he told her.

For the Feast of the Gods, Marshall had insisted that she order a dress from James Galanos. He had gone with her to choose it. Mr. Galanos himself had suggested a pale ombre *eau de nil* chiffon, simple, unstructured, one-shouldered evening gown. But Marshall preferred a more expensive, more complicated dress, a sky-blue beaded and jeweled crepe georgette, all bones, stays, snaps, hooks, zippers. She did not argue with him. He usually had the last word, especially if Corey was around.

This morning old California desert sky, smog-less and cloudless, was framed in the domed glass above Demetra's head. Not in a long while had she seen such blueness above her. Milly had taken the blue dress out of its special ivory satin bag and hung it on a gold peg in the dressing room. The dress was the same color as the sky, Demetra thought, as she held it close to her face, wondering if it would make her eyes appear bluer or greener, as they often changed with whatever she was wearing on a given day.

She drank some coffee and got ready as quickly as she could. Within an hour she was at the hotel.

The young valet parking attendant recognized her. "Good morning, Mrs. Killingsworth. You are early. Today's the big day, right?"

"Yes, tonight it will be all over. I'll be grateful for that moment."

He seemed surprised by her response. "Well, I guess that's one way of looking at it."

Inside, she was elated by the tall ionic columns forming an allée to the entrance of the circular ballroom, banked with gnarled olive trees in giant boxes and rows of tall dark cypress. The entire stage backdrop was an immense projection of the famous Titian-Bellini painting, *The Feast of the Gods*. Everyone agreed that this was a perfect theme for the Olympics year, since the guests attending the gala would be the gods and goddesses of the East and West sides of the Olympian city.

She had thought it might be effective to decorate the ballroom so the guests would feel that their party was an extension of *The Feast of the Gods*. Yesterday, as the engineer flashed the projection on the backdrop, the painting's massive scale overwhelmed her. The gods were all there. They would look out over the ballroom and the guests. Apollo, with his laurel leaf crown set upon his fair hair, sipping wine from a cup; drunken Dionysus leering at lovely Aphrodite, Hermes, the Trickster; and Ares, the god of War, Priapus, with his crown of blue chicory that she identified immediately. And there *was* something bulging under the tunic of Priapus as he stared at the beautiful sleeping Loti. She was sure it was not her imagination.

The setting was as close in feeling to the painting as Demetra and her committee could make it. The underwriters had been generous. A movie studio had lent props and sculptures of Greek and Roman goddesses to place around the ballroom and provided the ceiling-to-floor backdrop curtain, all blue sky and floating clouds. Olive and laurel trees surrounded the ballroom and halogen lights and filters created an ethereal, rosy-fingered dawn. Lighting experts had designed moonbeams to be cast on the seated guests. From the ceiling, silk parachute fabric was swaged and puffed to give the effect of dense, white clouds floating above Mount Olympus.

Guests were to dine in the mythical forest of Arcadia, at tables draped with pale green cloths, glazed terra cotta service plates marking each place. Some tables were centered with bowls heaped with pomegranates, others with figs and grapes entwined with ivy, or terra cotta bowls of tender, sprouted green wheat, the Gardens of Adonis that Demetra had read about somewhere and sown herself in the greenhouse. After all this painstaking effort, she hoped that Marshall would be pleased.

***

At two o'clock she left the ballroom. Everything was in place. She had set the last card behind its service plate. Now the time had come to go home and get ready.

Marshall had warned her when he had ordered the dress. "I don't want any last-minute disasters, Demi. You have to look drop-dead magnificent for this event. I want the other women to be envious of you." He had no patience for what he perceived as her lack of self-discipline. Yes, she was capable of organizing charity events like the Feast of the Gods, of running a house the way Marshall wanted it run, but when the time came to get ready, she always seemed to fall apart. It had occurred to her many times before that she did not want to go to these events, that she hated them.

Back in her bedroom, she inserted the *Goyescas* tape, fast-forwarded to *The Maja and the Nightingale*, then turned up the volume so that the music would engulf her.

The Galanos was steamed and pressed and ready to wear, every layer hanging separately from the elaborate tucked bodice, rigid with stays. Grosgrain ribbons were hooked beneath the breasts to lift them, more ribbon around the waist to pull the flesh in tight. As she took it from its quilted satin hanger, the dress seemed heavier in her hands than she had remembered. Somehow, she balked at constricting her flesh in whalebone.

Under the incandescent closet light, the pale blue georgette seemed strange, grayish, and disturbing. She held it up and gazed at it, turning the dress this way and that in the light, trying to fathom why it had seemed prettier and bluer this morning. Was it really grey now, or was it just her mind playing tricks on her eyes? She was aware that sometimes ideas fixed themselves in her head so that she would develop a stubborn mind-set about a color or shape or line. Yet she knew that she had developed a keen visual sense these past five years, as she learned the art of researching and conserving paintings and furniture. Always trust the eye, the instinct, the heart, she told herself.

She pushed open another mirrored door and pulled out dress after dress. They all looked the same. They were all wrong. She was not even sure what she was looking for. Maybe she would not have to attend the party. Maybe she could stay home. Her stomach did a turn. Maybe she would get sick. It was already dark, and the full moon bathed the room in silver as she stood there, naked under the skylight.

At that instant she was drawn to a drawer that she rarely ever opened. Inside, buried beneath a stack of silk scarves she found an olive-green satin bag, tied tightly by long silk cords. She untied them and pulled out the skein of knotted white fabric. She released the knots and shook out the finely pleated silk dress from its years of confinement. The Fortuny gown. She had bought it in Venice. Had never worn it. She would wear it tonight. She remembered the trip to Venice taken the summer before they moved to Los Angeles from Seattle. Corey was nine years old. They had not been back since.

She had spent hours looking at paintings in the Accademia. When she saw Titian's *Presentation of the Virgin,* it had brought back memories of her convent days. A replica used to hang on the wall above Sister Claire's desk. Although she loved all the nuns, she loved Sister Claire the most. After she died, just before Corey was born, Demetra lost contact with the convent.

One day while Marshall and Corey went off to swim on the Lido, there was a sudden cloudburst as she climbed the Accademia Bridge spanning the Grand Canal. By the time she left the Accademia, the rain had stopped, the sun was shining, and a rainbow arched the sky over Dorsoduro. Instead of returning to the Gritti, she followed the rainbow past Campo San Vio toward Santa Maria della Salute, the church she had been admiring from their hotel suite across the Grand Canal. When she reached a small *campo* just beyond the Guggenheim Collection, she paused by an antique shop, admiring its window display, a jumble of frolicking gilt-wood *amorini*, silver *exvotos of* arms and legs and breasts, and old ruby glass Venetian goblets with dolphin stems. The charming *antiquaire* had greeted her in perfect English and, during conversation, told her about all the famous people who had once lived in the neighborhood.

"The eccentric Marchesa Casati lived just beyond the *calle*, and La Duse trysted with the writer, Gabriele d'Annunzio, in a palazzo just across the way," she told Demetra, who then asked the question she often asked antique shop owners. "Which is your favorite object?"

"If you will give me just a minute, I can show it to you. I keep it upstairs in my apartment."

She soon returned holding an olive-green satin bag, which she drew open. Inside was a skein of finely pleated, twisted, and coiled white silk. The Fortuny gown.

"You see, this delphos, as the dress is called, must be twisted and tied to keep the pleats set." She unknotted the white hank and shook it out. "These white dresses were the last Mariano Fortuny made. They were sold for more than thirty years, until the early fifties when people lost interest in them. This dress once belonged to a woman who lived in the neighborhood. She died not too long ago, and I bought it from her estate."

"Can you tell me its provenance?"

"I wish I could, but the estate wishes privacy."

"I understand. "

"Signora, do you ever seen anyone wearing a Fortuny gown in America?"

"I don't think so, but now and then I do see women wearing similar dresses. Mary McFadden's designs remind me of this one."

"Ah—but no one has ever truly been successful in achieving Mariano Fortuny's extensive color range or the permanence of his silk pleating. That is still a secret. These are collectors' items. Fortuny is also known for his metallic printed velvets and the cotton damask he created for interior decoration, but most of all he is remembered for these exquisite pleated gowns. You might enjoy seeing Palazzo Pesaro degli Orfei, near the church of San Beneto. The palazzo has been turned into a museum—now it's called the Palazzo Fortuny."

Demetra had bought the white Fortuny without even trying it on, and as soon as she returned to the Gritti, she shook it out, put it on and adjusted the pleats. Corey had told her that she looked beautiful, but Marshall's reaction was seared in her memory. "Christ! Why the hell did you buy that shapeless old rag? You look like a nursing mother in a thrift shop special. Where would you wear a thing like that?"

Now as she made up her face for the Feast of the Gods, she was emboldened by these Venetian memories. Despite Marshall's harsh words, the rediscovery of the dress gave her courage. With great care she slipped it over her head, pushing the tiny bubbles of *millefiori* Venetian glass through the corded satin loops on each shoulder of the delphos. From her wall safe she took a red leather box holding a garland of dark green enamel and gold ivy leaves sprinkled with tiny diamond dewdrops.

She fastened the circlet around her neck and looked at herself in the full-length mirror. Somehow, she looked even taller. The dress fanned out around the floor as it was supposed to, hiding her feet in high gold sandals that Marshall forbade her to wear because they made them almost equal in height. Enlivened by the dress, exhilarated by the music, she put her arms above her head in a flamenco dancer's pose and spun around to face herself again in the glass. For the first time in her life she thought she looked beautiful.

Marshall's voice blaring out from the intercom broke the spell.

"Are you ready yet? It's time to leave. You've got to be on time to greet the guests."

"I 'm ready, Marshall," she said, knowing that her decisive answer would shock him. He usually had to push to get her out of the house.

In a few moments he entered the bedroom to see for himself. "Christ almighty! You said you were ready! Why the hell are you wearing that? Where's the new Galanos?"

"I decided to wear *this* dress. Don't you remember the day I bought it in Venice?"

She saw the impatience in his eyes, felt the hostility he could no longer hide.

"Are you joking? After spending all that money on the Galanos!" Marshall leaned into her face. "What the hell's the matter with you? Why would you want to wear a secondhand rag bought in a junk shop! Christ only knows who sweated in it before you! Why do we always have to go through a crisis whenever we go out? You did the same thing to me the night of that dinner in Hancock Park, although, now that I come to think of it, this is the dress you should have worn to *that* party."

Then, in a slightly cajoling voice, he said. "Let's go, where's the Galanos? Put it on. We are going to be late. Come on, make it fast. Since you're the one who's supposed to be running the show, you've got to be there on time."

"I'm ready to leave and I'm not going to wear the dress you picked out for me. It wasn't my choice."

He raised his hand to slap her face.

She did not flinch. He dropped his hand. It was as though she were clothed in protective armor— silken, gossamer armor.

"Things are going to change around here when this party is over. You'd better believe it! Where's the necklace?"

"I didn't pick it up at the bank because I never intended to wear it." She had never liked the diamond *riviere*. The stones were too large and flashy.

"You're really looking for trouble tonight! You know fucking well that you're intentionally provoking me. If I weren't... "

She turned on her golden sandals and left him standing there, mouthing his threats.

With a dark green velvet wrap over her arm, she stepped down the spiral staircase, her hand tracing the curve of the aged mahogany banister. Demetra felt the smoothness of the polished wood under her palm as she moved down the steps.

As she set her foot upon the limestone floor of the foyer, a narrow ribbon of yellowed paper fluttered to the floor. Demetra, who considered herself clumsy, swooped as gracefully as a swan to pick it up. Written in an obviously Italian hand she read, "*Ricordo di Venezia, 3 gennaio 1947*." Strange! She wondered if that was the last time the dress had been worn. It must have been at the bottom of the satin bag all these years.

The Bentley was waiting for them, motor running, warming the soft-pelted interior on this damp, foggy June night. A strange wind blew from the northeast bending the poplars along the drive of Greenhill House. The dark trees made her recall her nightmare.

As they neared the hotel, Klieg lights crisscrossed from ground to sky. Wilshire Boulevard was choked with limousines, black and white chariots.

Inside the ballroom, the Olympians projected on the screen gazed out at the gods, goddesses, maenads, and satyrs entering the sylvan setting. The effect was so powerful that these jaded guests could not be blasé. For once there was nothing they could sink their teeth in, pull apart, dismember. Demetra stood before the scene and marveled. At each place was a facsimile of the painting. "Do you identify with any of us?" read the card. "Make merry with us tonight at The Feast of the Gods."

"How amusing how perfectly original!" The guests exclaimed as they were transported to the Mount Olympus *mise en scène* Demetra and her committee had created. The tone was set. Together, they would enact the Feast of the Gods.

The orchestra struck up *Some Enchanted Evening*. She saw Marshall move through the crowd looking for Marina, who had come as Venus, swathed in diaphanous golden gauze. Her blonde hair was raked back on her head by a diadem of translucent seashells, sprigs of coral and *diamanté* dewdrops. On her feet were flat gold kid sandals, their straps wrapped around her slender ankles. Each of her perfect toes was tipped in conch shell nacre.

Marina usually made Demetra feel ungainly. But not tonight. Tonight, as she looked across to Marshall and Marina, she felt empowered by the white silk hugging her body.

Soon the ballroom was filled with guests caught up in the spirit of the party's invitation. Diana Victor arrived in tiger-striped Saint Laurent chiffon-The Lady of the Beasts. Statuesque June Cooper wore a silver lamé caftan, her neck looped with immense gold beads, the high golden *polos* on her head making her even taller and more regal, just to make sure that no one would mistake her for anyone but Juno. The goddesses froze their smiles for the paparazzi.

Because Demetra was terrified to speak before large groups, she had asked June to welcome the guests. After an orchestra fanfare, June made her way to the stage. Before she uttered a word, she surveyed her subjects. All chattering stopped as she demanded the adulation and respect owed her.

"Welcome to the Feast of the Gods." A theatrical pause. "And Goddesses. Don't you think we should change the title of that painting? We goddesses need equal billing in this new age of feminine consciousness. We must all thank Demetra Killingsworth for chairing our annual Never Too Late to Learn benefit and for creating this incredible setting. And there are certainly many others to thank." Her eyes scanned the ballroom. Each one of those members was anxious for a crumb of recognition from their queen, but she singled out no one else. "As for the rest of you who worked on this event," she paused, "You all *know* who you are. Now, let us feast! Eat, drink and make merry in the manner of goddesses and gods!"

Applause and cheers.

Marshall leaned to Demetra, "Now that is what I call a perfect welcome speech. Short and to the point. Only you should have made it, Demi. Why the hell didn't you get up there yourself?"

She turned away and watched Marina McFarland slither to the dance floor with Harcourt who, because of his limp, rarely danced.

After the first course, Marshall's important Japanese customer invited Demetra to dance a slow, romantic fox trot. She had a hard-enough time dancing with Marshall, but with other men it was even worse. Now, sensing that Marshall was pinning his steely, uncompromising eyes on her, she stumbled on Mr. Tokita's toes at every turn. When she returned to the table, Marshall stood up, all bows and smiles to Mr. Tokita. Then, grasping her elbow so tightly it hurt, he led her back to the dance floor.

"Christ," he muttered when dancers surrounded them. "Why are you so goddam ned clumsy? I saw you trampling all over Mr. Tokita. See that fat lady dancing behind me? Watch her. She must weigh twice as much as you, yet she's as light as a feather."

She checked her tears by flashing a wide smile.

When the musicians took their break, she was relieved that dinner was about to be served. The food was hot, delicious, every course passed in elegant Russian service, while more white-gloved waiters poured and re-poured a champagne of excellent vintage.

Orange sorbet and coconut ambrosia, food for the gods, was the finale.

Soon the music became louder, more demanding, throbbing, as women twirled, swiveling like frenzied maenads. A glittering, faceted ball spun overhead, flecking the dancers with rainbow colors. Demetra watched the dancers admiringly, wishing that she too had been blessed by the Muse Terpsichore.

Marshall had left the table immediately after dessert and had not returned. Even though she knew he was still angry with her for not wearing the blue Galanos, she had assumed he would ask her to dance one more time, if only for the sake of appearances.

As Greek dancers, men dressed in starched white skirts, began their dance to the music of the *bouzouki,* she thought it might be a good time to steal way from the scene for a few minutes. Since the ladies' room would surely be crowded, she decided to retreat to her complimentary office where she could sit down and try to gather up the pieces of her shattered self. As she made her way through the crowded ballroom, the orchestra was blaring as the guests danced in glaze-eyed abandon.

She walked down the corridor and opened the door of the office.

There they were. On the floor. Marshall and Marina.

Although startled, Marina did not move, her gold gauze dress trailed behind her Demetra felt the frozen panic of dreams. She opened her mouth to scream, but no scream would come out.

Demetra fled. She did not cry. Besides disgust and betrayal, she felt terror. Marshall was so skillful at turning around the blame. What might he do to her for invading his privacy? Should she go home, or should she return to the ballroom and act as if nothing had happened?

Then a sudden calm came over her, as though she had just passed through the eye of the storm. She returned to the ballroom, took her place at the table, and did her best to converse with Mr. Tokita.

Instants later she saw Marshall and Marina weaving their way through the ecstatic dancers, Marina looking fresh, innocent, dewy with a sweet fixed smile on her face as she joined her husband, patting his arm, whispering in his ear.

A leering bacchanal pulled Demetra from her chair and dragged her to the dance floor. When he spun her rigid body around the room, she heard a distant roar becoming louder, louder, as he pressed his body against hers. The ballroom shuddered. Thousands of glass prisms clinked as twenty chandeliers shuddered. Fruit, plates, glasses tumbled off tables. Guests leaped from their chairs and ran for the exits.

The crowd panicked.

"*Kataclysmos!!*" cried the Greek dancers."*Kataclysmos!!*"

Marshall turned on the radio as soon as they got into the Bentley. The earthquake damage appeared more extensive in the flats of Beverly Hills, along East Wilshire and the Miracle Mile. He was concerned with only one thing—the extent of the damage at Greenhill House.

"It's a damn good thing I had the base for the Degas bolted to the floor, but you told me not keep the porcelain wired into the cabinets. If anything is broken it's your fault, Demi."

Your fault.

Whatever went wrong at Greenhill House, it seemed, was always her fault. She had taught herself to be blind to his blame.

As they turned into the driveway, the lanterns glowed, the electric gates parted. Greenhill House had its own generator. Marshall had also made sure that his house was bolted down upon an earthquake-proof foundation, one that would not sway with the earth whenever it trembled.

The front entrance of the house looked as it had when they had left it, the fountain still gurgling in the courtyard, the ornate brass knobs still gleaming on over scaled black lacquered double doors. Demetra noticed the long, jagged cracks in the stucco facade, but said nothing.

Marshall dashed past the Degas sculpture and then ran straight to the Long Gallery to check on his porcelain.

As Demetra flicked plaster flakes from the dancer's tutu, she thought how distant, how removed from the real world, the dancer seemed, just the way she was beginning to feel.

The staff was in the library, sorting hundreds of books that had tumbled to the floor. Demetra threw her arms around Milly.

"Not to worry, Mrs. Killingsworth—we're all fine—just a bit shaken up. Corey called from San Diego earlier this evening, just after you left for the party. She drove there with the Hadesson boy. Here's the telephone number." She pulled out a scrap of paper from her pocket. "But now the telephone lines aren't working."

"There seems to be no structural damage to this part of the house, Madam," Kevin said, "and the furniture seems intact with one exception." He pointed to the Russian porphyry urns on either side of the staircase. One had toppled from its base and shattered into shards the color of dried blood. Kevin began sweeping the sharp, jagged fragments into a heap.

"Not one single piece was broken. It's a damned good thing I didn't listen to you, Demi." Marshall said when he returned to the library. "If I had, my porcelain collection would have been destroyed, and it would have been your fault. You'd better check out the bedrooms with Milly while I inspect the rest of west wing with Kevin."

Milly took her arm as she made her way through the Long Gallery. Apollonia's words kept ringing in the head. *Fight. Be strong. Stay until the kataclysmos. The kataclysmos will be your sign. At that point you must leave your husband. Do not wait! Flee.* It was tonight or never. She made her decision. And there would be no turning back.

The bedroom was as pristine as Demetra always left it. The paper scrap she had saved in her shoe went back into the green satin bag along with the dress. Milly unclasped the necklace and Demetra placed it in its red Cartier box to return to the safe. Before turning the combination, she took out her passport and her personal savings account checkbook.

She put her arms around Milly and said determinedly, "Milly dear, I'm leaving Greenhill House. Please get those big duffel bags in Corey's closet and bring them to me. Then, while I am packing, try to find some way to distract him. Keep him in the west wing. He might try to stop me."

"I'll do my best, Madam."

She got into a pullover and jeans. When Milly returned with the bags, she stuffed them with practical clothes and several pairs of flannel-encased shoes. She packed the album of her daughter's baby pictures, her Daytimer into which she had tucked Corey's San Diego number, along with a travel kit filled with make-up, prescriptions, and toiletries. Then, with duffel straps slung over each shoulder, she walked out of her luxurious bedroom for what she hoped was forever.

At the top of the staircase she paused. Was there anything she had forgotten? The Fortuny gown! That had to come with her. She dashed back to the bedroom for the satin bag, holding it to her cheek for a moment before stuffing it into a side flap of the duffel bag. Then she made her way quietly down the staircase, her heart hammering so hard she felt short of breath.

"Where the fuck do you think you're going?"

She stood on the fifth step. Marshall bounded up the stairs and pounced, tugging the duffel bag straps off her shoulders.

Demetra screamed.

He kicked her. He pounded her with his fists. Then he pushed her. She fell onto the heap of porphyry fragments.

Kevin and Milly came running.

"Get the fuck out of here! This is our business!" Marshall bellowed.

Red oozed through Demetra's pierced sleeve.

"Jesus, Mary and Joseph—she's bleeding! Can't you see?" Milly shouted back. She helped Demetra to stand, then rolled the sleeve away from the wound. "Calm yourself, calm yourself, my dear—it's not so bad as it looks."

Although the gash was hardly more than an inch long, it was deep. The shard had barely missed an artery. "Find the first aid kit while I bind it, Milly," Kevin said, wrapping a clean handkerchief tight around the cut. "Is it painful, Madam? I don't want to hurt you."

She winced. Her body trembled; her face had lost its color. "Don't worry, Kevin. I'll be all right."

He helped her to the hall bench. She shivered when he unwrapped the tourniquet so that Milly could pour peroxide over the cut and swab it with disinfectant before Kevin bound it tight with sterile gauze.

Marshall finally spoke. "Take Mrs. Killingsworth to her to her bathroom— I don't want her bleeding all over that silk damask."

"You don't have to worry, Marshall. I am leaving. Right now!" she replied in a voice controlled by defiance.

He glared at her and then turned to Milly. "You heard what I just said. Take my wife to the bedroom!"

"She doesn't want to go to her room, Sir."

"Consider yourself fired!"

"Thank you, Sir." Milly put her arm around Demetra. "Don't worry, Madam. I have only stayed on because of you. Let me help you to the car."

Milly picked up the duffel bags, turned to face Marshall, "If you dare try to stop us, I swear on my deceased mother's Holy Missal that I'll call the police. And the *Los Angeles Times* as well. I shall tell them exactly what has been going on at Greenhill House. That would not be good for your precious public image, would it, Sir?

She turned to Demetra. "Let us be off then, Madam. Be sure to take the first aid kit with you. You'll need to change the dressing."

This time Marshall did not try to stop them. He snarled more obscenities under his breath. "You'll be sorry, Demi! Mark my words, you'll be sorry."

Corey's abandoned Mustang was still in the garage. Because Marshall considered it to be nothing more than a jalopy, the keys were always left in the ignition.

Milly stowed the bags in the trunk. "If you need me, you have my sister's Dublin address. She can always reach me."

Demetra's voice caught. "I don't know how to thank you, Milly—for all the devotion, all the loyalty you've given me. I'm sorry that you found yourself having to make such a choice."

"I'm grateful that you helped me make it," Milly said with tears in her eyes. "Please don't worry, Madam, this too shall pass." The women embraced.

Demetra, stepped into the car, and as the engine revved up, she reached for her bag and pulled out the Cartier box. "I want you to have the necklace, Milly. Sell it for the severance pay you deserve." She closed the door before Milly could say a word. As the engine purred, harrowing scenarios she had written over and over in her mind became a reality. Now she was relieved that the experience of her flight was far less violent, far less wrenching than her horrible imaginings.

***

Westwood had electricity. The receptionist at the residential hotel was sympathetic when Demetra made up a story about how she was afraid to spend the night without any electricity in her extensively damaged house.

"You're lucky. Not only do you have our last room, but it's one we just re-carpeted yesterday." He set down a thermos container of ice cubes, and pointed out the mini bar proudly, in case she needed a drink.

The suite was furnished in fifties motel style. Draperies and bedspread printed in an over-scaled orange and green banana frond print, the new speckled shag wall-to-wall carpeting exuding a liver-invading chemical odor that made her stomach turn.

As soon as she was alone, she peeled the wrapper from the soap sliver and scrubbed her hands. Then she uncoiled the blood-soaked bandage and wrapped her arm in a fresh dressing. She turned back the bedspread. Maybe it was her imagination, but the sheets did not look fresh. She drew them all the way back. A pus-stained corn pad lay nestled between the sheets. She snatched it up with a Kleenex and tossed it in the toilet, watching it eddy then disappear into the blue.

Now, as in her dream, she felt as though she had been cut away. Dismembered. When she worked in her garden, she often wondered how a plant might feel when it was yanked up and tossed onto a compost heap. She fell into the bed and curled up, knees pressed against her chest, as if to make her uprooted, shattered body whole. When she closed her eyes, scenes of her almost twenty teen year marriage began to unreel in her head. Demetra Duval ushering Marshall to a table at Les Deux Cités, where, at sixteen, Sister Claire had allowed her to take a part-time job as a hostess. Marshall telling her how impressed he was with her French and asking her for a date.

How handsome he was, how sophisticated he seemed. His was the first attention she had ever had from a man

Marshall on their wedding day, handsome in his dark blue suit, double gold wedding bands in his breast pocket. The pride on his face when he first held just-born Corey in his arms, marveling at how much his daughter looked like him. Happier times, those years in Seattle, before Los Angeles. How could she ever wipe out those memories? But why would she want to? She had been the wife of Marshall's youth, he the husband of hers, a man who was at once her father, lover, father of her daughter. But Marshall was no longer the person she had married. Corey would surely understand why she had to leave him. She would have to.

The decision was hers. Demetra's. Yes. There would be no turning back. She had to risk the unknown to be able to breathe again. She had been stifled far too long.

Before dawn she woke up in a sweat wondering where she was. Even though the room was drafty and cold, her face felt hot, the skin on one side of her face was distended with hives, numb and swollen. The lids were stuck together.

Staggering out of bed, she dumped the thermos of ice cubes into the sink, dunked a washcloth in the cold water, squeezed it out then pressed it against her eye until the cloth turned warm. Soon a new crop of minor anxieties surfaced to displace her real desolation.

What would happen to her greenhouse plants, especially the rare blue Himalayan poppy seedlings that she had finally made to germinate after months of refrigeration? She would have to send Kevin instructions for their care. She knew she could count on him.

As she stood by the window and watched the sun rise, it occurred to her that although she had never lived one day in her life alone, she had lived with loneliness all her life. Especially after she married Marshall.

Around seven o'clock, someone shoved a newspaper under the door. The earthquake was 5.6 on the Richter scale according to the headlines. Since the epicenter was at least eighty miles away, damage had not been as extensive as feared.

Except, of course, at Greenhill House, where the damage was irreparable.

"Dad called me earlier this morning. He is *furious* with you. He said you humiliated him in front of the staff."

Demetra forced herself to be silent.

"Are you all right? Dad told me that you went completely hysterical—that you fought him and fell onto the floor and cut your arm on the broken urn."

"Don't worry, I'm all right." Demetra had always hidden Marshall's physical abuses from their daughter. Even now she wanted to shield Corey from the truth to protect her from disillusionment. Corey's voice took on a hardness Demetra had never heard before. She sounded like Marshall. "You've got to get back to Greenhill House or else Dad might never forgive you."

"Forgive me? For what?"

"Remember how you used to tell me that we didn't have any family but one another?"

"I do. But I can never go back to Greenhill House."

Corey raised her voice. "Please do not reject us, Mom. You keep talking about finding your parents, but can you not see how you are walking out on your *real* family. We're all you have."

"Listen to me Corey—*please*."

"Mom—I'll be moving out of Westwood tomorrow. Please don't ask me why."

"Where are you going?"

"Downtown L.A. We have rented a loft. But don't try to find me."

Demetra heard the phone click. She was trembling. When she stood, her world started to spin. She gagged. The rug's pernicious chemical odor had permeated every pore in her body. She bolted into the bathroom and heaved bile into the whirling blue abyss. As she stared into the vortex, she felt as though she were being drawn into the devouring whirlpool of Charybdis.

Book 11

CHAPTER IV

Most people were not convinced that Demetra's decision to divorce Marshall Killingsworth was the right one. How could she possibly be happier, they would ask, without that mansion of hers, without that good-looking husband, without the power that so much money brings?

Two days later she took the first step. Garland, Farquhar and Lean's sleek chrome and plush offices took up the ninth floor of a high-rise in Century City. Monica Garland, one of the first recipients of the Never Too Late scholarships, had become well-known as the organization's defender. Now in her forties, she was considered a tough adversary in the courtroom.

She greeted Demetra warmly, "Because of your reputation within the group, I feel as though I already know you. Now, tell me, Demetra, why you're here and what you want me to do for you."

"I want a divorce from Marshall Killingsworth."

"Are you sure? Despite my profession, I must always begin by saying I don't really approve of divorce. I see what it does to people. You have a daughter, don't you?"

"Yes. Corey is eighteen and lives away from home."

"How does she feel about the divorce?"

"Sadly, she's against it. But I've made up my mind."

"Do you have enough money to live on? In a personal account?"

"A few years ago, I decided to save part of what Marshall gave me in a secret bank account. What I have saved is not all that much, considering his enormous wealth, but it should be enough to live on for a while. I would like to buy myself a new station wagon. And I hope to use some of the money to open an antique shop. It's something I've always dreamed about."

"Having heard about your home I'm assuming that you mean fine French furniture. Amassing that kind of an inventory could mean millions."

"I don't want that kind of shop."

"Have you thought about working for someone else for a while to get some experience?"

"Experience?" Demetra smiled and shook her head. "I've had plenty of experience. These past twenty years I *have* been working for 'someone else. A tyrant."

After the meeting Demetra returned to the hotel and tried to reach Corey again. No luck. She was still reeling from their telephone confrontation. She heard her voice break as she left a message on Corey's machine. "You probably need your car so if you do, I'll call Kevin to come pick it up here at the hotel. Please, *please* return my message. I am desperate to talk to you. I am scared. I really need your support. I love you so much, Corey."

Then she dialed the telephone number for the convent in Minnesota. No such number. It had closed two years ago. When she finally reached the office of the Diocese, she was told that all inquiries were to be made strictly in writing to the parent order in

Toulouse. No telephone inquiries were ever accepted. She found some writing paper in the desk drawer and wrote a letter to the Convent. After sealing the envelope, she was starving. It was twenty-four hours since she had eaten. The receptionist sent her the menu from Gina's Pizzeria around the corner. Marshall had always derided pizza as "guinea food," but now, feeling defiant, she ordered a large margherita and, while watching Masterpiece Theatre, enjoyed every wedge. Finally, she fell asleep. When she got out of bed in the morning, she felt capable enough to lease a car and look at apartments in downtown Los Angeles.

If you lived here, you would already be home by now! Call 213-377-3777.

So boasted the banner advertising a housing complex overlooking the Harbor Freeway. The apartments were walking distance to the Music Center, the cultural and social center of Los Angeles. It had occurred to Demetra that the cluster of colonnaded stone buildings resembled an ancient Greek agora, with its nearby temples dedicated to light, power, and justice.

She leased the Bunker Hill furnished rental by the month. Monica had advised her not to use her savings to buy a house until she was sure where, in this mega-metropolis, she wanted to live. At least here she would be close to Corey, wherever she was since Corey lived in her downtown loft. With luck she might even run into her somewhere.

The small apartment was clean, bright, with simple but comfortable furniture and a well-equipped kitchen. Demetra craved the security of shelves lined with food, so that afternoon she headed to the Central Market where she bought all she needed and more. In the evening she made gallons of vegetable soup for the freezer while listening to opera tapes. She also felt the need for frugality. Since the rent was more than she thought she could afford, she began to feel those old gnawing money worries again, the kind that used to keep her awake at night. She remembered the times the telephone was cut off and the visits from threatening bill collectors, when Marshall risked, then lost everything in his first business venture, and their first home was repossessed.

One morning a week later Demetra had her second appointment with Monica Garland.

"What's your apartment like?" Monica asked, handing her a cup of coffee.

Demetra smiled. "It's quite different from Greenhill House. From the living room window, I have a view of freeway traffic, from the bedroom a close-up of concrete and windows. It's fine for a while but I need a house with a yard, a place where I can dig and watch seedlings push through the earth."

Monica nodded. Her face was grave. "Any news from or about Corey?"

Demetra shook her head and began to cry. "She seems so near and yet so far."

Monica got up from her desk and came over to put her arm around Demetra. "I'm sure she's fine. She is probably more like you than you think. By that I mean strong, tenacious—and very sensible."

Demetra wiped her eyes and, regaining her composure, said resolutely, "What's the next step?"

"I've been working on the disclosure, making sure your husband has come across with everything," Monica replied. "So far it does not look very good, I'm afraid. Let me read this to you."

"Furniture, paintings, sculpture—all owned by the MK Art Investment Company. Cars—all owned by the parent company."

"I suppose that includes the Degas ballet dancer."

Monica nodded. "At the very top of the list."

"So be it. The Degas would have been incongruous with my new life. I could never afford the insurance."

Monica went on. "Your couture clothing, your jewelry was all paid for by the MK Art Investment as well. Including Never Too Late annual dues, your books, even your cassettes. Almost everything it seems was or is owned by Marshall's business or was written off by his over-leveraged company."

Demetra slumped back in her chair as if the wind had been knocked out of her.

"And, to complicate things even further, I was surprised to learn that Greenhill House is in Corey's name. How come?"

Demetra nodded. "Because we had to fly together so often, Marshall decided to put the house in her name just in case something happened to us. Corey was only twelve or thirteen. Since there were no grandparents—and Marshall had only a few living relatives—it seemed like a good idea."

Monica shook her head and turned the ledger page. "You must know about Corey's foundation and her trust fund."

"I always encouraged Marshall to put as much as possible into the fund. I co-signed for them," she said defensively.

"You must also know about the insurance policies for which she is beneficiary. None of those monies can be divided, Demetra."

"I wouldn't want them to be."

"Your husband was very clever. The more money in Corey's name, the less money you can get your hands on, the less money to be divided should the occasion ever arise. Also, fewer taxes to pay. I'm sure he's got a wad in a secret Swiss bank account."

"He was always flying to Geneva or Zurich, but I know he doesn't have any factories there."

"You will, however, be relieved to know that Marshall's lawyer claims that he won't contest the divorce. In fact, I've been assured that he wants to facilitate matters."

Demetra sighed. "That's one hurdle overcome, at least."

"Still, I wish there were more I could do about the settlement. I am afraid you are going to have to make some serious financial adjustments in your life. Of course, we can always appeal."

Demetra sat up and straightened her back against the chair. "I never had any money when I was growing up and precious little when we were first married. It might be a challenge, even a relief, to try to make it on my own."

Could she really live *without* his money? But, more importantly, could she live *with* it?

She left Monica's office at ten-fifteen. She got into the car, strapped herself in, and exited the parking garage turning on to the Avenue of the Stars.

She clicked on the radio. Bach. The Brandenburg # 5. She raised the volume so that its harmonies and order could help fill the hollow she felt inside.

Come on—move, Demetra. Move. You have got to keep moving. You might even see Corey crossing a street.

Instead of heading for the Robertson Boulevard entrance to the Santa Monica Freeway, her usual fast route, she found herself roaming the vast gridiron of Los Angeles surface streets. Destination unknown. Finally, she turned on to Wilshire.

She stopped at almost every red light but did not notice.

She passed, but never saw the Los Angeles County Museum of Art, the Tar Pits.

She kept moving. Past the villas of Fremont Place, past the Masonic Scottish Rite Auditorium.

She kept moving. The motion kept the emotions at bay.

When, in the distance, she glimpsed the landmark art deco tower of Bullock's Wilshire, she realized how far she had driven.

At last she arrived at Wilshire and Flower. Not far from her new apartment. She drove past the public library, the California Club, past her favorite Caravan Books, past Brooks Brothers, the Biltmore Hotel. Finally, she turned onto Sixth Street. She remembered that the Los Angeles Flower Market was somewhere near Sixth and Wall. She had never been there before. Why not go there right now?

Turning quickly onto Wall Street, she found a parking space and hurried across the street to the building where cottage industry growers sold their wares. Inside, the counters were massed with lilacs and peonies.

"Do you grow these yourself?" she asked the young boy who was clearing up, getting ready to close shop since it was almost noon. "I've never been able to grow either peonies or lilacs here."

"They're grown in Cherry Valley where it gets real cold at night, sometimes heavy frosts, sometimes snow. That's how come you can't get 'em to grow around here. The earth has to freeze before they can bloom."

"I'd like a bunch of each, please." She paused. "How much do they cost?"

"Six dollars for the lilacs. Eight for the peonies. Do you have a resale license?"

"I've applied for one, but it hasn't arrived yet."

"Then I gotta charge you tax."

"Of course."

He wrapped them and handed them to her.

She buried her nose in the newsprint wrapping. The sweet, healing scent was balm to her soul. It occurred to her that so long as she could afford to buy a bouquet of peonies and lilacs, she was a rich woman.

She found herself driving through Chinatown, onto the Hill Avenue ramp that spills onto the Pasadena Freeway. Hugging its old, wide curves, she took it all the way, continuing up Arroyo Parkway, then turning left on Colorado Boulevard toward the Norton Simon museum. She had read about the recent acquisition, the Goya *Doña* in black lace embellished with jet beads. But the chains were across the entrance. It was Monday.

She drove up Linda Vista, past grand live oaks, and tucked-away ranch houses, finally arriving at Foothill, the boulevard that stretches north to the San Gabriel Mountain range. She drove through Flintridge, La Cañada, La Crescenta, toward Tujunga and Sunland, towns she had heard of but never seen, even though they were well within a fifteen-mile radius of Greenhill House.

The radio announced a smog alert. Before long, it seemed as though the surrounding mountains had vanished into sick, thick air. She kept driving.

Commerce Street, Tujunga. The sign over the door read *Chockablock Tujunga Junque*. She slowed down. The window was crammed with cloudy pressed glass, battered baskets, dented aluminum coffee pots, blackened iron skillets, rolls of emerald green fuzz-flocked wallpaper, a cuddly felt reindeer dressed in red and white polka dots, a plastic ice bucket emblazoned *Souvenir of Atlantic City*.

Not very promising. She was just about to drive off. Instead she jumped out of the car and opened the door.

Inside, worse yet. Paperback books piled high on a table next to stacks of fusty, faded coverlets and blankets, outdated light fixtures, racks of used clothes smelling of cleaning fluid. No one seemed to be around so she could make a quick getaway. She reached for the doorknob.

"Anything special you're looking for, ma'am?" A man's voice rose above the piled high counters. The elderly man came forward. "I'm just putting away some collectibles—my neighbors' consignments from the Senior Citizens' home where I live. Would you like to have the first peek?"

She did not have the heart to leave without looking. He folded back the cardboard box to let her rummage through pairs of salt and pepper shakers, plastic flowers, bits of crockery, glass, tarnished brass. At the bottom of the box she caught a glimpse of green. Her heart raced. She held her breath as she drew out a mottled green frog carved from nephrite, like a Fabergé frog Marshall had once been offered in Paris. "I hate frogs," he had announced. "Frogs, even Fabergé ones, give me the creeps."

Marshall's taste in Fabergé ran to more impressive gold and jewel-encrusted objects.

She placed the little frog in her palm and let her fingers stroke its cool, smooth skin, run over its bulging ivory eyes.

"Sure looks like a genuine Fabergé piece, doesn't it?" he asked.

'You must have been reading my mind."

"The lady next door told me she bought it from a stone carver in Mexico City years ago."

"How much does it cost?"

"$50.00. I'm sure she paid less than a dollar for it in those days, so she's making a real good profit after my small commission."

"I'll take it."

She paid him the cash he asked for. He blanketed the frog in cotton batting and placed it respectfully in a bright blue Tiffany box.

The next few weeks she pored over classified ads, spent hours scouring antique flea markets and thrift shops. From Long Beach to Thousand Oaks, from Altadena to Garden Grove she searched. Leaving the apartment in the early morning, she returned only after the shops had closed and she had stored her larger finds in a rental storage bin. Finding small treasures for her new business seemed to subdue her sadness. In searching for *things*, she sensed she was acting out the search for her parents. At Goodwill she found a nest of Chinese export black and gold lacquered tables and at the Pasadena Salvation Army a cache of Boucher costume jewelry that looked so genuine that at first glance she was convinced it might be Cartier or Van Cleef.

After dinner, while listening to opera tapes on her Walkman, Demetra cleaned and polished each object, mended, washed, starched, and ironed every piece of old linen and lace. At the convent, the nuns had taught her to how to mend and embroider and to care for linen. When she opened her shop, she planned to have a corner reserved for beautiful old textiles.

Six weeks had passed since she left Greenhill House. Still no call from Corey. And the letter from the convent was taking longer to arrive than she had planned. Soon she found herself regulating her entire day around the mail delivery. Some days she would drive back to check the mail. She pictured herself tearing the letter open, but, as time went by, she imagined another scene, one in slow motion. First, she would put the envelope to her nose, then she would study its postmark, its stamp. Then calmly, deliberately, cherishing every gesture, she would open it with an antique mother-of-pearl handled letter-opener, one bought for that very purpose. She tried to block her greatest fear from her mind—the fear that her mother and father might be dead.

CHAPTER V

If a member of Never Too Late to Learn came upon her shop on Melrose, she would never have believed that it belonged to Demetra Killingsworth. At *Choses* there was no fine furniture, no rare porcelain, no Georgian silver. Here there were no priceless Old Master paintings, drawings, or sculpture. *Choses* meant "things" in French. But the implication was more: this was the new life Demetra *chose* for herself.

She had, in six months of leaving Greenhill House, and with very little money, stocked her shop, and with a few gallons of paint and a roller completely transformed the space, painting the walls, stenciling the floor. All by herself.

Choses' mullioned windows were tassel-swaged with vintage velvet portieres bought from a house off West Adams in downtown Los Angeles. Faux bamboo étagères and oak Welsh cupboards displayed majolica plates and pitchers. She heaped needlepoint and Victorian beaded cushions on a divan she had upholstered in paisley shawls, poured rose water into silver-topped antique crystal bottles. Paper lace valentines and postcards she tucked into English toast racks.

In an attic trunk in West Covina she had found some Carrickmacross lace which she tossed over a comfortable Victorian tufted chair where she could sit and read if there were no customers.

Farrell Minton, the Arts and Crafts dealer, owned the shop next door. His shop window was sparsely dressed in masculine Stickley furniture, Dirk Van Erp brass and bronze objects, in contrast to the more romantic Victorian-Edwardian profusion of *Choses*. The day she had moved in, Farrell came by with a pot of hyacinths and welcomed her to the neighborhood. He was slender, rangy, red-haired and spoke in a lazy Alabama drawl, and although he was usually dressed in coat and tie, he still managed to look casual. Demetra guessed that he might be about forty-five.

"I remember seeing you in Jack Carlson's shop in Laguna Beach. If I'm not mistaken, you bought that fabulous Regency penwork cabinet from him. Your taste has taken a real turn!"

"My taste and my pocketbook. I'm separated now."

"But your voice tells me that you're a lot happier. I hope you don't mind my saying so, but the very first time I saw you looking over the shop with the real estate agent, I recognized your face."

"I used my maiden name on my business cards, hoping that no one around here would associate me with Marshall." She twisted the button on her cardigan until she felt the string snap.

"Come on, don't kid yourself! Everyone knows who you are. Most of the dealers, anyway. Maybe some of your customers don't."

"May I have a look at your shop?" she asked.

"Come right on over. You know, we should make some sort of an arrangement to keep an eye on each other's stuff," he said holding the door open for her.

She looked around. A large painting of eucalyptus trees and

smoky purple mountains hung on one wall. "I come across these California *plein air* paintings all the time. If you would like, I will let you know whenever I see one that might be worth buying," she said.

"I'll do the same for you." He took a small red address book from his jacket and wrote in her apartment telephone. She wrote his in her Day Timer.

One evening a week later he called at home to tell her that he had just come across some seashell and seaweed American majolica.

She was pleased. "My favorite pattern—do you think it's a good buy?"

"Sure do. I hardly ever see the stuff around anymore."

"Please put a hold on it and I'll go by the shop tomorrow. Thanks, Farrell." Obviously, he wanted to be her friend. And Demetra felt in need of a friend. When they met again, she would tell him all about Corey. And about her letter to the convent.

One afternoon, while listening to Bizet's The Pearl Fishers, she arranged what she called a "tablescape" a collection of little carved quartz turtles marching across a lawn sprouted from wheat seeds she'd sown on cotton batting, the little green stone frog with ivory eyes floating on a real lily pad in a shallow Rookwood bowl. Since the frog was her first purchase, she had decided to keep it for good luck.

She glanced out the window. A long white limousine had stretched itself out in front of *Choses*.

The chauffeur opened the door and out stepped Ethel Hadesson, Basil Hadesson's wife, followed by Diana Victor, in black from head to shiny patent leather toe. Diana had become Ethel's new best friend since Basil had bought a Gulfstream jet.

Ethel, whose face and body showed the lizard-like effects of lounging around too many pools in Palm Springs and Vegas, was a vision in Pepto-Bismol pink, her favorite color. The boxy Chanel jacket hid her wide hips, but that was all it did for her. Her hair, processed the color of Rice Crispies, looked as if might snap crackle and pop should anyone touch it.

Diana threw her arms around Demetra. "Darling, how nice to see you again! June and I missed you at the opening night of Turandot. Ethel and I decided to pop in for a glimpse of your shop. Ethel is a new member of Never Too Late. You do know each other, don't you?"

Demetra folded her arms and unconsciously took a step backward, "My daughter and Ethel's son are...friends."

"*Used* to be," flashed Ethel, as though she were relieved. "They broke up a few weeks ago." Her heavily made-up lips set in a smirk, she picked up a lace pillow, turning it this way and that as she pretended to look for a price tag.

Elated, Demetra squelched the urge to ask what happened.

A long silence. Diana's jet bead eyes darted from corner to corner. "Your resignation was the main topic of yesterday's board meeting: we were all so distressed. You are *sorely* missed, Demetra. By the way, those arrangements you did for The Feast of the Gods benefit were *divine.*" She pronounced it *deveen.*

"I heard they were *amazing*—fabulous, *totally* fabulous," Ethel piped up, "We were in Vegas so we couldn't go, but Diana told Basil and *I* all about them."

Your grammar isn't correct, Ethel— it's not "Diana told Basil and I," it's Diana told Basil and me. "Demetra thought but didn't say. Instead she turned away and murmured, "Feel free to browse, ladies. I have some work to finish in 'the office." She retreated to the back room, happily mulling over Corey's break-up with Harley Hadesson. Maybe it would not be much longer before she would have a call from her daughter.

Meanwhile, in the shop, Diana and Ethel were exclaiming over the merchandise. Even the opera chorus was not loud enough to mask Ethel's squeals. "Oh, look! How *cu-u-ute!* Whaddaya think, Di, do you think I oughta get it?"

"You don't really need that ugly little *grenouille*. It's *not* a quality accessory," Diana replied. "Now if you want a really fine *objet de vertu I'll take* you to *La Vielle Russie* next time we're in New York. Or the next time we fly to London I'll introduce you to Wartski."

Demetra wondered what it was out there that was not up to Ethel's quality. She had seen magazine lay-outs of Ethel's bogus Italian, palazzo-sized house with its wall to wall shags and Las Vegas style family room lined up with slot machines.

A few minutes later Diana peeked into the office. "We've got to move on. There is an important meeting at The Secret Garden. The King of Spain is coming to town, and we're preparing the A-list guest list for a magnificent, world- class formal dinner."

As Diana opened the door for Ethel, she said, "Too bad we cannot add your name to the list, Demetra, but you know how it is. Marshall will be attending."

Demetra smiled and said, "Thank you for thinking of me. I have dined with the King of Spain. He's a charming man." And certainly not the snob you are, Diana, she thought.

"Let's have lunch one of these days." Diana said holding the door open to allow Ethel to sweep out. "Why don't I give you a ring as soon as all the festivities are over?"

Sure. Same old insincere Diana. So, what did it matter that she, Demetra, was no longer on the Los Angeles A-List. She was relieved to be past all that. It simply did not matter anymore.

To hell with them!

The limo drove off.

As she went back to complete the table-setting, she saw at once that something was missing. The little green frog with the ivory eyes no longer floated on the lily pad in the Rookwood pottery bowl.

Now this did matter!

Farrell had warned her about shoplifters.

So it *must* have been Ethel. But was it worth having a confrontation with her? Basil Hadesson was a dangerous man.

CHAPTER VI

"House for rent near Music Center" read the advertisement in the Los Angeles Times. "Private situation in secluded wooded grove, reached by an unpaved road. Please write: Box 386, LA. Describe your needs concisely. Perhaps my house will suit you; good rental for proper, loving tenant."

Thinking that the house might be in the Mt. Washington area between Pasadena and downtown Los Angeles, Demetra answered the ad.

Dear Owner of the House in the Woods,

I have been looking for a small house and garden to rent in downtown Los Angeles, preferably close to the Music Center, not too far from the antique shop I've just opened on Melrose. This fall I hope to work, part time, towards a degree in art history at USC. At present I am living in a temporary furnished apartment. If you would like to interview me, please call 213-271-1100 or write to the above address.

Yours truly,
Demetra Duval

In a few days she found a terse message on her answering machine. "H.T. Skidmore, calling here. If you would like to see the house, come by at 4:00 on Friday."

She copied the address.

On the day she set out for her appointment, the rain had not yet stopped, those early autumn rains that last for days, pounding hard, soaking deep into needy, summer-baked earth.

She turned off the freeway at Echo Park driving by past *botanicas* and *carnicerias* following Mr. Skidmore's directions scotch-taped to the dashboard:

Avenue 51 all the way up, past Elysian Park. Take the left fork at the top, and when you see the dense trees and a row of mailboxes, you will know you have arrived. Follow the unpaved road to the third house, the one with the blue door.

She had not expected to come upon the thicket of live oaks so suddenly. The unpaved road was only a wide muddy footpath, carved with wheel ruts and with her wide station wagon she was not sure she would get through. The wheels balked as they crushed fallen branches littering the lane. Although it was only late afternoon, the autumn sky was already dark. A lantern shone over the door of Mr. Skidmore's house half-hidden by a stand of Italian umbrella pines. The house was built in the Craftsman adobe style, the idealized bungalow, the California Dream.

She rang the bell, heard carpet slippers shuffling, then a bolt sliding out of its hasp. The door was opened by a man with a shock of white hair, a man older than she would have expected judging from the voice on the telephone. "Demetra Duval?"

She extended her hand. His clasp was firm. "Thank you for giving me the chance to interview for your rental."

"Come in, won't you?"

She scraped her muddy boots against the stoop.

"Don't worry, my floors are all gym-finished hardwood," Mr. Skidmore said peering down at her through steel-rimmed glasses that had slipped down over his nose. He was dressed in a plaid flannel shirt and baggy corduroy trousers.

As she followed him through the entry alcove into the living room, she guessed he was well over eighty years old. Music periodicals were strewn over the tables, *Opera News* magazines and *New York Times* "*Arts*" and *Leisure*" sections were stacked everywhere.

"Please sit down and let us talk for a few minutes. I want to tell you about the house to find out if it is for you or not. Then I will show you around later, if you'd like."

She sat on the beat-up leather hassock. "I've passed the freeway turn off sign for Elysian Fields many times, but I'd no idea this compound existed. It's like being in another world."

"You should see the city view at night, through the trees. Here you are, surrounded by dense woods, yet you look down upon a sea of twinkling lights, and, if it is a clear night, you are beneath a sky full of stars. You would never believe you are right in the middle of downtown Los Angeles. Elysian Park gives us privacy that's such a luxury these days." He smiled. "We like to think we're the best kept secret in town."

"When these houses were built in the early thirties, Brendan Gill, the architecture critic, thought it an enchanted place. So do all of us who live up here. So please do not tell too many people about it, just your closest friends, should you decide to rent the house."

Surely, he would be the one to decide whether she was the right tenant. Perhaps he was trying to read her mind, or test her out, she thought.

"I think you'd like it up here—it's very peaceful. We never have any problems. A few years ago, one of the neighbors had a TV set stolen, but other than that, there have been no major burglaries, no violence, if you're worried about that sort of thing."

She did not dare tell him that since she left Greenhill House, there was already far less violence in her life.

"Please allow me to show you around. You'll see that the place needs a good paint job, and you'll have to buy yourself a new stove and refrigerator."

"Are you moving out of state?"

"I'm off to Ojai to live with my sister. She is all involved with the local music festival and I will be helping her out—finding the right musicians, choosing the programs. But I don't intend to sell this place just yet."

"I'm not looking for a house to buy. I'm just starting out in business."

"The antique shop on Melrose that you mentioned in the letter?"

She nodded. "Is your work close by?"

He touched a match to the bowl of his pipe and took a deep drag. "I work at home, as a music historian and critic. I free-lance for a lot of these periodicals you see piled up around here." He told her that his family was originally from Boston, that his father had moved to California to work with Collis Huntington, the railroad tycoon, in the twenties.

"So you've decided to go back to school?" he asked.

"I'll be taking a course in Renaissance Art at USC."

"That was one of the things I liked about your letter. The other was your wish to be near the Music Center. *Music* was the magic word." He picked up a copy of *Opera News*. "Music is—has always been my life. Can you believe that I had twenty-three replies last week? And they keep arriving every day."

"I hope I have half a chance to rent your house."

"You've more than that. It's yours if you want it. Come on, let me show you around before you make your final decision. We'll have a look at the kitchen first."

There were no dishes in the sink, but the room, though neat, needed a floor-to-ceiling scrub. Mr. Skidmore was clearly oblivious to the spattered grease over the stove, to the grimy cupboards and split butcher-block counters. An old gas range was stacked with black iron skillets; singed potholders stuck to the refrigerator.

"There's a nice-size bedroom, and my little office can be used as another bedroom if you like. The niche in the living room where I keep my big worktable is supposed to be your dining area." A hooded fireplace took up part of the other wall. "It has a gas jet to start it up. There is plenty of wood in the bin outside. You will need a fire here at night. The temperature can drop thirty degrees in a day. You'll feel the cool nights up here under the trees, sometimes even in summer."

"I like having a real fire. I used to live in a house where there were only gas fires with fake logs and heaps of fake cinders!"

He laughed. "Some people will do anything for effect!"

His bedroom was sparsely furnished with a tubular brown metal bed covered with a faded patchwork quilt. The closets were small but cedar-lined, as he pointed out with pride. There was one bathroom, obviously recently modernized.

"Well, what do you think, Mrs. Duval?"

"I like it very much. I can imagine living here."

"You wouldn't be afraid to drive up here alone at night?"

She shook her head. "I'll get used to it."

"You'll get to know the neighbors. I'm the oldest one up here by far." They discussed the rent. It was far less than the small apartment near Melrose she had been considering. She inquired about a lease. He wanted three years.

"When would you like to move in?"

"As soon as possible. Shall we set the date for two weeks? "

"I can be out of here in ten days. The movers are all signed up to come and pack up my books. They tell me one day should do it."

"That sounds about right to me." They shook hands. The house in the woods was hers.

After a week of scrubbing, disinfecting, rolling on fresh white paint coat after coat, the cottage began to look and feel as though it belonged to her. She had scoured grease from the walls and ceiling, sanded woodblock counters, soaked black-crusted stove burners in ammonia water. By the end of the third day, the kitchen was clean enough to cook in.

Her arms ached, but her heart glowed after polishing the second-hand furniture with linseed oil, turpentine, and beeswax polish concocted from a recipe once given to her by a Williamsburg curator. She pinned Indian flowered and paisley spreads from Pier One on the old sofa and club chairs. With a buffing machine rented from the supermarket, she polished the hardware floors until they gleamed.

She felt like Snow White mopping up the cottage in the woods and remembered her own convent childhood. When winter was over and the empty coal bins in the basement were swept out, the nuns allowed the orphans to transform the dusty cubicles into "summer houses."

The girls would happily sweep out the bins and, after they had scrubbed them with soapy water, they decorated the "walls" with scraps of fabric remnants and magazine cutouts. She always dreaded that day in late September when the nuns ordered the girls to clear out the bins. Then the trucks would drive up and surly men would shove coal chutes through the basement windows. Sometimes she cried as the jet lumps rumbled down the metal slide, gradually filling their "summer houses" with black from floor to ceiling.

Now it did not matter that her fingernails were splitting, that her hands were rough and chafed. She felt the same satisfaction she had felt as a child scrubbing out the coal bin. Cleansed, purified. As though she had been reborn, as though she was Snow White.

From time to time a "runner" dropped by *Choses* to peddle treasures gleaned from out of -town swap meets or the classified tag sales; old ladies in retirement homes came by to sell cherished treasures—yellowed lace fans, bugle-beaded shimmy dresses from the twenties, costume jewelry from the thirties and forties.

She'd read somewhere that collecting was sublimation, sometimes for sex, but for her it was more like a setting of things in harmony, gathering up bits and pieces from an engulfing chaos to create another world of her own—a world where things of disparate and distant origins were juxtaposed in an original way to give the illusion of order, the notion of oneness in her micro-universe.

One evening a few weeks later, Farrell came by *Choses* for the early dinner she had ordered from a take-out place in nearby Thai Town.

"Still no news from Corey?"

She shook her head. "You'd be the first to hear."

As they ate the sticky honey noodles with nephrite jade chopsticks provided by Farrell, he said, "You used to amuse the trade, Demetra. The top dealers knew you were a real quick study. All you needed was a few weeks and you seemed to be an expert on any subject. Ted Granger, the auctioneer, is an old friend of mine and told me that you had an incredible eye."

"That's high praise, coming from him." She kept rolling and re-rolling the edge of her napkin. "But no wonder he was so complimentary. He knocked down the hammer on many of our purchases. Including a Degas bronze ballet dancer."

"I was surprised to hear that Marshall intends to marry Marina McFarland."

Even with her impending divorce, learning that Marshall was going to marry Marina thrust a knife in her side. She put down her chopsticks and never picked them up again.

"Yeah—she's supposedly after Marshall to simplify the place," he said, "I hear she is not buying anything, though. Just selling stuff. At least that is the message the tom-toms are beating along Melrose Place and La Cienega. My friend who owns a fabric shop in the Blue Whale told me there is some Greenhill House furniture coming up at Christie's New York."

"I wish her luck," she said feeling her stomach tighten up, her back stiffen against the chair.

"Luck? Come on, now! Be honest with yourself."

She shrugged. "She may be just the kind of woman Marshall needed. He has set his sights high on the social ladder. That's why he didn't fight the divorce."

"Do you want to talk about her?"

"Maybe...someday."

"Why not now?"

She took a deep breath. "May I have some wine?"

He poured her another glass. "How do you feel about Marina?"

"You mean how does she *make* me feel?" She folded her arms as if to contain herself. "Inferior, inadequate. She always has. Marina loves men while I have always been afraid of them. Except for you, Farrell,"

He fidgeted with the sunglasses in his jacket pocket. "If you don't mind my asking, how is it that you're not better off financially?"

"For one, Marshall isn't as rich as he seems. Most of the property was owned by his over-leveraged business. Besides, I decided that to be free, truly free, I had to sever all ties with him and his money. Whatever I receive in settlement I will put into trust for Corey. Luckily, I opened a savings account a few years ago, so at least I had enough to start a business. And I still have enough to live on until I make a success of it."

She saw the disbelief on his face.

"You must think it's cavalier of me to talk about money this way—it may be hard for anyone else to understand, but I don't want any of his money."

"Why the hell not? You're due your fair share."

"I have a fixation about it. I know if I were using his money, I'd still have him watching over my shoulder trying his best to control me."

"Well, you're really something else! The first divorced woman I've ever heard of who turned her back on money."

"I was around it long enough to learn that it wasn't money that made me happy."

"For those of us who've never had any, that's kind of hard to understand."

"Maybe it's irrational, but that's the way I feel."

"Does your daughter know about the trust you'll put in her name?"

"No. I won't tell her until she's twenty-five."

"When did you speak to her last?"

"In June. I have not seen or spoken to her since. I never told her about the women." She blushed. "Or how I'd found him with Marina..."

"You don't have to go there. I get the picture."

"Corey blamed me for walking out. I tried convincing her that it was Marshall I was leaving, not her. I had never expected her to react that way. I'd hoped she'd understand." Her voice faltered. "But she wouldn't listen. Oh, Farrell," she began to cry. "What did I say, what did I do that was so terrible?"

He reached for her hand and held it tight. "It's you who has to get over a rejection. Why do you want to take all the blame for what went wrong between the two of you? Where is she now?"

"I've tried tracking her down. One of her girlfriends told me that when she and her boyfriend broke up, she took off for San Bernardino, so I drove there the same day, but I just missed her. She'd moved on from the antique flea market where supposedly she had a stand."

"Like mother, like daughter."

Demetra eyes were pensive. "Strange. That never occurred to me! Maybe she does have a little of me, after all." She smiled. "But that's *not* the way she likes to see herself. It is more likely that she's run out of money and had to sell things. She probably couldn't find an acting job."

He laughed. "Who knows, maybe she'll turn up at the Pasadena Rose Bowl Swap Meet one of these Sundays."

"Farrell, have you ever been married?"

"Yes." He paused. "I'm married now."

"You never told me! You don't wear a wedding ring."

He put down his chopsticks. "I'm married, Demetra, but not in the traditional way." He paused and searched her face before he spoke. "I'm gay."

"I didn't think you were, somehow."

He smiled. "How long have we known each other?"

"Is it almost two months?"

"Don't you think if I weren't gay, I would have made a pass at you by now?"

"I don't think about such things..."

"Why not? You're a gorgeous woman."

"Because I've got too much on my plate these days." She sighed deeply. "A failing relationship with my daughter, trying to find my parents, trying to make a success of my shop."

He searched her face. "Come on, Demetra, don't play the martyr. You've tried your best, now get on with your life." He scowled. "And for God's sake don't go pouring your heart out to any of those freakin' Freudians!"

She heaved a sigh that seemed to rise all the way from her toes.

He blushed. "I'm sorry—I've had some bad experiences with psychiatrists. Relax. I know that Corey will come back to you one day. When the time is right. Mark my words."

She began to pick at a bleeding hangnail that was making her hand throb.

He scowled. "That's a nasty habit. You have beautiful hands— such long tapered fingers. What makes you bite your nails so ferociously?"

She grinned. "I've *never* let anyone catch me at it. I've let down my guard with you, Farrell."

He reached over for her hand and held it tight. "Go find yourself a gym, or better yet take a dance class. It would do you a world of good to get some physical exercise."

"I dig in my garden."

"So do I. But that is not enough. I used to be a dancer. On Broadway. But then I developed a back problem, so I changed careers."

"Do you still dance?"

"Sure—only at home. Once you know what it's like to move your body, it's hard not to dance. If I don't dance, I'm not in touch with myself or my feelings. Dance gives me energy—even when I'm tired and must force myself. Have you ever taken ballet classes?"

"I've never had any desire to, although I do enjoy watching ballet. When we were first married, Marshall and I used to laugh about my ungainliness. And then, as the years passed, he became downright hostile about it." She paused. "Come to think of it, there *is* one kind of dance I seem to be drawn to."

"What's that?"

"Spanish dance." She smiled. "And flamenco. From the very first time I saw it on *The Ed Sullivan Show*. The nuns loved Ed Sullivan."

"Supposedly there are some really good Spanish dance teachers around L.A. why not have a go at it?"

"You're *crazy*, Farrell. *Never*, not even in my wildest dreams have I *ever* seen myself as a Spanish dancer." She laughed.

"It's nice hearing you laugh, Demetra."

She reflected for a moment. "Come to think of it, maybe the thought did flash through my mind. Just once. The night I wore the Fortuny gown."

The Return to Granada 1946

Mariano Fortuny y Madrazo, striking in his long robes, pauses on the patio of the Alhambra palace, surrounded by tall cypresses. Fountains arched high over beds of purple iris scenting the air. He looks out over the city of Granada, waiting for the sun to set behind the mountains, but tonight there will be no moon to light the sky.

Mrs. Elsie McNeill Lee, his American patron, with the help of Italian Ambassador, has arranged a publicity tour to celebrate Fortuny's new collection of unique designs to be available in New York, at her Madison Avenue shop, Fortuny, Inc. The room is filling with the crème *de la* crème of society—-Spanish, French, Italian and Moroccan as well as many of his American aficionados, some who had worn his exotic clothing for years.

Mariano is overcome with nostalgia. He was three years old when he lost his father, the celebrated painter Mariano Fortuny y Marsal. From time to time he loses himself in memories, heart-warming flashes, perched on his father's shoulders, strolling through the studio garden, his strong legs wrapped around his father's neck, his little hands grasped tight in his father's hands, stained from pigments. He admires his own streaked palms. "Look papa! Now I have hands like yours!" This episode became a game for father and son, an image so embedded in his memory that it would never leave him.

Fortuny sighs, turns his head to his patron and avoids her eyes, not wanting her to see them wet and gleaming. Reaching for her hand, he says, "Because of you, dear friend, I am here tonight in my hometown. I must confess that although I have a great love for Italy, I have always felt that I am a Spaniard. And I shall always be a Spaniard, a Spaniard from Granada. Tonight, my mind is flooded with images, memories, deep feelings as glimpses of my childhood rise to the surface of my mind.

"And so, I thank you, Senora Elsie, for planning this event. My beloved father would have been pleased—and proud that I have inherited his artistic sensibility, his passion for painting." Elsie takes his hand and holds it tight.

Mariano reads the mention in the program in his hand—an announcement that the noted soprano, Atena Valli, is scheduled to appear in London, at Covent Garden. She will sing the title role of Norma, the Celtic priestess.

Tonight, she would enchant the audience with an aria in Spanish. *The Maja and the Nightingale* from Goyescas, by Enrique Granados. She had chosen to wear one of Fortuny's most precious ensembles, the pleated cerulean silk gown with its brocade coat shimmering with Moorish patterns inspired by these very rooms. And later, after dinner, he would have the pleasure of meeting Madame Valli. He has never forgotten her stage performances, La Tosca in Roma and in Napoli, the Princess in Turandot. He has never seen her as Norma.

Then, suddenly, the room is quiet as Atena Valli makes her entrance. The audience leaps to its feet, applauding until La Valli bows her head and presses her palms together with her fingers pointed up, her way of gracefully silencing her devoted fans.

Before she sings, Mme Valli thanks the Italian Ambassador, who proceeds to dedicate the aria to Mariano Fortuny, the guest of honor. "He is child of Granada," says the Ambassador, gesturing to Fortuny, "a great artist who has continued the fame of his brilliant father. But Mariano Fortuny y Madraz has not only used his easel, he has also created textiles and apparel for the 20th century. His invention of theater lighting has enabled the stages of the world to turn from night into day and clouds to float in the sky. Madame Valli now dedicates this aria to you Quejas La Maja Y El Ruiseñor."

Atena nods to her accompanist, and begins:
Why in the shadows does the nightingale
Sing its harmonious songs,
Hoping to find comfort in the shadows,
Sadly singing her songs of love?

The poignant song of the Maiden, is soothing in its melody and lyrics, yet Fortuny's mind wanders to an image of Atena as Norma at the altar of the Druid priests, performing her rituals as she sings her hymn, Casta Diva, beseeching the goddess, with arms stretched wide as though to embrace the moon.

Tonight, the audience is enchanted by Atena's voice, by her glamour, her artistry," and again there is enthusiastic applause. She leaves the stage and the concert continues with classical guitar and the music of Manuel Villa Lobos.

Dazzled by the performance, "memorable," the guests murmur their praise, with many asking, "How could it not be, with the presence of Mariano Fortuny?"

Afterward, the Italian ambassador and his wife greet their guests in the reception line; Mariano and Senora Elsie McNeill Lee appear first; they are presented to their hosts and profusely thank them, then move on to the buffet laden with Spanish specialties.

Mariano approaches Atena. "I must admit that as you sang so beautifully, I could not help but think of Norma," he says. "You see, Madame, I have often envisioned you as Norma. "The next time you are in Venice, please come by my studio at the Palazzo Pesaro degli Orfei. I would be happy if you would accept my gift, a white delphos made just for you. Perhaps—and I repeat perhaps—you might wear it when you sing your Casta Diva in London."

After supper, the Italian Ambassador had arranged entertainment in one of the whitewashed "caves," a flamenco *jeurga* of gypsy dancers, guitarists, and the most esteemed *cantaor* in Granada.

Elsie McNeill is delighted.

And so is Mariano. "It will give me great pleasure to enjoy flamenco in the city of my birth. When I was a young man living in Paris, I was awestruck by a work of the American artist, John Singer Sargent who had painted, *El Jaleo*, his masterpiece, when he was in his twenties, after his introduction to the culture of Andalusia, by its gypsies and their music. At the time Sargent was studying in Paris with the famous Carolus Duran, a friend of my late father, Fortuny y Marsal, also a celebrated painter."

The Ambassador replies, "I too have admired Signor Sargent's painting. *El Jaleo*, now so beautifully displayed in the Boston palazzo of my good friend, la Signora Isabella Stewart Gardner. Tonight, the most famous flamenco dancer in Granada will make Sargent's painting come alive for us. And as our o*les* and *miras* and *palmas* encourage the dancer, so we become her Jaleo.

CHAPTER VII

It was two weeks since she had enrolled in her extension course, "The Art of Renaissance Venice." Demetra always sat in the corner of the very last row, but no matter how casually she dressed, she still stood out.

On her first day in class she had overheard a student about Corey's age say something admiring about her to a friend. Since Corey rarely saw beauty in older generations, Demetra was flattered.

Professor Anthony Tradland, renowned iconographer of Italian painting, closed the door behind him, his respected presence immediately silencing the chatter. Mid-forties, dark-haired and boyish, he cast a spell over his students, especially his women students.

"Did any of you see the program on PBS last night? The one on the Venetian restorations? Those of you who did had a good close-up of one of Titian's greatest paintings, *The Presentation of the Virgin*. Today I want to talk about that picture. And about the egg as a symbol in Renaissance painting. Turn off the lights, please.

"As you can see in this slide, there is a basket of eggs at the foot of the Crone who sits in the foreground of the painting. Mary, as a young girl of perhaps seven or eight years old, is mounting the temple steps to be presented to the priests."

Demetra knew the painting well and used to imagine herself in the replica on the wall over Sister Claire's desk. In the picture the young Virgin being presented at the temple looked so confident, so radiant, not in the least bit awestruck by the patriarchs the way Demetra had been on Confirmation Day as she bent with shaking knees to kiss the Archbishop's ring.

When the bell rang, Professor Tradland, his tall, statuesque frame rising above the podium, answered questions posed by the women admirers crowding around him. She had never had the courage to ask one, but she always listened to his replies before leaving and driving straight home, anxious to check the mailbox.

It was always the same whenever she flipped open the lid. The tightness in the stomach, her heart pounding in anticipation, the feeling of stifled frenzy. She was beginning to lose hope that a letter would ever arrive from the convent.

Jammed into the box was the usual pack of weekend supermarket specials. As she yanked them out, her heart vaulted when she saw an envelope with a foreign stamp. At first, she was disheartened when the letter was not from Toulouse, but then she was pleased that it was a reply from Claudia, her English friend, the Countess of Cherwell. There was no mistaking that distinctive grey writing paper embossed with entwined triple C's beneath a tiny gilded coronet and her lingering powder-puff fragrance. She had always assumed that Claudia would drop out of her life after learning about the divorce.

She would save the letter to read with her tea.

The kitchen still smelled of cinnamon and apples from the muffins she had baked early that morning. She took one from the bread drawer, took a big bite and put the kettle on to boil.

Dearest Demetra,

It has been almost two months since I received your last letter, and I hope you will forgive my silence. But I do want you to know that a long-time friend of mine will be arriving in Los Angeles in a month or so. He is the writer Thomas Pierson. You may have read some of his books, Patterans, and Hazard among others, bestsellers here in England. He does not know a soul in Los Angeles, and I know that you would find him interesting. He is working on a screenplay of his new novel, so if it is all right with you, I shall give him your telephone number and address. He seemed so eager to meet you after he saw your photograph on our piano "picture gallery." I told him all about you. He seemed intrigued.

I do run into Marshall occasionally, at Annabel's. I have not invited him to Cherwell Castle—I just do not want to entertain him. We will discuss it sometime when we are together.

Please let me know about Thomas P. Write me or else ring me at Cherwell Castle on weekends, Belgrave Square otherwise. We are longing see you again. Come with Corey this summer if you can. You name the date. Rupert sends his love, and lots more comes from me.

Claudia

P.S. I rang up Heywood Hill for a copy of Morris Dance, Thomas' latest book—it should be arriving soon.

Thomas Pierson. She had read *Patterans,* his acclaimed first novel several years ago. She remembered admiring his picture on the book cover. How rugged he looked standing atop a windswept moor wearing a toggled pea jacket, the archetypal North Countryman, she remembered thinking.

She slid the letter into its tissue-lined envelope, resisting the urge to pick up the phone to call Claudia. It was already past midnight in England. Besides, she had to quell her extravagant urges to use the phone so freely the way she used to at Greenhill House.

The bills she left unopened. Saturday was early enough to sit down to figure out which to pay first. After that, she would dig around in the garden, and in the afternoon, she would drive to Westwood to see an old French film; she missed hearing and speaking her childhood language.

The telephone rang and she lunged to answer it, always hoping that it might be Corey. But it was only Hunter's Books. *Symbols in Art,* her reference book for Dr. Tradland's class, had arrived. She told them she would pick it up on Saturday.

On Saturday morning, the late autumn winter rains beat down, shattering the first, fragile Iceland poppies, knocking over the Michaelmas daisies. Most people in Southern California disliked rainy weekends. No tennis, no mountain hikes, no surfing, and, for Demetra, no gardening. Weekends were the loneliest. She had tried keeping *Choses* open. Not worth it. On Saturday there were so few serious customers on Melrose.

Eleven-fifteen. She had almost forgotten to turn on the Metropolitan opera broadcast, one of the few rituals from her former life.

The curtain had just fallen on the first act of *Turandot* and the Opera Quiz panel was introduced. Today's chat was about famous sopranos who had sung the title role. She turned down the sound until it was barely audible. Opera trivia did not interest her. Better to use the time browsing through her notes and looking over Tradland's reading list. She sat at her desk and leafed through some papers. Nothing sank into her brain. She looked out at the rain pouring from the gutters, sluicing the patios. If only she could have dug around in the earth or pruned her roses, she might not have felt listless, so at odds with herself. Greenhill House kept looming up. She wondered what the rains might have done to the perennial flower borders. Marshall had never liked them because they were not in constant bloom. Maybe he had had them all ripped out.

Alone. And lonely, she admitted to herself, but the choice had been her own. She turned up the volume and wandered into the kitchen to seek solace in the refrigerator. With limp celery stalks, a few wizened carrots, half a withering cabbage, a few mushy tomatoes, bits of leftover dinners from the past week she would have vegetable soup. In the cupboard she found half a bag of barley.

She wrapped herself in an apron and in half an hour a pot of soup simmered away as Prince Calf and Princess Turandot sang the demanding "Riddle" exchange, the ruin of many a soprano voice. How much better she felt stirring the pot and listening to those soaring voices, how much more in tune with herself.

After bravos and curtain calls, she changed into loose jersey trousers and an old cashmere turtleneck sweater. She should try to savor her newfound freedom by doing exactly as she pleased for the rest of the day. Maybe she would drive to Santa Monica.

The rain had stopped and the gusts blowing across Wilshire Boulevard smelled of wet concrete and the Pacific. Sometimes she wondered why she had chosen to live near the Music Center instead of Santa Monica and the ocean.

After picking up her book at Hunter's, she walked to the movie theater, then stood in line for one of the simple pleasures of her new life. "A small popcorn, no butter, and an orange soda, please."

She heard a voice behind her.

"Are you planning to sit in the very last row?"

She turned to face the man who had made this brazen remark. Her eyes met Professor Tradland's. She smiled. "I was about to give you a very rude answer."

"I'm surprised you didn't recognize my voice. You've been hearing me drone on and on twice a week for the past two months."

She had never stood so close to him before, nor had she ever noticed his gentle hazel-brown eyes. In the classroom he was simply a font of knowledge.

"May I join you?"

"Only if you buy your own popcorn. And I prefer sitting close to the screen." She heard the awkwardness in her voice.

"Then you should do the same thing in my lecture room."

They found their seats in the half-empty theater and hardly had a chance to speak again before the lights dimmed.

The film was a re-run of the *Umbrellas of Cherbourg*. She'd seen it at fourteen when Sister Claire had taken her. She had never forgotten the bittersweet story about a beautiful girl, her mother, and the rich jeweler who wanted to marry the young woman even though she was pregnant with another man's child. At the end, when the girl's mother died, Demetra let the tears roll down her cheeks unchecked, lest Tradland notice her wiping them away. By the time the film was over, however, she had regained her composure, and her tears dried without blotting.

"Well, that was a tear-jerker all right," he said, "I must admit I cried a bit myself. Do you have any plans for dinner?"

She paused, hoping that he would not ask her to join him.

"I know an Italian restaurant in Hancock Park. Not one of those noisy places with Milanese high-tech decor, but a real trattoria with Papa in the kitchen and Mama at the cash register. I don't need to book in advance."

She hesitated, groping for a reasonable excuse. "I live downtown."

"I live in the Los Feliz area, which isn't far, so you can follow me."
There was no way out. "Well, thank you, Professor Tradland."
"Please call me Tony."
"My name is Demetra."
"Of course, I know your name."

The host led them to a quiet corner table. A pianist was playing
Come Back to Sorrento.

He ordered a bottle of *Lacrima Christi* from Naples. As they
touched glasses he looked straight into her eyes. "Do you think I do
this regularly?"

"Do what?"

"Invite my beautiful students to dinner?"

"I'm not at all sure of your habits, but I'm delighted you invited
me," she said, crossing her arms in her lap.

The waiter appeared. When she asked Tony to order what dishes
the restaurant did best, he ordered dinner as though he'd lived in
Italy for years: pasta with zucchini and some local sand dabs sautéed
with white wine and lemon and capers, Livorno style.

"Tell me why you're taking my class," he said.

"I wanted to get beyond what I'd learned on my own from art
books and auction catalogues. So I guess the past years haven't been a
total loss. Seems that I've done a fairly good job educating myself."
She blushed. "I hope I don't sound too smug! I don't mean to."

"Not at all. I can tell from your papers that you have a solid art
history background. Where did you grow up?"

"Minnesota, St. Paul."

"Where did you meet your husband?"

Demetra hesitated, surprised at so direct and so personal a
question. "One day he came in for lunch in a restaurant where I

worked part-time as a hostess. As he was walking out the door, he told me that he was impressed with my French. It was my first language, you see. He asked me out on a date. I thought he was very handsome, very sophisticated. I was flattered because I'd never had any attention from a man before."

"You had my attention long before you signed for my class. From time to time I used to come across a picture of you in those society magazines I flip through in the dentist's office."

"I suppose I should be flattered, but I want to forget that part of my life. I don't even look like that woman anymore."

"It's hard to make less of a face like yours. I have a hard time avoiding you from where I stand in the lecture room. You know you give Bellini's Madonna a lot of competition."

She laughed. "If I am that much of a distraction, then I should be wearing a veil to class. Now what can you tell me about yourself that I have not already learned from the jacket of your last book on Veronese? I know that you've been to Oxford, Princeton, and Yale, and because you're sitting across from me on a Saturday night, I'm assuming you're not married."

"My wife died about six months ago."

"I'm sorry."

"It was over very quickly—pancreatic cancer. Our marriage was already on the rocks. It had been for a long time. We were about to file for divorce when she found out her days were numbered. It was not an easy time for either of us because of the pain, and her anger and resentment about dying. So that I could make her last days comfortable, I took a sabbatical and we flew to Venice. Do you know it?"

"I've been there. Only once. I'd love to see Venice again, but for now it's out of the question."

"She died in a little flat near the Ca' d'Oro. It belonged to an Italian colleague." He stopped. His eyes glistened.

She wanted to reach out to touch him, but she checked herself. "Do you have children?"

"My wife kept putting off having a child. I always wanted one, but she insisted that she finish her monumental Caltech project first. She was a biologist working on DNA research."

The waiter appeared with the wine and poured a glass. Tony took a sip and, after nodding his approval, said, "What happened to your marriage to Marshall Killingsworth?"

"My divorce should be final in December. Marshall has plans to remarry." She tried to sound detached, matter of fact. "A woman from Pasadena, Marina McFarland, a socialite from one of the old pioneer families. Just the kind of woman he wanted, someone from a good background, an Ivy League school. She speaks several languages. She's also exceptionally beautiful."

"Do you have any children?"

"An eighteen-year-old daughter. I was about her age when she was born."

"That makes you around your mid-thirties. I will be forty-one this winter. The 25th of December." He smiled. "Jesus Christ and I— both Capricorns!"

"I wonder why your mother didn't call you Noel."

"She wanted to, but my father insisted I be named after his father. But she got her way with my middle name."

"Noel?"

"No, Natale. My parents were Italian Immigrants. I was brought up in Bridgeport, Connecticut."

"I never knew my parents, but I was told that my mother was Greek."

"I'm not surprised. Demetra, after the Greek goddess of harvest."

She nodded, wanting to stop it right there. Why she should tell him too much about herself? He was, after all, her teacher and if she revealed her entire life's story, she wondered how she could ever face him in class.

The main course arrived.

During dinner Tony changed the subject to travel and film and books. Over coffee, he asked her what sports she enjoyed.

"Sports?" She shook her head. "Every now and then I've skated on the rink in Santa Monica. I learned on the pond across from the convent—taught by a nun who was a former champion figure skater. I'm afraid I'm still frozen in figure eights."

There was a long silence. Finally, he glanced at his watch.

She looked at hers. It was almost midnight. He insisted on following her home, again reassuring her that he lived only ten minutes away. At her door she felt obliged to offer him a drink, hoping that he would not accept.

"No thanks. Wine with dinner is all I need of an evening." He put his arms around her shoulders, took a long deep breath and held her close.

"I'm not going to kiss you on your lovely mouth, although I've thought about it all evening."

She looked up at him, arching her head back from his embrace and pulling away. "Are you so sure that I would have let you even if you wanted to?" She was sorry when she saw the embarrassment in his eyes.

"What are your plans for tomorrow?" he said.

"I'm going to write part of the paper you assigned. And work on my flower border. My flowers need pruning and staking after all this rain."

"May I come by to give you a hand?"

She hesitated. "O.K if you'd like. Sundays are the longest days for me."

"Saturday nights are for me, so maybe we can work something out for weekends. What time tomorrow?"

"Around twelve-thirty. Oh—I almost forgot! Tomorrow's the second Sunday of the month. I had planned to go to The Rose Bowl Swap meet, but I'm usually back by noon. I'll be happy be to cook brunch for you if you help me tidy up the garden."

"I accept." He kissed her forehead.

She bolted the door and waited for a few minutes until she heard his car drive away. Tradland was a dynamic personality in class, but not nearly as forceful across a table. She went straight to bed, mulling the evening over and over again in her mind before she fell asleep and dreamed.

The house by the sea is built in the Craftsman style, like a house designed by Greene and Greene. It belongs to Paul Mellon who has an illustrious, well-respected American name. Demetra walks in. The owner tells her the kitchen is much older than the rest of the house.

Demetra asks to see the garden. A woman kneels, digging in the earth. She pulls up an iridescent oyster shell. Mother-of-pearl, she says.

Demetra asks if the Indians once used this place as a dumping ground. The woman smiles. "This is a far, far older place than that." She pulls up another shell from the gravelly earth.

Demetra speaks to the woman. "Perlmutter, madre di perla, mother-of-pearl." She does not know why she speaks these words, but she does.

The radio alarm rang at five o'clock. A soprano was singing the Villa-Lobos *Bachianas Brasilieras Number Five.* She turned the sound up to hear the harmonies of cellos and soprano voice that never failed to give her pleasurable shivers, all the while reflecting on the vivid dream.

When she arrived at the Pasadena Rose Bowl, the waxing moon was still high in the sky. December mornings could be cold, and, with the heavy rain, the San Gabriel Mountains were laced-edged with snow. She pulled up to a giant camper near Portal 10, checked her parka for a flashlight and gloves, and zipped her wallet and checkbook into a hidden pocket—Farrell had warned her about pickpockets. Now she was ready to circle the world of the Rose Bowl. She prayed that this would be the day she would find Corey. One of Farrell's friends had seen her at the indoor Flea Market in Long Beach; she might at this very moment be milling around among all these dealers and bargain hunters.

One section of the bowl's perimeter was given over to so-called antiques and collectibles; otherwise much of the merchandise was junk. Still, her eye was so trained that she often found saleable objects and furniture for *Choses* in far less likely places.

She walked briskly, her eyes sweeping over the throngs in the morning gloom. When the sun came up it would be easier to recognize faces. At one stall, she looked over freshly cast white plaster copies of Greek and Roman statues—Apollo, Artemis, and Aphrodite torsos, Winged Victories, The Boy on a Dolphin. As she looked them over, her favorite of the lot was a finely cast statue of Hermes, wearing his winged cap.

Other less glamorous wares lay on blankets spread on the ground: old pop-up toasters and other "early" appliances sold in the thirties, rolls of antique barbed wire, stalls filled with Hummel figurines, stalls offering early Barbie dolls.

Over another booth, a sign proclaimed, "One man's trash is another man's treasure."

"May I have a look at this?" she asked before she picked up a ceramic plate.

"Sure, but if you break it, it's yours." the dealer replied.

She examined the 19th century copy of the 17th century potter, Bernard Palissy. A snake, in relief, curled around the plate's surface of rough, textured faience grass. Not a particularly rare piece, but interesting, nonetheless. For a moment she forgot her quest. "Are you Demetra Killingsworth?" the dealer asked.

"Let's say I used to be. Now I use Duval, my maiden name. Your plate is a genuinely nice nineteenth century copy. Probably Portuguese."

"Yeah, but nowadays even these copies go for a lot," he said defensively. The tag read $450. A retail price—a bit too steep for a dealer, but certainly worth the money, she thought.

He read her mind. "Of course, I can do better on it, that is if you want it. I'd like to know that my plate belonged to you."

"Thanks, that's very generous, but if I bought it, it would be for resale, not for my own personal collection. I come here to buy for my shop." Then she heard herself blurt out. "I've really come here looking for my daughter. Someone told me that she does the swap meets—that she has been seen here. So far, I've not been able to find her. I keep hoping she'll turn up one of these Sundays." She stopped and took a deep breath.

"I haven't seen anyone with your name in the list of dealers who sell here. Does she look like you?"

"She doesn't look like me at all. She has long, reddish-blonde hair and lots of freckles across her nose."

"Well, from now on, I'll be sure to keep an eye out for a freckled blonde at swap meets. I'll tell her to call her mother." He chuckled.

"I may return for your plate, but if I don't—you shouldn't lower the price too much. It's certainly worth what you're asking for it."

"Thanks. You are an honest lady. I really hope you find your daughter."

The jostling crowd had become so dense that she was pushed along by the hordes, past piles of automobile parts, rusted valves, tatty chenille bedspreads and hooked rugs, past tables crammed with opalescent amber carnival glass, strands of poppit beads and Bakelite bracelets.

She began to rummage through some racks of vintage clothing still reeking of cleaning solvent. One dress looked like one Marshall had bought her. She had been married in the dress; a sleeveless white pique printed with sprays of tiny pink roses. She read the label, *The Clothes Tree. St. Paul.* Shivers ran up her arms.

Where on earth had it come from? Maybe from one of the boxes in the basement, the ones she had given to Corey when she moved in with Harley Hadesson. Heart hammering away, she found the woman who ran the stall.

"Can you tell me anything about this dress?"

"Whaddya wanna know?" The woman took a drag on her cigarette, "The price is written right there on the sleeve but I'm sure I can do better on it."

"I wondered where it came from."

"Try reading the label."

"May I ask where—and when you bought it?"

"From a girl in Leucadia. At a swap meet. Couple of weeks ago."

"I've never heard of Leucadia before—where is it?"

"About 100 miles from here—not far from San Diego."

"What did the girl look like?"

"Tall, with long, straight reddish hair. Good lookin' girl."

Demetra glanced at her watch. She would drive there right away. Her heart beat hard at the thought that she might soon find Corey— at least to reason with her, to reassure her of her love.

"Now if you're thinkin' about drivin' there to look for her, you're outa luck. She was selling everything out. She spoke about having an acting job somewhere. Her boyfriend was called Michael. Nice lookin' fella, tall, dark hair."

Michael? Who was Michael? Demetra wondered as she paid for the dress. Then, trying to hold back the tears, she pushed against the jostling crowds. There was nothing to do but follow Farrell's advice and be patient.

She checked her watch. Eleven thirty already. She was sorry Tony Tradland was coming by for lunch. All she wanted to do was go home, have a good cry, and sleep off her despair.

***

Tradland was sitting on the doorstep reading the Sunday *Los Angeles Times*. He was dressed for outside work, in old Levis and a plaid flannel shirt under a heavy grey Shetland sweater. "Did you find any bargains?"

She pulled the dress from the bag and held it up. "Hardly a bargain since this once belonged to me!" She did not tell him that she was married in the dress. He might ask too many questions.

"You mean you found a dress that actually belonged to you at the Rose Bowl?"

"The dealer must have bought it from my daughter. At a swap meet in Leucadia. I was about to drive there, but then she told me that the girl she bought it from had sold out and left with a boyfriend. Someone I've never heard of."

"She's probably having a great time. Why do you seem so worried about her?"

"I feel the terrible breach between us. The way we parted was so ugly. Of course, I want her to be happy, to live her own life. I am the problem, you see. She won't forgive me for divorcing Marshall."

"Why won't she listen to your side of the story? She is almost twenty years old, after all. She's a big girl."

"I can't bear to tell her what really happened—she worships her father so."

He shook his head. "You're far too charitable. You cannot protect her all her life. She is old enough to know the truth—whatever it is. Come on, tell me where you keep the garden tools. I'll do some cleaning up while you make brunch."

"You'll find them in the garage closet. Start by raking the grass beyond the trees and be sure to toss whatever you rake up ion the compost heap beyond the shed."

"Cook plenty of everything. I guarantee you I'll be famished by the time I'm finished."

When brunch was ready, she tapped on the window and motioned to him.

She watched him wiping the mud from his feet meticulously before walking in.

As she was pouring his cup of coffee he said, "You're not at all what I expected, Demetra."

"Oh? What did you expect?"

He sighed. "A woman not nearly so serious."

He pressed her to talk about herself; she kept changing the subject. "Sometimes I wonder why I did not move to another city, but I love warm weather and sunshine, so I decided to stay right here. One weekend before I opened *Choses,* I drove to Mexico, to an inn near Ensenada where I felt so at home. Since then I've been listening to Spanish language tapes in my car."

"I'll drive down with you one weekend, if you'd like."

She laughed. "As long as you bring along your own books and find another palm tree for your shade."

When they had eaten, drunk enough coffee, he began to stack the newspapers in a neat pile.

"I'll straighten up after you leave," she said.

"You're not going to get rid of me so easily."

"Well then, I'll put you to work in the kitchen."

As she was rinsing the plates, he came behind her and wrapped his arms around her waist. She pulled away faced him.

"I want you, Demetra. I hope you feel the same about me."

Her heart pounded, she stood stiffly, but said nothing.

He put his lips gently to her. "Your mouth tastes like orange marmalade."

They stood there for a few moments. She felt his arms tremble. He seemed afraid to go further without her permission.

He kissed her forehead. "Such a lovely brow. Like the 'Young Woman' in the portrait by Pollaioulo. I want to make love to you—but lately—it's been difficult." He squeezed her hand and put it to his lips.

"I feel I know a lot about you sitting in your class these past months and after our long talk last night, but I can't make love to you. I am much too confused. I would not feel a thing. I thought being free from Marshall would really make me free about sex, but it has not. I am confused. I really don't know what I feel."

"And I'm still battered from my wife's death. Who knows, maybe if we keep enjoying each other's company, and if our feelings grow, then it will happen. That way neither of us will wake up with regret. I wouldn't want you avoiding my eyes in class."

He picked up his sweater and walked to the door. Demetra followed, then, turning, he kissed her lightly on the lips.

"See you in class on Tuesday."

"What's the lecture?"

"Titian's 'Venus'. The one in Dresden."

"I'll be there."

"In the back row?"

"In my usual seat."

"I've had a wonderful Sunday, Demetra. It's been such a relief not to spend another weekend alone."

"For me, as well. Thanks for tidying the garden." She waved goodbye as he backed out of the driveway and into the wooded lane. He was a charming, sensitive man, but she was not yet sure if a relationship could ever develop.

As she stacked the rest of Sunday's papers in the kitchen closet, she noticed a fragile blue airmail envelope lying between the classifieds. She turned it over. It was postmarked "Toulouse, France," the postmark so blurred she could not decipher the date. Her head reeling, she staggered to the counter for the mother-of-pearl opener, and, just as she had done again and again in her imagination, sliced sharply through the flap with the blade. Inside she found one thin sheet of folded paper.

November 1984
Dear Miss Duval,
   We apologize for the delay in our response to you since the archives are closed during the months of July and August. We have found the document to which, by law, you are entitled, in Albi, Provence.
   According to the entry, you were delivered to the Convent of the Divine Transfiguration in St. Paul, Minnesota (defunct since January 20, 1978) on October 3, 1948. Your name was listed as Demetra Duval. You were a foundling brought to the convent by Monsieur Charles Duval of New York City. Although Mr. Duval claimed not to be your father, he allowed you to be given his name and The Mother Superior of the Convent saw no reason to disbelieve his story. The doctor who examined you said that you were about two weeks old. We cannot offer you more than this information, which we hope will be useful to you.
   Sister Antoinette Agathe
   Secretary, Order of the Divine Transfiguration,
   Rue de la Tour 28, Toulouse, France

Reaching for a chair to steady herself, she burst into wild tears. With this terse, dismissive letter she had arrived at the end of her search. Why would Sister Claire have led her to believe that her mother was Greek? She had to have known something! Suddenly her throat felt itchy and dry, her mouth parched. She filled a glass with tap water and drank it down in one swallow. She drank another glassful. The cold water flooded her stomach, nauseating her. Knowing she would never make it to the bathroom, she leaned over the kitchen sink, retching until she heaved dry.

She fell into a chair and cradled her head in her arms on the kitchen table until there were no more tears.

Who was Charles Duval? Maybe he was dead. Dead or alive, what would have been the reason for giving her his name? She called New York City Information. Only two Charles Duvals listed in the boroughs. She called Duval in the Bronx, leaving her message on the answering machine. A young Haitian returned her call an hour later. He told her that he had arrived in New York only four years ago. The other Charles Duval was a plumber who claimed he'd never heard of Demetra Duval. Questions kept raging in her head. How could she find him? Where should she begin to look? And where was Corey when she needed her so much? She tried calling Farrell, but there was no answer. He had talked about driving his partner to Monument Valley for the weekend. Most likely he would be back in the shop tomorrow morning. Feeling a throbbing pain in her hands, she looked down at her fingernails—they had been bitten down to the quick.

On Monday morning she was at the Los Angeles Main Library steps fifteen minutes before it opened. She wanted to look up Charles Duval in as many city directories as she could.

When she finished, she drove straight to Choses although she had the urge to keep on driving.

Farrell had returned.

"My God—you look like hell! What happened?" He threw his arms around her "The letter arrived."

"What did you learn? "She spoke calmly in a flat, resolute voice. "That I was a foundling—brought to the orphanage by someone called Charles Duval of New York City. They have no idea who my parents were. That was all the information they had."

"Charles Duval. Strange—I seem to have heard the name, but I don't know where or when."

"I've already tried finding him in New York. No luck. I have a few more names to call. One in St. Paul, one in Salt Lake City. Another in Chicago."

"Remember what I told you the first night we had dinner together?"

"About finding myself?"

"I still believe what I told you before, Demetra. If you would only try finding yourself, it wouldn't be nearly so important for you to find your parents."

She spent most of the next morning, trying to track down Charles Duval. When Tony Tradland called to ask her to spend the next Saturday afternoon and evening with him, she balked, but then thought she might feel better if she went out. There was nothing she could do to change the contents of the letter and she vowed not to discuss it further.

Tony lived in a garden apartment of *Il Posto Incantato,* an old Italian Baroque style residence in the Los Feliz section of Los Angeles. He unlocked the grillwork gate to a small shaded courtyard centered by a white marble sculpture of a woman. Her throat was looped with beads carved in relief; her lips turned up in a sweet, archaic smile. In her outstretched hands she held a bowl from which a fountain bubbled then trickled over into a surrounding pool where lily pads floated.

"She's Astargatis, goddess of the springs, Aphrodite in her earlier guise," he said. "Seventeenth century B.C. from the ancient Syrian city of Mari. The original is in a museum in Aleppo. While I was there I took some good photos and her measurements and when I came home I found an Italian stone-cutter in the San Fernando Valley to copy her."

"She's beautiful," Demetra responded, "already with a patina of time past!"

"That's because she lives outside. The original is glowing white marble." In his donnish way, Tony began to detail the sculpture technique as though he were standing before his class. He went on for at least five minutes until he stopped himself. "Forgive me! This is no way to welcome you. Let us go in!"

He led her into the small entry hall opening to a large, high-ceilinged living room. Between its oak beams the ceiling was painted midnight blue with a field of golden stars and moons in various degrees of waxing and waning.

"I've always liked ceilings painted to look like sky, but I've never seen one as beautiful as this, Tony."

"A few years ago, when I went to a Leonardo conference in Krakow, I admired a ceiling like this at the University—in the library of Copernicus. Well, you can see the results for yourself."

An antique walnut neoclassic bookcase crammed full took up one entire wall. The room faced still an enclosed garden, its walls faced with clipped ivy, against which was placed yet another marble sculpture, a copy of the Aphrodite of Knidos. The other walls were lined ceiling to dado with paintings, watercolors, etchings, drawings. Tabletops were massed with more framed sketches and bits of sculpture.

Demetra moved closer to have a look. The pictures were of women, goddesses all.

"I've been collecting for a long time, gathering up material for my next book. It is about Aphrodite's first appearance in the West until her demise with the advent of Christianity. And then her re-emergence in Renaissance *poesia* painting."

She laughed. "How did your wife feel about having another woman's image plastered all over the walls?"

"So long as wasn't on the kitchen wall, she didn't mind." He smiled. "But then Aphrodite wouldn't have been comfortable in the kitchen. She never claimed to be a cook. And speaking of cooking, I hope you will help me with dinner. We're going to make pasta from scratch."

"I've never made pasta before."

"My mother taught me how. And I will teach you. His kitchen was tiny, but well lighted and well equipped.

"What kind of pasta will we make?" she asked.

"*Lo scrigno di Venere.*" He said. "Venus' jewel box." Marcella Hazan's recipe. First, we will make some regular pasta, then we'll add some pureed spinach to half of it."

He set a wooden board on top of the stove burners that he'd temporarily covered with plastic, put his hands under the water tap and scrubbed them vigorously, as though he were a doctor preparing to operate, or a pagan priest about to perform a purification ritual

She thought she had better do the same.

He dusted the board with flour then heaped more flour into a mound dug into its center into which he sprinkled salt. Then he deftly cracked five whole eggs into the crater without smearing the yokes. Finally, he pierced the yolks with a fork and stirred the mass with his fingers and rolled it into a ball that he kneaded with the heel of his hands.

She took turns, pushing, patting, punching. When the dough was shiny and elastic, Tony covered it with a fresh white linen cloth.

"We'll let it rest, divide it in two and add spinach puree to half of it."

He showed her how to use the yard long and narrow rolling pin. Soon there were two circles of dough, one pale yellow, the other pale green, ready to be cut. He neatly sliced the green pasta into fine ribbons, then cut several five-inch discs of dough from the yellow.

Demetra, who enjoyed cooking, had never concocted anything so elaborate or time-consuming. "I must be a peasant at heart," she said, "because whatever I cook is tossed into one pot."

While the dough "rested" he uncorked a bottle of vintage Biondi-Santi Brunello into a long-necked glass flask and tied a red napkin around its neck. After filling two balloon glasses, he offered one to her.

"Now let's relax." He beckoned with his little finger and said in a come-with-me-to-the-Casbah tone of voice, "Let us now go to the bedroom where I show you sexy slides for my new book."

She laughed, then obligingly followed him down the hall to the bedroom. She sank down onto the dark green velvet love seat and surveyed the room. The bed's four spiraled and carved gilt wood columns supported a white linen canopy. It was covered with a lustrous velvet leopard skin duvet and tossed enticingly with cushions made from antique textiles.

Tony pulled down a screen from the wall opposite his bed, dimmed the light and began to click the cartridge wheel. The first image was of a tiny figure with bulbous haunches, a rippling belly, and huge pendulous breasts. "The Venus of Willendorf, the famous Neolithic fertility goddess, discovered in 1908."

He projected slide after slide of female figures from pre-historic sites in Malta and Turkey. More slides on the goddess of love as Innana in Babylonia, as Astarte in Phoenicia and Canaan, and in Cyprus where Aphrodite was said to have been born.

Although she enjoyed mythology, she found Tony's relentless interest unsettling. It verged on the obsessive.

Finally, he arrived at representations of Venus and Adonis.

"Adonis was a youth beloved of Aphrodite. In ancient Greece, there were cults to Adonis. His women devotees planted fast growing seeds in little pots and left them on rooftops to sprout. Gardens of Adonis, they were called."

"I'd read about them somewhere, so I grew some to use as party centerpieces for an Olympic benefit called the Feast of the Gods. A woman criticized me for using them. Not decorative enough, she said."

"Obviously, these gardens didn't ring a bell in her psyche," he said, smiling. "Maybe it's the Greekness in you that led you to use them."

"I'd never thought of that. I was only following the party theme."

As he droned on and on showing slide after slide, she felt herself nodding.

Demetra was asleep when she felt Tony's hand on her shoulder. She leapt up.

"Dinner's ready." He took her hand and sat her at a small round table. A single fat candle, surrounded by greenery with small, creamy white flowers, burned in the center of the starched white cloth.

When Demetra admired the blossoms, Tony told her that they were myrtle, sacred to Aphrodite.

The first course, a mixed seafood salad, was heaped on white china plates molded like a giant scallop shell.

After that he returned with the oven-golden pasta pouches placed side by side on two Chinese sang-de-boeuf plates. Each little *"scrigno"* looked as if it had been tied with a green noodle "string." The steam burst through as he slashed the pouch. Inside, the noodles, bound by a wild mushroom and cream sauce, looked like pale green seaweed.

"I've never eaten pasta so delicious," she said as she tasted hers.

All during dinner they talked about Aphrodite. Or, at least Tony did. Demetra could not have interrupted him, even if she had wanted to.

He would not let her near the kitchen afterwards. "Don't worry. I'll clean up tomorrow."

Why, she thought, was Tony so much more obsessed in his own environment than he was in hers? She knew there was no way she could compete with his dream goddess or with another set of male obsessions. Marshall's womanizing had been enough. She had not even told Tony about the letter from France, but then he didn't give her a chance: he was so caught up with admiring and describing Aphrodite, the unobtainable love of his life.

THE PAINTER,
THE JOURNALIST
AND THE GYPSY
Segovia, Spain, May 1948

-

The English Painter parks the new Morris Minor by the dusty roadside. He and his wife, an American journalist, have chosen this tranquil site for a picnic. From the high hill they look down upon the Roman aqueduct and the meandering river; from above, perched on high granite cliffs, they admire the breathtaking panorama of the towers and turrets of a medieval castle, El Alcazar.

They have both come here to work, the Painter to sketch the Alcazar, the Journalist to write an article for the New York Times—her assessment of Spain at the end of the Civil War and the restoration of the Kingdom.

The woman spreads a white sheet over the meadow grass strewn with buttercups and bluets. With great ceremony, the Painter opens an elegant fitted picnic hamper from Asprey, London, a Christmas present from his parents. His pretty blonde wife has packed it with sherry from Jerez, a sack of Marcona almonds, a jar of olives. The rest of the meal will come later and finish with a bowl of blood oranges macerated in orange liqueur. Then the woman will open the box of her favorite Whitman's Sampler Chocolates, a present sent from New York.

He searches his canvas bag for pencils, a sketch book for himself, and for his wife a notebook. As they sip their sherry, they are quiet, lost in their separate worlds. An hour passes: the stillness is broken by shouts, the distant rumble of wagon wheels, the neighing of horses. The Englishman leaps to his feet, eager to have a closer look at the caravans and the raggle-taggle of gypsies. He must sketch these nomadic Rom, who seem so different from the gypsy families who dance for tourists in the white-washed caves of Granada or the *gitanes* of the Camargue who worship their patron Saint Sara in her church at Les Saintes Maries de la Mer. While the Rom are setting up camp under the ample shade of cork trees, the couple share their lunch. When they have finished the oranges, the Journalist reaches for the Whitman Sampler. As she is about to open the box, she notices a gypsy woman moving toward them. She becomes uneasy, wondering what the woman will say. Or what she might do.

The gypsy greets them in heavily accented Spanish the Journalist barely understands, but she smiles as though she does, and offers the Gypsy the box of chocolates.

Wary of the *gorgio's* uncommon generosity, the gypsy fixes her dark eyes on the Journalist, then turns the box upside down, as if to assure herself that it has never been opened. She smiles, nods her acceptance, and muttering in the language of the Rom, she leaves the couple and trudges up the road holding her candy box in both hands like a new-found treasure.

The picnic is over, time to leave. As the couple are making their way to the car, the Gypsy returns, a towheaded, fair-skinned boy, about two years old, held against her hip. She asks the *gorgio* if she has children. She replies that she has not. Although they have always wanted them, they have not been so blessed.

The Gypsy moves closer and tries to thrust the child in the arms of the Journalist, "Take pickaninny, take pickaninny," she urges in archaic-sounding English. The Journalist asks in Spanish why she wants to give away her child. *"No es Rom - tome pequeños niño. Él es rubio como tú. Tome, tome."*

Suddenly two *guardia civil,* the younger with bayonet fixed, arrive on the scene, having come to inspect the *quinqui* encampment. When the older guard takes the child from the Gypsy's arms, she does not protest. Instead she says, *"Tome la senora , dir il mejor vida al pequeño niño."*

The Journalist and the Painter are overwhelmed with sadness for this dear child, a beautiful blond boy looking so much like the Journalist that he could easily be her son. She begins to cry, heartsore for what might happen to this unwanted *pequeno nino.*

One of the *guardia civil* offers the child to the Journalist to hold. The little boy's huge blue eyes gaze into hers in fascination, as though in recognition.

The Painter wraps his arms around his wife and the child.

The *guardia civil* orders the Gypsy, the Painter and the Journalist to follow him. The matter will be settled at *la estación de la guardia civil.*

CHAPTER VIII

A week later, Demetra stuck in freeway traffic, was late for work. Before opening *Choses*, she stopped by Farrell's shop. They had a mutual call-forwarding telephone arrangement.

"Any important messages?"

He shook his head. "I *know* what you mean by important. But you *do* have two messages. One from American Express, the other from Thomas Pierson. He said he had tried reaching you at home first. Was I ever impressed! I couldn't *believe* what I was hearing. The master's voice! I told him I had borrowed all his books from the library. He blushed. "I hope I didn't gush too much. Have you ever read any of his novels?"

"I hardly ever read novels—but I did read *Patterans* a long time ago."

"Pierson is one of my favorite contemporary English writers along with John Fowles and Lawrence Durrell."

"You think he's *that* good? What message did he leave for me?"

"He wants you to call him."

"Didn't he leave an address? It costs a lot to call England."

"Hell! The guy's right here in Santa Monica. He's already rented a furnished condo in Venice."

"What was he like over the phone?"

"Sounds more like an actor than a writer. If you want, I will go by the library to check out *Morris Dance*, his latest book, so you can have a look at him on the book jacket."

"My English friend Claudia has already sent me a copy, although I haven't had time to read it."

"I'll bet you anything she's trying to fix you up with him."

"Farrell, you're a hopelessly incurable romantic."

"What's wrong with romance? You could use a little in your life. You are way too standoffish. I see how you react to people who don't know you, and you don't send out any messages to men."

"I've got enough going on in my life. I'm not ready for romance or for too many acquaintances, for that matter," she snapped back. "I'll wait to call him

toward the end of the day."

He reached for a Bullock's Wilshire shopping bag and handed it to her." I bought you a present yesterday from that resale shop in Santa Monica. I could not resist. You'll look great in it."

She held her breath as she lifted the scarlet dress from the white tissue folds. When she held it up, its multi-layered silk chiffon skirt floated as if wafted by a slight breeze. A garland of red silk poppies encircled the halter-top.

"How beautiful! I have not worn a red dress in years. Is it really mine?"

"It's yours for keeps, Demetra."

"Thank you, Farrell," she sighed. "But I wonder where on earth I'd ever wear it."

"You'll find just the right occasion. Come on—try it on for me."

"Right now?"

"Sure, why not? I'm dying to see how it fits you."

She stepped behind the curtain to undress, but he hardly waited for her to put it on. He drew the curtain open.

"The back needs still needs hooking up." she said, blushing, "but I can't do it myself."

"I'll do it for you."

He fastened the hooks. The dress fit perfectly.

"See how the poppies light up your face! And what a beautiful straight back you have, Demetra." Wistfully his hands traveled along her arms, her bare back. "Your skin's so smooth. You have a dancer's back."

She shivered slightly, hoping he had not noticed. It had been a long time since she had felt a loving, gentle hand caress her body. She wondered if Farrell had ever stroked a woman's body before. She wondered if…

Then he lifted her hair and deftly coiled it to the top of her head. "See how great the dress looks with your hair upswept. Or you could even draw it back tight for a more Spanish look. It would suit you that way. And absolutely *no* jewelry." He thought for a moment. "Well—maybe some diamond studs in your ears. Or pearls. But that is it. Halston claims that too much jewelry is aging for a woman. I tend to agree with him."

She threw her arms around him. "Oh Farrell—Thank you! You're the most thoughtful, wonderful friend." She kissed his cheek. "I love you!"

"I love you, too, Demetra." Then he brushed her lips gently with a kiss and stepped away. "Now please don't forget to call Thomas Pierson. He seemed anxious to talk to you."

She did not know why she wanted to put off answering Thomas Pierson's call. Certainly, she did not want to appear overly eager, but more to the point, she wanted no more intrusions on her freedom, no more invasions of her privacy. And writers were so discerning, so scrutinizing. She had no desire to be grist for his word mill.

***

A week later she drove to Little Tokyo to a shop where Farrell had discovered some old yet inexpensive Imari porcelain. Parking her car on a side street near the New Otani Hotel, she stood at the corner daydreaming about Corey while waiting for the light to turn green. Suddenly she heard someone shout, "Mom!" Startled, she looked across. Corey was standing on the opposite side, waving. Mother and daughter ran toward one another embracing in the middle of the street. They walked arm in arm to the sidewalk. Demetra did her best to hold back tears of joy. Corey seemed genuinely happy to see her mother.

It had been some time since Demetra had seen her looking so well and in something other than frayed jeans. She was wearing an ankle length velvet skirt with boots, and a burgundy long-sleeved jersey.

Come on, Corey, my car is parked just around the corner. Since it's almost lunch time, why don't I drive you to the cute little house I've rented—it's my very own" Even before Corey replied, Demetra caught the fleeting, unresponsive glance before her daughter averted her eyes.

"I'd love to, Mom, but I don't have time. I was just on my way to Gorky's for a bowl of borscht." She checked her watch. "I've got an audition in an hour and a half."

"Where are you living?"

"A few blocks from here, in a loft."

Corey must have noticed the hurt on her mother's face. She sighed and, shaking her head, she relented. "Okay, if you really want to. Come on, let's go. Michael, the guy I'm living with, drove to San Diego this morning."

As they walked toward Santee Alley, Demetra, put her arm through her daughter's and, tightly clasping Corey's fingers. She said, "Tell me about your friend Michael."

"He's a set designer and incredibly talented. He worked with George Strehler on *The Tempest* for the Olympics. Now he is helping to re-work the sets for *The Beggars' Opera.* After that, who knows where he'll be off to."

"How did you meet him?"

"When I was trying out for a part I didn't get."

"When can I meet him?"

"We're not ready for that yet. At least I'm not."

"Have you introduced him to your father?

She shook her head. "Oh my God no! Will Dad hit the roof!" She grimaced. "You know how prejudiced he is. Michael's last name is Rosiello. He's Italian."

"Does he speak it?"

"With his parents he does. Michael was surprised that I knew so much about painting and sculpture. I told him I owed it all to you—being dragged around to museums and cathedrals in Europe."

"That's nice to hear."

"And remember how I used to hate it when you spoke to me in French? Now I am glad you did. Having an authentic accent was valuable during some of my auditions." She stopped and pulling out some keys from her shoulder bag proclaimed, *"Voila, Maman, nous sommes arrivées!"*

Demetra smiled. *"Merci, ma chère."*

The loft was in an old brick building that housed a textile manufacturers' outlet. A freight elevator lifted them to the second floor. When they walked into the loft, the first thing Demetra saw was the rumpled bed, set defiantly in the center of the room, as though Corey were trying to prove something. A few coarse army surplus blankets were heaped on the floor.

In the corner were boxes had been crammed with books and clothes. Demetra recognized a sleeve of one of her old cotton batik blouses sticking out from one of them.

Rolled up canvases were stacked the floor, others propped along the walls. Easels displayed preliminary sketches. Metal folding tables, all loaded with open paint cans, linseed oil, brushes soaking in turpentine, took up the rest of the space. The place reeked. When Demetra's stomach did a turn, she hoped that her face had not shown it. "*Oh, my darling daughter, doesn't living with this terrible odor bother you?*" she pleaded silently.

Corey, as though she were testing her mother said with more than a tinge of hostility in her voice, "You don't even have to say a word, Mom. I know exactly what you are thinking. By the way, the toilet's down the hall if you need it. A bunch of us share it." She laughed. "Michael says the smell reminds him of the latrines in Tripoli, so I hope you don't have to use it."

Demetra instinctively folded her arms and drew them in against her body.

"But we do have a sink over in the corner behind the screen where we get water for cleaning the brushes and hot-plate cooking. That reminds me—I'd better eat something before the auditions." She pulled open a drawer and took out a loaf of bread, a jar of peanut butter and some jelly.

"Want one?"

"No, thanks, I'm not the least bit hungry," Demetra said as Corey smeared tan globs on thick seven grain slices.

Corey must have read her mother's body familiar body language as well as the look on her face. "I should have known better than to have brought you here. Now I'm sorry I did."

"Please don't say that, Corey. You have no idea how happy I am to be here."

"Oh sure! I will bet you can't wait to get your hands on this place to clean it up. I can just hear you." She mimicked her mother's voice. "*Ma chère*, don't you have any respect for your property? How can you possibly live in such a hideous mess?" She laughed. "I'll bet you've already figured out how you could transform it into something more to your liking."

Demetra felt the jab. "I can't help what I feel. At least I'm truthful when I say I couldn't live in this kind of chaos."

"Chaos! It is always the same. You have never been able to accept me the way I am. Maybe it's a good idea if we let things cool off before we meet again."

"Please, Corey, one day I'd like you to come with me to see my house and the antique shop on Melrose. I wrote to you about it."

"At the moment I haven't got the time or the inclination to see your perfect paradise. Or your little junk shop, for that matter."

Demetra felt her wounds deepen but mustered enough composure not to show it.

Corey kept on. "Harley Hadesson's mother told one of my friends about it. As far as I'm concerned, you left me, Dad, and your home for a junk shop on Melrose. That is really what it's all about, Mom."

"Yes—I have gone from riches to rags. But now I've gone on to riches of a different sort." She looked around at Corey's surroundings. "Of all people, I thought you might have understood this."

Demetra saw that the steely look in her daughter's eyes had softened.

"While you finish your lunch, I have something important I want to tell you, so please listen, please *hear* me."

Corey frowned and put down her sandwich. "Don't tell me you're getting married."

Demetra shook her head. "Right after I left Greenhill House I wrote to the parent convent in Toulouse. A letter finally arrived a few weeks ago. I wanted to talk to you, to tell you what I'd learned, but I didn't know how or where to find you."

"What did it say?"

Demetra repeated the contents of the letter from memory, then told her daughter about the so-far futile search for Charles Duval.

Corey's eyes brimmed with tears. She threw her arms around her mother and held her close as they cried together.

"Mom, this has given you so much pain. Dad was right when he told you not to make the search. Now you have finally learned. We are all the family you have. Come back to Greenhill House. *Please.* Dad may have made plans to marry Marina, but I know he wants you back. Please, Mom."

Demetra shook her head. "No, Corey, I love you very much, you know I do. But I've taken this path and I'm sticking to it."

"Then just answer one question for me, Mom. Have you been going out on dates?"

"I've been seeing a college professor. We're just friends…"

"The idea of your seeing other men bothers me, Mom."

"You don't have to worry. I know I am not the right woman for him. Or, for that matter, that he is the right man for me. But we've become good friends."

Cory, visibly relieved reached out to put her arm around her mother's shoulder. Then she withdrew abruptly, and without any softness in her voice, said, "But I'm still upset that you're so intent on making the search. Come on—we'd better get out of here. I don't want to be late."

CHAPTER IX

Demetra wondered how she could get through the Christmas holidays alone. Still no word from Corey after their unsatisfying downtown meeting. Farrell had gone off to Phuket with his friend. Tony had already left for Connecticut to spend the holidays with his ailing mother and his many relatives. He had invited Demetra to join them: although she was tempted, she did not have the heart to accept. It would not have been fair to either Tony or his family to tag along. Why should they share their festive Italian Natale with a woman who rarely laughed, a woman who kept hearing the sadness in her own voice? So, as if to console herself, she bought a bowl of fragrant paperwhites from a flower shop on Melrose.

The closer to December 25, Christmas, the more she thought of Seattle and happier times. Family times.

On Sunday before Christmas she made a red-ribbon spray from ivy runners she'd cut from the banks behind the house, just as she used to do in Seattle. She gathered up pinecones to heap in a polished copper pot beside the small pile of holiday cards sent from customers, dealers and suppliers.

Finally, the night before Christmas Eve, she mustered up the courage to call Kevin's line at Greenhill House.

"Mrs. Killingsworth, I'm so happy to hear from you!"

"I was hoping you'd pick up the phone. I'm relieved that you still have your job—and that makes me happy too."

"So far, so good. Mr. K's been out of the country a good deal."

"Has Corey been by to see him?"

"She came by often after you left, but after she broke up with Harley Hadesson she hasn't been back. I've been told she'll be dropping by on Christmas Eve. Then she'll be off to Malibu for Christmas Eve dinner with her boyfriend Michael's parents."

"Do you know what time she arrives?"

"Around six o'clock. Mr. K. told Cook to prepare a platter of smoked salmon and caviar, and I've been given orders to polish the Georgian wine coolers for the champagne."

"Thank you, you've no idea how happy you've made me."

"Please don't tell a soul or else I might lose my job."

"Don't worry, Kevin! You know how discreet I am."

Christmas business was dismal. Yesterday she had made only two sales. Demetra began to doubt her judgment, her taste, her choices. Maybe Diana was right about it all being all junk; maybe people preferred buying presents in a place like Bullock's Wilshire or the Broadway where they could be exchanged for pots, pans, perfume, or pantyhose.

Early on Christmas Eve she washed and dried her hair, brushed it and clasped it back with a barrette. The weather report predicted light frost. She tossed her second-hand fake fur over her old but flattering apricot cashmere turtleneck and matching wool skirt.

Lipstick neither too red nor too pale, Demetra, she told herself, and only a hint of liner around the eyes. Corey had never liked her to wear much make-up.

Just after the sun had fallen on the year's shortest day, Demetra parked her station wagon across from Greenhill House's gates which were hung with two huge holly wreaths. Red, white, and pink cyclamen bordered the drive. From the car window she saw tiny white lights blink on illuminating the façade of Greenhill House.

She turned on a tape of Puccini arias, then sat back to listen and wait.

At seven-thirty a Bel Air police patrol car slowed down and came to a halt beside her station wagon. The guard signaled for her to open her window.

"Good evening, Officer Daley," she said, lowering the volume on her car radio.

"Mrs. Killingsworth! I haven't seen you in a long time."

"I'm waiting for my daughter."

"I saw her drive up to the house earlier today. Must have been around four o'clock when I came on duty."

"I'm going to stay here until she leaves this house, Officer."

"I understand. Take real good care of yourself, Ma'am. It's sure nice to see you again. Merry Christmas!"

She closed the window and turned up the tape, all the while keeping her eyes focused on the house. By the flash of light from the open front door, she saw that Marshall was saying goodbye to Corey.

She got out of the car to stand by the gates so her daughter would be sure to see her.

Corey got into her car and revved up the engine. Marshall waved and went back into the house. The car made its way around the circular drive and waited for the gates to part. Demetra waved. Her eyes met Corey's in the headlights' glare, but the car drove on.

"Stop—stop—Corey—it's me! Mom! "

Corey's car disappeared.

Staggering back to the car, Demetra slid into the driver's seat and lay her head on the steering wheel, hugging it tight as though it might keep her from shattering. Although her insides screamed, she was dry-eyed.

She heard a tap on the window.

She looked up.

It was Kevin.

He opened the door. He was out of breath.

She leaped out and flung her arms around him. She began to cry.

"I'm so sorry, Mrs. Killingsworth. I saw her, but she did not stop the car. I saw it all from the second floor. You'd better move on! Mr. Killingsworth is leaving!"

She could hardly get the words out. "Please, take care he doesn't see you. I'm afraid for your job."

"I'll dash around to the service entrance. Good luck!" He gave her a hug and ran off.

An instant later she heard a car engine. Headlights beamed in the drive.

She turned her ignition key. Click. She tried again. Lights flickered on her dashboard, as a car made its way to the parting gates. The Bentley. She sat rooted in her seat, hoping Marshall would not notice her station wagon. She flicked the car lock and pressed her forehead against the wheel and waited, her heart hammering as though it wanted to break out from her chest. She heard the motor turn off and a car door slam.

Tap-tap on the window. "Demetra! It's you, isn't it?"

She looked up into Marshall's eyes, relieved that a solid glass sheet protected her. He was even more handsome than she had let herself remember, as though he had just spent a holiday in the sun.

He knocked on the window. "Open up! I want to talk to you—please, Demetra. Let us be civilized about this." His voice was pleading, even gentle. Maybe he was more like the old Marshall again.

She shook her head. No words would come out of her mouth.

"I signed the papers today. I was going to call you tomorrow. They're my Christmas present to you." He smiled.

She sat stricken by the malice in his face.

"Don't you want to thank me?"

She was tempted to open the door to slap his face.

"Or maybe it's the other way around. I should be thanking you, Demetra. You made things easy for me."

She reached for the ignition, her hand shaking so hard she was afraid she would not get the engine started, but this time it turned over. She put the gear into drive and drove off, her body in a sweat, tears streaming. From her rear-view mirror she could see Marshall standing in the road looking after her car.

As soon as Demetra unlocked her front door, she yanked off the ivy spray. Then she touched a match to the gas starter. When flame licks darted from the burning logs, she dumped the pinecones into the fire, comforted by the glowing sparks. One by one she tossed in the Christmas cards, all except the card of thanks from grateful Milly. Then came the ivy, last the mistletoe. She wanted no reminders of this so-called sacred night

Although she rarely drank alone, she opened a bottle of red wine. Christmases past, Cristal champagne from a Baccarat flute; this Christmas, Chianti from a kitchen tumbler. She sat by the fire, staring into the leaping flames, fireworks of hissing, sputtering sparks. No cards, no carols, no music, no midnight mass.

She reached for the photo album and turned to Corey at eight years old.

Was this the girl who drove right past me, my daughter? The daughter who helped me knead dough and line muffin tins, who scattered wild-flower seeds in our back yard? No, it could not have been my Corey. It had to have been someone else.

She relived Christmases Past. Baking gingerbread ornaments with Corey, finding the perfect blue spruce that Marshall felled so swiftly, so deftly with his well-honed ax. All three-driving home in the beat-up pickup truck heaped with forest greenery and mistletoe. After dinner she and Marshall untangled Christmas lights which he would weave through the boughs and, without fail announce, "Not enough lights—I'll drive to the hardware store for a few more strings." And when the tree was decorated, he would always say, "It still needs a few more ornaments." Then he would lift Corey high so she could pin her star to the top.

She checked her watch. An hour had passed. She had guzzled down all the wine knowing that it might be the only way to get through Christmas Eve. Then she fell into her unmade bed and slept until two o'clock on Christmas Day.

She tried to find something to eat in her half-empty refrigerator—her raw stomach needed solace, but the only food she felt like eating was bread. Whole wheat bread. Two by two she toasted the slices, until more than half the loaf was gone.

That afternoon because she felt the need to be among people, she drove to Pasadena to see *Amadeus,* the new film about Mozart. For Christmas night dinner she bought herself a giant tub of popcorn. With butter.

By the time New Year's Eve turned into the end of New Year's Day, she had seen all the movies in the multiplex, every one of them with giant buttered popcorn. And in only a few days she had finished the box of See's Candies that Tony had given her before he went off to Boston. Her clothes were tight. Even her shoes were tight. She had gained seven pounds over the holidays. The luster in her eyes had dimmed, her face looked puffy, her skin blotchy. She became careless about washing her hair.

Didn't care.

Her sheets had not been changed in almost three weeks.

Didn't care.

The kitchen table was stacked with unread newspapers, the sink heaped with dirty dishes. When she passed the mirror, she hardly recognized herself.

Didn't care.

On January 15 she re-opened *Choses*. She turned on the Granados *Goyescas* to break the stillness and, at the same time, still her mind.

The rest of the day was slow. Only one sale.

On January 16, two sales and one exchange.

When she got home, she found an airmail letter from Corey, postmarked Papeete, French Polynesia.

Dear Mother,

On Christmas Eve Dad told me about the divorce going through. I was terribly upset as I was leaving Greenhill House. It was probably around seven-thirty, and a woman was standing by the gates. When I saw her waving her arms and shouting, I drove right by, thinking she was probably one of those people hanging around outside the gates waiting for movie stars. I was on my way to spend Christmas Eve dinner with Michael's family. We all left for Moorea after Christmas Day lunch.

This morning I had a flash. It suddenly hit me that the woman could have been you, Mom. You know I am not that bad a person so, even though I'm still upset with you, the least I can do is say I'm really sorry if it was you standing there. Maybe something inside me knew it was you. But then you probably did not realize what was going on inside me *that night. I felt my world had blown up and I blamed you for it. Michael has insisted that I call you to wish you Merry Christmas, but I decided that I was not going to see you or talk to you until I worked things out with him. Michael's parents seem to approve of me. They are Catholic and have been urging us to get married, but I do not want to. Not yet, anyway.*

Dad still has not come to grips with the idea of Michael being Italian. His parents are lots of fun. They love scuba diving and fishing and at night we all get together while his Mom makes spaghetti sauce with the clams we dig up. My dream is that someday we could all be one big happy family again *and that you and Dad will make up.*

You will be glad to know that I'm speaking French daily. Thanks again for teaching me, Mom. Michael is calling me to go sailing
Happy New Year and lots of love,
Corey xxxx,

P.S. I got your address from Kevin. We may be back in Los Angeles in a week or two. We found another loft with better light and this should please you—also better "facilities". I promise to call the minute we are back in town. "

How many times had she read the letter? By the time she put it away, she had studied every phrase, every word, every implication.

That night she changed the sheets, cleaned up the house and instead of going to bed at seven-thirty as she had since Christmas, she went to bed at midnight and had the best night's sleep in months.

***

The rest of the week Demetra scoured the classified ads for Friday morning garage and house sales.

She was becoming aware that lately her search for "things" bordered on mania, mostly because the quest for Duval had produced nothing. She had simply exchanged one obsession for another. More than once she had phoned the convent in Toulouse begging for more information, but even with her fluent French, she got nowhere. Nothing more was known about this shadowy Charles Duval, the Mother Superior insisted.

As she scanned the newspapers, she intuitively checked off a few ads to follow up. She had begun to trust her instincts, but she knew that it was usually a key word or phrase that set her imagination into motion. "*Faded carpets bought in Damascus*"—or "*Victorian treasure trove.*" Ads clearly written to seduce. In Thursday's *Los Angeles Times* she read:

Contents of old Pasadena estate. Owner-collector formerly in consular service. Fourteen rooms crammed with antique furniture, Chinese ceramics, bronzes, oil paintings, old perfume bottles. Doors open on Friday morning. No one allowed entry before 10:00. a.m.

She thought she would be the first to arrive at the mansion, but a line had already formed. After helping herself to a complimentary cup of coffee, she stood at the end of the long queue and waved to Farrell who must have arrived before dawn.

At last the door opened after what seemed an endless wait, and the crowd jostled and shoved its way into the house. Antique dealers and compulsive collectors scurried about for bargains, yanking off price tags, just in case, since a tag in hand meant the right to buy the merchandise.

By the time she reached the living room, most of the items had been claimed but no one seemed to have noticed the primitive painting of the Cuzco Madonna hanging in the passage. The wistful Virgin held a rose in her hand, swags of painted pearls looped across the skirt of her wide dress. She stood, smiling sweetly, upon a crescent moon.

The price tag read $1200. Although she had never spent that much on any single item for *Choses*, why not mull it over and decide whether to buy the painting after looking through the entire house?

Inside a kitchen cupboard she found six black and white sun and moon faced Fornasetti plates from the fifties. Twenty-five dollars for six plates. Not bad, she thought. People were beginning to collect pieces from Fornasetti's Milan studio. She yanked off the tag just in case Farrell had not noticed them.

Prowling around, she found some old Guerlain perfume bottles from the thirties on a bedroom dresser. *Mitsouko, Shalimar, l'Heure Bleue.*

The crowd had gone for the big stakes—the Second Empire Boulle furniture, a questionable Rosa Bonheur, garish cloisonné enamels, and florid nineteenth century *animalier* bronzes. Farrell appeared with a small Vienna Secession rug over his arm.

They stood together in the long payment queue.

"How did I ever miss those plates? Thanks, Demetra! Did you find anything for yourself?"

"I'm going to splurge on the Cuzco School Madonna."

"She's charming, but pricey. My colleagues say they do not do very well with religious stuff. Strange that Santos and Italian crèche figures just don't move in L.A."

"I wonder why not. After all, this is the city of the Queen of the Angels. Besides, I do not find her so 'religious' with festooned with all those roses and pearls. I can hardly wait to give her a place of honor in my window."

***

Friday was never a busy day for *Choses* since it was on that day women usually did their weekend marketing or cooking.

For Demetra it was a good day for changing the window display.

Out came the bamboo-cane shelves laden with Edwardian majolica and the fern-filled glass and brass Wardian case. When the window was cleared, she stacked some bricks in the center, propping the painting against them. Around the base she swirled an ivory-fringed Spanish shawl floss-embroidered with pink roses and a meandering jasmine vine. Its colors matched those in the Madonna's dress.

Farrell ran out to buy some roses from the boy who always stood by the off-ramp of the Hollywood Freeway. He then arranged them in an old crystal vase to set before the painting.

All afternoon she walked in and out of the shop admiring the window's effect from the street. She would put an outrageous price on the painting as insurance that it would not be sold for a long, long time.

It was almost three o'clock by the time she finished her sandwich, and the doorbell announced the day's first customer. Demetra peeked through the curtain.

Gail Claiborne, of all people. Today she wore an ankle length skirt in a colorful flower-splashed print, a tucked-in wood-rose cashmere sweater, and around her small waist, a burgundy leather belt edged in gold coins. An olive green and cream woven shawl was draped over one shoulder. It was decidedly one of Gail's signature semi-bohemian getups.

She threw her arms around Demetra as though they were long lost friends. "I've wondered what on earth had become of you! It's such a while since we've seen each another—I think the last time was at the reception you gave at..."

Demetra drew back slightly. "I'm happy to see you, Gail."

"This is your shop?"

She nodded. "Have a look around if you'd like."

"One of our Never Too Late members mentioned that you'd opened an antique shop and I've been meaning to find out where. Then when I saw that Peruvian Madonna in the window, I came to a screeching halt and almost got rear ended!"

"I hope you think she was worth the risk."

"Depends. Do you think she's might be one of those official government fakes from Peru?"

"I don't know much about Spanish Colonial art, but I *do* know she's old because I went over it with a black light and examined the canvas very carefully."

"If she's for sale, may I make an offer?"

"I just put her in the window this afternoon. I'd hoped she stay there for a while."

"How about $6000?"

Demetra took a deep breath. Six thousand dollars was five times more than what she had paid for the painting. She had obviously made a good buy.

"I sense your hesitation. Maybe I did not offer you enough. Name your price then, and we'll negotiate."

"I was only taken aback by your instant decision."

Gail pushed back her glasses and looked straight into Demetra's eyes. "That's the only way to buy anything. The Madonna just screamed out to me from your window. *Buy me!*"

"Do you collect Cuzco Madonnas?"

She shook her head. "Not really, I buy only what knocks me out."

"What the French call *le coup de foudre*. The Madonna is yours then." She felt her heart thud: she had to accept Gail's offer.

Gail pulled out her checkbook while Demetra wrote a receipt.

"Do you want to take the painting with you? I can wrap it in newspaper and twine."

"No need—just some newspaper to line the car trunk. I cannot wait to get her home. By the way, I thought your Feast of the Gods theme was brilliant. I told you that in my note."

"I was touched that you took the time to send it to me. I should have written to thank you."

"I was sorry to hear about your divorce."

"It should have happened long ago but..." she hesitated and smiled. "Here's another instance when it's never too late."

"Is there a day when you might be free for lunch?"

"I can't leave the shop. Lunch hour is my busiest time."

Gail pulled out an oversized agenda from her shoulder bag. "Let us make a dinner date, then. I have my calendar right here". She laughed. "Doubles as my dream journal, as well."

"Dream journal?"

"Yes, I record my dreams," she said, as though she might be talking about composing her grocery lists. "It's the very first thing I do in the morning. I keep the book by my bedside, right under my dream- catcher. When I woke up this morning, I knew that I had to drive down Melrose, just as I had done in last night's dream."

Gail thumbed through her date book. "How about next Friday night—January 18? I know that Chris has invited Simon Heath, the director of his new movie. If you are free, we would love to have you join us. Then you can see where I've hung your Madonna of the Roses."

Demetra hesitated. On the freeway, downtown Los Angeles was only twenty minutes from Sierra Madre, where Gail lived. She had not been to a dinner party in a long time, and she wouldn't know a soul there. Besides, actors were usually so self-centered.

"Thank you, Gail," she said, "Although I'd really like to accept, I don't think I should."

"Don't worry. I'll send someone to fetch you, so you won't have to drive."

"I have no problem driving—it's just that I've..."

"Good. I'll expect you then. Around eight o'clock?" She opened her notebook and handed her a map with clearly printed directions. "Dress casually and bring a sweater. It gets chilly in the foothills." She glanced at her watch. "It's past 2:30! Time to hit the freeway before the traffic gets bad." She took Demetra's hands in hers.

Demetra hoped she didn't notice her bitten fingers.

"Are you happier now in this new life of yours?"

"Happier? No. Freer, yes." She was surprised how easy it was to answer Gail.

"Let us save our long talk for next week. What a lovely afternoon it has been, finding my Madonna here with you." She kissed Demetra's cheek. "I always felt you were different, that you stood apart from the rest of the group."

"I thought the same about you, Gail." Despite her exuberance, Demetra felt Gail's serenity, her directness, her completeness. "I'll always remember today."

"Yes, synchronicity, wasn't it?" She revved up the engine then drove off waving.

"*Synchronicity.*" What did that word mean? Maybe it was like serendipity—the Indian word for wondrous happenstance. But maybe it meant more than that. She must remember to look it up.

When she returned to *Choses,* she set about straightening the window, overcome with an unexpected sense of loss as she gazed at the stack of bare bricks still draped with the Spanish shawl. Maybe she should have kept the painting, for a few months at least. True, she had made an enormous profit and the painting would have a good home because Gail loved it, but still she wished she hadn't sold it; it was as though she had traded part of herself for money.

***

She turned the arrows on the paper clock. "Back at 2:30." She would visit Farrell next door for jubilation or for consolation, she was not quite sure which.

He was sitting in his favorite Morris chair reading a Christie's catalogue. "What's up? You look worried."

"I suppose I should be ecstatic, but I'm not. I just sold the Cuzco painting."

"Who bought it?"

"Gail Claiborne. An acquaintance from my Never Too Late days."

"Her husband is Chris Claiborne, the actor, right?"

"She was so happy to find it that she offered me $6,000."

"Wow! An offer you could not refuse. What did you pay for it?"

"Twelve hundred dollars."

"Hell—you made out like a bandit! You got five times what you paid. In only one day! Every antique dealer's dream. Be happy!"

"I'm not sure I should have sold it in the first place."

"Come off it, Demetra. Are you going to be a dealer or are you not going to be a dealer? Besides, more stuff—even better stuff—will come your way. Wait and see. That's what makes this business so incredible. Please don't think I'm a New Age weirdo when I tell you about my little theory."

She laughed. "I could never think that, so what is it?"

"Sometimes I have this sense that a certain shop is urging me to stop by, and if it is a strong enough feeling, I go out of my way to follow it. Most of my best finds were made that way. Usually it's an object I've consciously thought about, which makes it even stranger."

"I wonder if that's what Gail meant when she called finding the Cuzco painting 'synchronicity.' "

"That's exactly the word my friend uses. *Synchronicity.* It's supposed to mean much more than coincidence. My friend says that whenever he has deep dreams, or when he is into meditation, he finds that these 'meaningful coincidences' occur."

"I hardly ever recall my dreams," she said, "but whenever I do, they stay with me for a long time."

"He told me that whenever you have one of these synchronistic experiences, look back and try to remember and reflect on what you've been dreaming."

She smiled. "You, Farrell, of all people, should know how busy I am. In my world there's no time for silly dream reflections." The moment these words were out of her mouth, a little frisson of fear traveled along her spine as her dream surfaced.

She is now in an ancient place, way back in time. She pulls up another shell from the gravelly earth and turns it over in her hand "This is a far, far older place than that." She pulls up another shell from the gravelly earth. She speaks to the woman. "Perlmutter, madre di perla, mother- of- pearl." She does not know why she speaks these words, but she does.

She checked her watch. "I'd better get back to the shop."

"You're not leaving until you sit down and have a cup of tea with me. I haven't seen enough of you lately."

CHAPTER X

The sign at the gate read *"Mountain Mists."* Gail's house nestled into the curve of a mesa in the San Gabriel Mountains, the last of the private acres before protected forest reserve. A white rail fence surrounded the property, and stands of tall poplars and live oaks bordered both sides of the long gravel drive winding up to the hacienda-style adobe house

She pushed the buzzer and announced herself into the gate speakerphone, something she had not done since Greenhill House. The gates yawned open. She parked the station wagon in the courtyard where, although it was still light, gas lights flickered. A *copa de oro* vine, a thick garland of enameled green leaves and blaring yellow trumpets, festooned the house's arcaded facade.

Chris Claiborne greeted her at the door. He wasn't nearly as tall as she thought he'd be, but that was usually the way with larger-than-life stars. "Welcome, Demetra. Gail's so happy that you could join us tonight and so am I."

As he hung her coat, Demetra paused to admire a still life on the console table. A white rose in a pearly Roman glass bottle, a blade of ripened barley, a pomegranate, and an olive branch lay on the worm-eaten walnut.

"Gail's just finishing up in the kitchen so I'll tend to the introductions." He took her arm to lead her to the guests.

This was the first dinner party she had attended on her own. Ever. Marshall had never allowed her to accept a dinner invitation when he was out of town—even with a safe male escort, even with a woman. Her stomach churned, her tongue felt dry, she was not sure what sounds would come out of her mouth. It was as though she had to compose and memorize sentences in her head before uttering them.

As they stepped down into the sunken living room, she tripped, lunging forward to seize Chris's arm to keep from landing on her bottom. Her face flooded with color. She heaved a sigh and drew herself together, thankful that at least there were only two other guests in the room.

"I'd like you to meet Simon Heath," Chris said as he introduced her to a callow looking Scot with scant hair, bulging forehead and pale blue eyes. Heath made a reluctant effort to rise from the deep-down sofa to shake her hand.

She was obviously an intrusion.

"And this is Maeve Peters. Maeve just arrived from Manchester this afternoon. We begin shooting some scenes together next week."

Maeve, who seemed not much older than Corey, had long straight hair, a wide face with high cheekbones, and eyes unusually slanted for a blonde. A Finnish face. Her teeth were almost too small for her full lips, giving her a slightly feral look. After the introductions, the young woman turned her attention back to Simon Heath and continued their intense conversation, making Demetra feel even more unwelcome.

"What would you like to drink, Demetra?" Chris asked.

Her mind went blank. "White wine if you have it, thank you," she finally stammered even though she had never liked drinking white wine on an empty stomach.

As Chris opened a bottle of white Burgundy, Demetra took in the beauty of the room. Faded kilims covered the herringbone hardwood floors. Bunches of orange and peach Iceland poppies were massed in glass bubble bowls, wheat sheaves in a Chinese stoneware pot. Votive lights flickered on the Tuscan credenza. The effect was warm, mysterious, womb-like.

Gail, wrapped in a huge white apron over her long pale green cashmere dress, hugged Demetra. "You see, it wasn't so hard to find us after all. I half expected an SOS call from some pay phone."

"I'm so happy to be here with you in your beautiful home."

"After dinner I shall give you The Grand Tour if you feel like it. I have some last -minute stirring to do. Why don't you come on into the kitchen with me?"

A fire burned in the fireplace on the sitting room side of the kitchen. The walls and cupboards were waxed pine, the terra cotta floors inset with blue and white Portuguese tiles. Copper pots hung from an oval ring over the scrubbed oak refectory table.

Demetra inhaled the fragrance of nutmeg and vanilla, mixed with the thick, winy odor of simmering stew. Lifting the lid, Gail said, "*Navarin* of lamb, a variation on my English mother's lamb stew." A long rolling pin stuck with bits of dough and flour lay on the floury marble pastry counter. A deep, sugar-crusted pie sat cooling on a wire rack. "Apple-sultana pie for dessert."

"I'd live in this kitchen if it were mine. Marshall had such a neurotic compulsion for order. Every utensil had to be stashed away in a drawer or cupboard."

"I can't imagine living with such a controlling man. How did you take it as long as you did?"

"I often ask myself that same question."

Gail looked up at the wall clock. "I hope our other guest isn't lost somewhere in the mountains. We will just have to sit tight and wait. Before we join the others, I have something I would like to give to you, without anyone else around."

She handed Demetra a folder made of coarse, mottled paper, the recycled kind.

She pulled it open. "How lovely! Like antique Venetian *arte povera*. Wherever did you find it?"

"I made it. For *you*. This is what I do to keep busy when I'm on location with Chris. Or at home alone when he's away. Our children are married or in graduate school, so now I have the time to be creative."

"Where do you find the materials?"

"I'm always on the lookout for old pages from nineteenth century botanicals and prints. You know, those nature series with butterflies, fruits, vegetables, flowers, fish, seashells. I cut them up and turn them into pictures along with cutouts from auction catalogues and art magazines."

The design was a powerfully surreal seascape. In the deep transparent water, exotic fish swam, and fantastic sea flora bloomed. A small boat skimmed the water. Pennants, on which were embossed strange symbols, fluttered from the masthead. A beautiful woman reclined in the boat, her long, fair tresses billowing behind her in the wind. An iridescent full moon glowed in the sky.

"The moon is a life-size color photograph of a giant 18-millimeter pearl. I cut it out from a Christie's jewelry catalogue. Doesn't it have an ethereal glow? "

"I'll always treasure this—thank you." She wanted to kiss Gail's cheek, but she thought that it might seem too familiar.

"Turn it over and read what it says."

To Demetra,
Thank you for my Madonna.
I look at her every morning
When I open my eyes.
Love, Gail

She tried to keep her voice from breaking. "I hardly know what to say or how to thank you enough." For an instant she thought she might tell Gail about the disheartening letter from the convent. And about Charles Duval. She longed to unburden her feelings, but she pushed away the impulse.

They rejoined the group in the living room.

Fifteen minutes later the bell rang. Chris went to the door and reappeared with a tall, familiar-looking man with grey-streaked dark hair. He was wearing a heather tweed jacket, a teal shirt, a knit tie. "I apologize for being late, but I was abysmally lost. My terrible sense of direction. Never fails me," he said with a broad smile. "Not typical for someone of my ancestry." He laughed as though Gail might have understood what he meant.

"Demetra, I'd like you to meet the writer of *Morris Dance*." Gail said. "I *know* he's been looking forward to meeting you. Surprise!" She grinned.

Demetra felt the blood flushing her face as she extended her hand.

Thomas Pierson was much taller than he appeared on the book jacket. His face was strong and ruddy as though he spent a lot of time in the wind. He had a long, Celtic upper lip, a square cleft chin, and his serious blue eyes sought hers as he grasped her hands. "At last! Why haven't you returned my calls?"

"I really meant to, but sometimes I'm a terrible procrastinator. I'm sorry."

"Don't apologize. It was in the cards to happen this way."

Chris offered him a drink.

"No thanks. I will not hold up Gail's dinner. I have a feeling it's ready."

Gail nodded and led them to the dining room where she seated Demetra between Chris and Thomas.

On each stoneware plate lay an oversized white linen napkin pushed through a ring made of terra cotta. Demetra complimented the table setting. "Your napkin rings look like ancient pottery."

"What an eye!" Gail said. "They're Roman—at least third century. Our archaeologist friend in Israel digs them up by the barrelful. Thousands of them. At the end of summer, they toss them all on the rubbish heap. After all, how many jug handles can a museum use? I asked him to save some for me."

Chris laughed. "Gail loves anything made of earth—clay tiles, terra cotta pots, adobe houses like ours," Chris said, filling Demetra's glass with wine. As she sipped the mellow claret, she felt as though she had come to a tranquil and protected place.

The table conversation was mostly about film and *Morris Dance*.

"I thought that writers didn't have much to say about their story once shooting gets under way," Demetra said to Chris.

"That's usually the case, but Tom and Simon were classmates at Oxford, so they decided to work together in mutual respect."

Demetra was quiet, still feeling the outsider. At least be honest with Pierson, she urged herself. "I'm embarrassed to admit that I haven't read your new novel. But I did read *Patterans*. What's *Morris Dance about*?"

"It's the story of three generations of gentlemen farmers from 1875 to 1963. Takes place in the north of England."

"When I was a child, I used to play the Morris Dance on the piano." She laughed. "Whenever I heard it, I imagined little green gnomes hopping around a campfire. I've always wondered why it was called 'Morris Dance'."

"Now that's a good question. We'll let the director answer that one."

Simon turned to Demetra. "A Morris Dance is an English folk dance sometimes danced around a maypole, but there are scholars like Frazer who say it was danced in early pagan nature rites."

Thomas added, "Some say it's the dance of gypsies or tinkers wandering about England. Chris plays the rich landowner at the end of the last century: he is unaware that his mother is part gypsy. That is all I will tell you for now, but if you like I'll give you the script to read."

Demetra thought she saw Maeve's eyes darken; her full lips tighten slightly against her perfect white teeth.

"Tomorrow I'm going to ring up Claudia to tell her that we've finally met." Thomas said, "I want to catch her before she runs off for the Seychelles."

"If I were Claudia, I'd never leave Cherwell Castle," Demetra said, "It's so cozy and comfortable and her lovely gardens with all those billowing perennial borders."

"But didn't you leave your beautiful house and..." His eyes clouded. "I'm sorry. That was boorish of me." He reached over and placed his hand over hers.

She thought his touch over-familiar, unusual for an Englishman she had just met. "I'm not sure what you've heard about me."

"Claudia told me about your leaving, and your circumstances."

"It was entirely my decision to leave Greenhill House. No one forced me out." She took another swallow of wine. "Are you writing another novel?"

He nodded." It's due to be released next year, and then we hope to start film production soon after."

"What's this one about?"

"A Victorian romance. About Ruskin and Rose La Touche, the much younger woman in his life. "

"I once read *Effie in Venice*, about Ruskin and his first wife."

"So you know that Ruskin had more than a little difficulty with sex."

"I remember very clearly," she said turning her eyes away from his.

"My book is about Ruskin's forays into spiritualism after Rose La Touche dies. By the way, you know that picture of you on Claudia's piano. The photographer did not capture your wistful quality. I think I may have fallen in love with you long before I got on the plane to Los Angeles."

She felt the blood rush again. "Good heavens what a line! You must surely be Irish, not English!" She laughed.

He helped himself to another of Gail's homemade rolls and spread it lavishly with butter. "I wasn't born in England 'though I grew up in Yorkshire. My brother, his wife, and sons, still live in the family house. I live in East Riding, not too far from Scarborough."

"I've never been quite that far north."

"My house is built in the middle of wild dunes on a cliff overlooking the sea. A Victorian gentleman's Moorish fantasy built about 1880. I live there alone."

"You're not married then?"

"No. I lived with a woman for almost six years. A dancer from the Royal Ballet. Although we had finally set the wedding date, she walked out on me. That was about three years ago. We had no children. She didn't want any." He buttered a piece of Gail's homemade bread. "Now she's married to a rich sheep baron in Australia and I'm happy for her. I do not blame her for leaving me. It's not easy living with a writer."

He poured more wine in Demetra's glass. "Since then I've had a few distractions from my work, but they didn't amount to much." He looked straight into her eyes. "I admit I need a woman in my life."

She felt color rising to her face. "How did we ever get on this subject? Excuse me, I didn't mean to...."

"What's to excuse? It is normal. No! I take that back. It is *abnormal*. Two people our age, each living alone. Don't you mind living alone?"

"I don't because I'm not always lonely. But even if I were, it's still a small price to pay for one's freedom."

"I suspect your host would enjoy a chance to talk with you so why don't we continue our conversation another time? I've discovered a place in downtown Los Angeles, on lower Sunset. *Sevilla de Oro.* There's a flamenco guitarist and dancing on weekends"

"I've driven past it but have never been there. I have always loved flamenco. Do you?"

He nodded. "I visit Andalusia at least once a year. Why don't I come by for you at eight o'clock tomorrow night? We'll have dinner and see the show."

"It's very nice of you, but…"

"I'll get your phone number and address before we leave."

During the rest of the dinner whenever Demetra looked at Maeve, she tried to ignore the jealous twinges she was feeling. In the candlelight the actress's profile seemed so refined, so angelically pre-Raphaelite as she leaned across the dinner table intent in conversation with Thomas.

Demetra turned to Chris, almost afraid to overhear them, while her mind formed pictures. *There she was, Demetra, sitting with Thomas Pierson at Sevilla de Oro, sipping a glass of amontillado, applauding the dancers.*

It was as though Maeve had been reading her thoughts. The next instant, the actress excused herself from the table. Demetra's eyes followed her as she passed the full-length mirror in the hallway and paused to stare at herself admiringly, lifting her long, thick, almost waist length hair up and away from her face and smiling. Then she stepped. back, her eyes still fixed, unwaveringly, on her own reflection.

CHAPTER XI

On Saturday afternoon she wondered what she should wear for her dinner with Thomas, waiting until the very last minute to decide, just as she had always done at Greenhill House. Some habits must never change, she thought, as she tucked an old red silk blouse into a black velvet skirt, wrapping and tying a black crushed leather belt around her waist. She was relieved that the skirt still fit. The weight was coming off gradually.

How right the fringed and embroidered Spanish shawl at *Choses* would have been with this outfit, but then she quickly dismissed the idea as being too thought-out, too much like s costume.

After brushing her hair from her forehead, she tied it back loosely with a black velvet ribbon and stood back to study the effect, wondering why she'd never before worn this dramatic, very Spanish combination of red and black. She flung her arms high above her head in what she imagined to be a flamenco pose. Then, embarrassed by her silliness, turned away abruptly from her reflection.

She turned on her new tape; Puccini's *Turandot* starring Placido Domingo who had sung the role of Calaf in the Los Angeles Olympics production at the Music Center only a few days after the

Feast of the Gods gala. The tape was her consolation prize for missing the performance.

When she opened the door for Thomas, he handed her a bouquet of striped yellow and red parrot tulips and kissed her on both cheeks.

"Thank you—how beautiful! Like the tulips in a Dutch painting. I was afraid you might not find your way up here."

"Your directions were brilliant."

"Please make yourself comfortable while I put these in a vase."

This was a great Old Masters sale," he said, leafing through the old Christie's catalogue Demetra had left on the table. He held up the double page color photograph. "My brother sold this one."

She recognized the Titian. A painting of Venus.

"It fetched a tidy sum, bought by a British museum."

"I just saw a slide of a similar painting only a week ago. I loved the vase in the corner." She pointed to the vase with a single blue iris. "Why did your brother sell it?"

"He's not the least bit interested in art. Neither is his wife. He's obsessed with his old Bugattis and Ferraris and he has to keep up the house."

"What kind of house?"

"Elizabethan—it's been in my father's family for centuries."

She reached into the cupboard for a bottle of *nouveau* Beaujolais.

He opened the bottle deftly and poured some into tumblers.

They sank down on the sofa. "Welcome to my cottage," she said, raising her glass.

"To our friendship, Demetra. I'm happy, at long last, to be here —sitting next to you."

The voice of Gwyneth Jones filled the room with its presence, commanding them to listen.

"Turandot, the icy princess. Isn't that the famous riddle scene?" he asked.

She turned up the volume. "Turandot is explaining the riddle to Calaf. She's warning him about what will happen if he doesn't give her the right answers to the three questions."

"He'll die like the other suitors who failed," he said, "Knocked off by the frigid princess."

"I guess you'd call her that." She was annoyed by the warm flush she was feeling. "If our reservation is at 8:30, we'd better be leaving— it's almost nine o'clock."

They finished their wine and drove down toward the flickering lights of East Los Angeles to *Sevilla de Oro.*

Since it was a balmy evening *El Patron* led them to a corner table on the patio. "You're in luck tonight because the legendary Conchita del Lago is filling in for Rosita Triana, our principal dancer who called in sick."

"What's the specialty of the house?" Thomas asked the waiter in Spanish.

"I usually recommend *paella,* but there's at least a half hour wait while it cooks. Since the first show will be starting in a few minutes, I recommend the grilled shrimp."

Demetra loved hearing the Castilian lisp, the *th* sound that softened the language.

During dinner she kept the conversation to England, Claudia and Gail. As they were waiting for custard flan she said, "You mentioned your research in the south of France…"

"I'm researching the Gypsies of the Camargue."

"Another book about gypsies?"

"Yes, after I finish the Ruskin story. The plot has been churning around in my head for a long time now."

"I've always wondered how novelists begin to write. It must be like creating a world from chaos."

"It's no great mystery. I can tell you exactly how I begin—always with a visual image, an image that grabs hold of me and will not let go. An obsession."

"But then what do you do with that image?"

"I think about it a lot. I may even do some research on the period, the time, or a place that I don't know much about. When the image becomes fleshed out, I leave it alone for a while, let it incubate. You see, the story is already there in the unconscious, already written, ready to be mined out. Gradually I begin to fit together all the pieces to create a world."

"I try to do more or less the same thing with the bits and pieces I find and put together in my shop."

"Writing is a craft which gets better as you go along. Some people are born with a voice, others develop one as they gain self-confidence by writing, and re-writing. That is really what it's all about. And one more thing. The hardest thing of all—never push the pen over the page unless you are pushing your heart as well as your mind. How do you like to spend your time?"

She took a sip of wine. "By using my eye and whatever taste I've developed during the years at Greenhill House, trying to make a success of *Choses*, my little semi-antique shop. When I put my mind to something, I can be determined."

"And you're also beautiful."

"I've never ever thought so."

"Why aren't you more confident about your looks?"

She took a deep breath. "Marshall always found fault with my appearance. Especially toward the end of our marriage. He got tired of looking at me, I guess."

"He must have been blind."

"He wanted me to change myself."

"Change yourself?"

"I don't want to talk about it. Now —why don't you tell me how you start your day in Yorkshire."

"I get up before dawn, saddle my horse and ride along the beach if it's low tide. If not, I take the high road through the dunes so that I can look down over the sea crashing against the rocks. I love the ocean. I can't imagine living away from it." He sat back in his chair and looked at her for a long moment before he said, "By all accounts I'm not supposed to like the sea."

"Why not?"

He grinned. "Gypsies supposedly hate water. I cannot tell you why. It's in their bones, in the collective unconscious." He searched her eyes, as though he had expected a reaction, and reached for her hand as distant castanets clicked louder, more insistently.

Then, as the guitarist began stroking his guitar, there was a burst of enthusiastic applause for Conchita del Lago who appeared in the center of the patio, castanets arched over her head. She was neither young nor pretty, but she was striking. Her body was slender, long waisted. She was wearing a flounced white skirt, a black bodice, a red silk flower tucked into her chignon. When she danced, her shapely, graceful arms made half-circled swoops, her fingers clicking, rolling castanets.

"She's dancing the *sevillanas*," he whispered. "Traditional Andalusian, =happy, festive dance. Sometimes with castanets. Not flamenco."

As she watched the dancer, her thoughts flew to the time when Marshall was negotiating for a steel mill near Bilbao. The owners had flown them down to Andalusia in their company plane. In the caves of Granada the gypsies had danced for them. Marshall seemed bored during the entire performance, his mind obviously full of spreadsheet figures, but she had never forgotten those spotless whitewashed caves hung with burnished copper, the dancers, the music, so foreign, yet so strangely familiar. And so were the sounds…she remembered *mira, mira!*

She was startled out of her reverie when the dancer made her exit to *olés* and a burst of applause.

"Conchita del Lago is an incredibly good dancer," Thomas said." As good as I have ever seen in this country. Later on, she'll be dancing her alegrias for us—and if we're lucky, the more somber *as a finale*. Did you enjoy her Sevillianas?"

"I did—very much—in her black and white dress she reminds me of the dancer in Sargent's *El Jaleo*. When I was in Boston for the first time I headed straight for the Gardner—and when I stood before the painting I could almost hear the shouting, the clapping as though a real woman were dancing across the enormous canvas 'stage.'"

"The painting is also great favorite of mine. Most people think the dance is called *El Jaleo*, but *jaleo* is really the clapping and shouting, *mira, mira* or *ole'* —encouraging the dancer to give it her all. Imagine the sound of those two guitarists strumming hard — the *cantaor's* voice, full of passion as he sings of sorrow, betrayal, life, death –the plight of his people, a once despised minority."

"In my mind's eye I can still see the dancer flipping her skirt back so eloquently. But she doesn't have castanets in her hands."

"She's most likely dancing the *soleares*, where the dancer pours out her heart and soul—and never with castanets."

She resisted pouring out her own heart by telling him that she'd never learned to dance in the convent, never attended a prom; about Marshall, begrudgingly shuffling her around a dance floor but only when he had to. He kept reminding her that she was clumsy, with no sense of rhythm.

"I've always loved Spanish music. Farrell, my antique dealer friend next door keeps after me to take dance lessons." Shaking her head, she laughed. "But I'm a hopeless case. I could never be a dancer. Certainly not a flamenco dancer!"

"Why not? You are strong and healthy. Why don't you have a go at it, Demetra. It is never too late, you know.

She grinned. "*Never too late?* I've heard that phrase before!"

After dinner Thomas drove Demetra straight home. When he asked to come in, she made no excuses about Sunday being a work-at-home day, as she'd planned. Instead, she went to the kitchen for some wine, and turned on the *Turandot* tape.

The fire had burned out. He quickly started another blaze, with very little smoke and hardly any kindling, as if he were used to building fires every day of his life.

She complimented him on his skill.

"Comes from being a gypsy," he laughed." And from living in an old house without central heating."

"Why do you keep making jokes about being a gypsy? Soon you'll have me believing you,"

"I'm not joking," he said, pinning his eyes on hers so she sensed that he really meant what he said.

Shaking her head, she said, "You've been writing too many romantic novels."

"You told me that you'd read *Patterans*. You must know that first novels usually contain more than a bit of autobiography. Can you remember anything about the story?"

"Only that it was about a well-bred boy who ran away from home to live with the gypsies. With the approval of his parents."

"I suppose you thought it was the work of a florid British imagination, latter-day D.H. Lawrence. How do you think you'd feel about me if you thought it were true?" His tone had become serious.

She smiled. "Something about you *does* remind me of Heathcliff."

"I'm a much nicer bloke than he was. My parents saw to that."

"Tell me about your background, then."

"You want the truth? Keep in mind the old cliché that truth is often stranger than fiction. I have never discussed this with anyone. Not Claudia. Not even Chris."

They settled back on the sofa.

"I'm adopted. From my very first memory of them, my parents always referred to me as their 'gypsy child,' so it was not a shock when I came of age and they explained my origins to me. At least what they knew about them."

"Do you know where you were born?"

"Probably Spain, or the south of France. My mother was an American journalist working in Madrid during the civil war, my father an Anglo-Irish painter living in Cordoba. They met, fell in love, married, and lived in Spain until about 1954 when I was six years old. You may have seen my father's paintings. Very much in the style of Flint who was a mentor and friend."

She nodded. "I've seen many Flints come up at auction."

"As my mother told the story, one day during the spring *Feria,* my father wanted to sketch a view of Segovia, so she packed a picnic lunch to eat on the hill overlooking the Roman aqueduct. Some gypsies were camped there. Nomadic gypsies—*quinqui,* she called them. That folk are not the same as those who have the flamenco tradition in Spain and southern France. Spanish gypsies, the *Calò,* are more integrated into the fabric of Spanish society."

Demetra rapt but amused and smiling inside, was still convinced that this was a tall tale.

"A gypsy woman stepped out of her wagon and approached my parents, urging them to take me, the tow-headed *rubio.* She implored them, insisting that they would be able to give the child a better life. 'Here, *senora,* take *pickaninny*—take *pickaninny,*' she kept urging my mother. I always thought the word came from America, but I have learned since that its origin is Spanish. *pequeno nino*—little child. In any case, my father went to fetch the *Guardia Civil.* Even after the war you saw them on every street corner. They went to the authorities together and my new parents got permission to take me, a two-year-old boy, back to England. They' had tried without luck to have children..."

"You mentioned a brother..."

"In the way it often turns out when children are adopted, my brother was born a year later. And because I am adopted, he is my father's heir and will have his title, became the lord of the manor. "

"Your parents must have given you lots of love. Although I do not know you very well, you seem so well-adjusted."

"I may seem that way," he chuckled. "But I can assure you I'm not. No fiction writer is ever entirely normal."

"What about your parents' families? How did they feel about your parents adopting a gypsy child?"

"My grandparents were close friends of Augustus John, the artist who founded The Gypsy Lore Society, so my mother had grown up hearing about gypsies. They had concluded, though, that I am not a real *Rom* because if I were, the woman would have never given me away. But my would-be wife could not cope with my anonymous background. She was a middle-class English snob, worried about bloodlines as though I were stud breeder. I'm convinced that she didn't want me to be the father of her child."

"We have something in common, then," she said.

"What's that?"

"I don't know who my parents were either." She told him about her thwarted quest ending with the mysterious Charles Duval. When she was finished, he put his arm around her. "Whoever your parents were, you were born with an instinctive love of art and music."

"These past few years I've often found myself wondering what's more important in shaping a person, genes or one's upbringing."

"With writers, I'm all for nature—-heredity over environment. As far back as I can trace there have been no novelists, in my adoptive parents' families. So I've picked up the writing gene from someone."

He grinned. "I like to think it might have come from a writer who came to Spain during the Civil War."

"Someone like Hemingway?"

"You've got it!" His face turned red and he laughed. "Everyone has fantasies. But fiction writers must really depend on them. Now tell me about yours."

"I don't have fantasies. Or I should say I do not allow myself to have them. Only goals."

"You mean you've never daydreamed about living in Shangri-La? Or conducting a symphony orchestra? "

She shook her head.

"Or dancing a *pas de deux* in *Swan Lake*?"

"Sometimes when I listen to opera, I have imagined myself on a stage, but I've never allowed myself to dwell on what I know I can't do. And you already know how I feel about dancing."

He drew her close, brushed his lips against her hair and ran his fingers through its length. Her hair had not been cut since she left Greenhill House.

Then he kissed her hard and tried to find her tongue. She pulled away. She enjoyed his closeness, his touch, but she could not respond. She fell back against the cushions.

"Because of Claudia, I feel I know you better than you know me," he said. "I tried to remedy that by telling you the truth about me. I'm sorry if I disturbed you."

"Don't apologize. I suppose I could get up and walk away from you—but I'm not sure I really want to."

He again pulled her closer.

She drew back and looked at him intently. "I admit there's not much desire left in me, but maybe I've never known desire. I remember needing—wanting—to be close to Marshall when we were first married. But those feelings vanished and, as time went by, I came to dread his so-called lovemaking. It was all about power and control."

She wondered why she had begun to talk about Marshall again. After all, this man had only kissed her.

Gwyneth Jones was singing "In Questa Reggia." "Maybe I'm as frigid as the Princess Turandot," she blurted out. Again, feeling a loss of control.

"You've obviously never made love with the right man."

She started to stand up. "This conversation is far too intimate for people who've been together only twice."

He grabbed her hand and held it tight. "Two lonely people enjoying each other's company—then why not communicate our feelings as well? Remember what I once told you. What are we waiting for?"

"It's still painful. I begged Marshall to see a therapist years ago, but he did not want anyone, not even a doctor, to hear about his sadistic streak. He wanted nothing to mar his public image. He even threatened me if I told anyone about our so-called love life, so I went to see a psychiatrist without his knowing. The doctor urged me to leave him but like a fool I stayed on, too afraid of his anger, always desperately seeking his approval. I was terrified that he might discard me if I made him angry. It is as simple as that. It was not just the wealth and the creature comforts. I simply couldn't face rejection."

"Surely you *must* have seen something in him when you married him."

"During those first years he was charming, courtly. And impetuous. I was so shy and hesitant that I was drawn to him. He was also obsessively ambitious. Ambition can be exciting to someone so young. I was just a simple, convent-bred girl, without any sophistication at all, and I enjoyed having him transform me into a woman he felt was more acceptable, more desirable.

"Sort of like Galatea to Pygmalion. And when did you fall out of love with him?"

"After I saw the gradual, subtle changes in his character. As he gained money and power, he seemed to lose both his love for me and his compassion. I became his chattel, part of his property. No matter what I did, it was never enough."

"It's a wonder you didn't get sick or have a breakdown."

"He took out so much of his anger on me during those last few years of our marriage that I did become physically ill and accident-prone."

"How did you rebel?"

"I stopped sharing a bed with him. At first, he would not allow me to sleep alone for fear the servants would catch on that something was not right between us, although surely they must have known what was going on."

"It's amazing that you stayed as long as you did."

"I was stupid to have put up with it for so long. Although at first I protected him for my daughter's sake, I began to realize that I must have been sick as well. Then the night of the Olympic benefit I walked in on him with a woman."

He took her hand and kissed it. "Don't you have any men friends?'

"The antique dealer next door. A loyal, loving friend."

"Someone you could fall in love with?"

"He's gay. I love him as if he were the brother I never had, and I know he cares for me a lot. And I have seen one man—he's an art history professor, but he has his own problems and we're too much alike in temperament for our relationship to go anywhere. She moved away from him and said, "We both have to be up early, and you have a long ride to Santa Monica."

He stood to leave. "And I have to be at the studio by six o'clock. Maeve is shooting an important interior scene with Chris, and I want to be there to make sure Simon directs it the way I wrote it. It's a struggle writers always have with directors, but we seem to be working it out very nicely."

They walked to the door together hand in hand, Demetra suddenly disturbed by the thought of the lovely Maeve and what she might mean to Thomas.

He kissed her gently on the lips and told her that he would call her again. Very soon.

But his phone calls stopped after that night and Demetra was convinced that whatever he had seen in her photograph was obliterated by her flesh and blood closeness. Of course, he had found something wrong with her. Or maybe she had said something that had hurt him. And she should never had spoken so freely or so much about herself, about her absence of desire. No wonder she had driven him away.

One night she impulsively picked up the phone and dialed his number. But before he answered, she slammed the phone back into its cradle. She should wait for him to call her.

Two weeks later she found Gail's message on her answering machine. "Thank you for your lovely note. On Thursday morning I have some errands to run on La Cienega so why don't we plan to have lunch at *Choses?* Let me bring it."

She rang Gail right away.

"Thursday's fine, but don't bring lunch. I'll order it from the deli down the street."

"Keep it simple then. By the way, I'm crazy about grilled cheese sandwiches."

On Thursday morning Demetra was at home packing a hamper. She had decided that the best way to have grilled cheese sandwiches was to make them in the shop.

The phone rang. When a foreign operator's voice came on the line, she hoped it might be Thomas.

She heard a faint voice. "Mom, it's Corey. I'm calling from Sydney. This connection is bad, but I wanted you to know that we will be in Australia for a while. Tomorrow morning we'll be on our way to Alice Springs."

"You told me that you'd be back here in a couple of weeks!" Demetra tried to hide her disappointment.

"Michael's giving a presentation of some of his sketches for a ballet in Adelaide. Is everything okay with you, Mom? Here—he wants to say hello."

She heard a pleasant voice say, "Hello, Mrs. Killingsworth, this is Michael."

"Hello, Michael. I'm happy to meet you, if only by telephone."

"And I've been looking forward to speaking to you…" Then all she heard was a disheartening dial tone.

Even though they had hardly spoken, she was gratified by the call, happy that Michael had wanted to speak to her.

She went back to the hamper, adding the thermos of watercress and potato soup she had made the night before. She sliced some cheddar cheese and placed it between slices of bread buttered on the outside, wrapped each sandwich in aluminum foil and packed them along with her travel iron. She planned to "grill" them flat with the sizzling hot iron. When the nuns were not looking, the girls made such sandwiches in their rooms.

Why, she wondered, had it never occurred to her to make "ironed grill cheese" sandwiches for Corey when she was a little girl?

"Lo and behold! Convent style!" Demetra said. There, on the peeled-back foil, lay a perfectly toasted cheese sandwich oozing melted cheddar. "Quite a change from those fancy tea sandwiches at Greenhill House, isn't it?"

"Definitely a change for the better. Delicious!" Gail said.

"I've always found something strange about Thomas. He seems like a man who is guarding a secret past. Do you feel that way about him?"

"Not at all. I thought he was both outgoing and forthcoming." She offered Gail a brownie, feeling privileged that Thomas had confided in her. Then she told Gail about the airport phone call from Corey.

"I'm glad you have one less worry, Demetra. Even though you have been missing your daughter, at least you know that she's well and happy. Now you can relax. Michael's obviously a good influence, and she is well on her way to a serious acting career. Count your blessings! And for heaven's sake do not try to make Corey a clone of you. The more you leave her alone, the more likely she *will* turn out like you—at least the best part of you. Now—what about Thomas?"

"What about him?"

"I've been waiting for you to bring up his name. Of course, you must know he was called back to England. Before he left, he told me he had rung you up and left a message, but you never returned his call. I assumed you didn't get on with him."

"I never got any message! I was sure he'd lost interest in *me*." Although her pride was assuaged, she felt a sense of loss. Careless, irreparable loss.

"You might want to check your answering machine. Sometimes messages don't record if the tape needs re-winding."

"How long do you think the crew will be in England?"

"Several months, at least. They are supposed to be shooting all the romantic exteriors, but the weather's been cold and rainy. Chris leaves next week. When the crew returns to LA, they will shoot the major interiors. And the love scenes. But it will be a closed set which means that even I do not watch. Not that I care to."

"I don't know how you can stand watching your husband in bed with another woman. I'm still shell-shocked from finding Marshall with Marina, even though I was no longer in love with him."

"I'll admit that when Chris first began his acting career, it *was* hard on me but after all our years together I feel secure enough."

"I've often wondered if Thomas might be in love with Maeve."

"Maeve's one and only lover is a don at Cambridge. A woman." She shook her head and smiled. "Demetra, I wish you could see the look on your face."

Demetra laughed. "That's a relief! I'm glad I can count Maeve out as a rival."

CHAPTER XII

When she got home the first thing she did was to replay the entire message tape.

"Demetra, Thomas here—on Monday morning. Thank you for a wonderful evening. It has been a long, long time since I have felt this way about a woman. Please call me today or tomorrow because I'II be off to East Riding on Friday. They will be shooting some scenes for *Morris Dance,* and I want to talk to you before I leave. I don't know yet when I'll be returning."

There was another message from him. Almost the same, but with guardedness in his voice. She dialed Gail's number: maybe she knew where Thomas could be reached in England. No answer. She felt like throwing the answering machine on the floor and kicking the living daylights out of it.

FERIA DE FLAMENCO, CORDOBA, 1922

A few days later Demetra was at *Choses,* dressing the window with an old flamenco poster she had found at a swap meet in Azuza.

After that Saturday night with Thomas Pierson, the poster had taken on a new meaning. She propped it up against some bricks and stood back to admire it, wondering if Thomas would approve.

It was quiet that morning. She was able to read at least forty pages of Vasari, *Lives of the Painters*. Around noon she heard the doorbell and looked out from the storeroom to see who had entered. She recognized the stunning dancer from *Sevilla de Oro*. Today she was dressed in a short black, nipped-in jacket with an Art Deco diamante brooch perched on the lapel. Her long black hair was coiled into a black chenille snood, large pearls studded her ears. She was not pretty in a conventional way with her high-bridged nose and slightly protruding teeth, but she was elegant, and *muy* Spanish.

"Good morning. I'm Conchita del Lago." Her voice had a pleasing timbre; her Spanish-accented English was almost perfect, with just an occasional grammatical error that made it charming. "You are the owner of the shop?"

Demetra extended her hand. "I saw you dance at Sevilla de Oro. You must have heard the applause from our table."

"I did, and I thank you for it. When I mentioned your enthusiasm to *el patron,* he told me that Mr. Pierson mentioned that you had a shop nearby."

"Is there anything I can help you with?"

"I was just admiring your Cordoba poster. I have some similar flamenco memorabilia. I have been collecting since I was thirteen years old, but now I want to sell my collection. My landlord wants to raise my rent which I cannot afford. I have found something nice; it's much smaller and without a little garden which I shall miss. I will not have enough room to keep my collection, so I am forced into selling."

"Tell me about the sort of things you have, and I'll try to tell you whether or not they're saleable."

"I have lots of costume jewelry from the 20's, 30's, 40's, antique clothing, shawls, brocades—but I will not be selling any of my vintage clothing because I am still wearing it, but there are fans, some Chinese robes, a few pieces of furniture."

Trying to hide her excitement Demetra said, "I'd be happy to look over your collection, but you should know that I generally take things on a consignment basis, especially the higher priced items. Is that all right with you?"

Conchita agreed and gave her a business card with her studio and home addresses. She opened the door for the dancer and as she walked out, she noticed a tear on the shoulder of her black velvet jacket, so beautifully mended with tiny stitches that it was hardly visible.

Only a few customers dropped by that morning but Demetra didn't worry. If the collection was as Conchita del Lago described it, she had come across a treasure trove and her rent would be guaranteed for months. And Conchita might not have to leave her *pequeño jardin*.

Demetra pressed the buzzer marked Maria C. del Lago and looked around. A bank of tall calla lilies flanked each side of the door. A bee darted by, then moved into the depths of a lily. She watched in fascination as it buzzed and bumbled its way out of the white velvet tunnel, all fuzzy and drunk with yellow pollen.

Heels clicked against the tiled steps. Conchita greeted her wearing a saffron yellow Chinese silk embroidered dressing gown, red silk mules on her feet. "I am sorry you had to wait. I was on the telephone to Spain ordering castanets for one of my students. Come in, please."

As Demetra followed the dancer up two flights, she stared at the dragon, breathing red and purple fire, coiled seductively on the back her dressing gown.

The apartment was dark and smelled of green cypress candles. Demetra recognized the poignant lament, the haunting arabesques of

Goyescas sung by a soprano. "That's *The Maiden and the Nightingale* from *Goyescas,* isn't it? I've never heard it sung before."

Conchita turned down the volume. "You are hearing the operatic version. I purchased it in Spain. If you like I would be happy to have a copy made for you. Please sit down. I have just brewed some coffee. May I offer you a cup?"

"Thanks. I'd love to have one—without cream and sugar, please."

While Conchita was in the kitchen, her eyes swept over the book titles: they all appeared to be books in Spanish or books in English about Spain. On another shelf, rows of opera cassettes were packed in tight.

When Conchita returned with a small silver tray Demetra recognized the cups as Sevres porcelain. "I couldn't help but notice your book titles—and your collection of opera cassettes."

"I read a great deal—especially poetry, Garcia Lorca, Calderon de la Barca—and I adore opera—including Spanish opera, the *zarzuela.* Did the flamenco presentation at Sevilla de Oro please you?" Her slight Spanish accent and the lilting formality of her speech added to her charm.

"I've enjoyed flamenco ever since I saw the gypsies dance in Granada. I wish I knew more about it." She thought of Thomas and a feeling of loss swept over her.

Conchita went on. "Flamenco has very ancient origins. I tell my students that its roots go back to Cadiz, in the days of the ancient Carthaginians. Then later on you will have other influences— Moorish, Hebrew, Gypsy."

"But what gives the music that special sound? Is it in a particular key?"

"It is the *compas,* the beat, all of which gives it its special sound. All the real flamenco dances are based Arabic twelve beats. Listen!" She clapped twelve beats, emphasizing the third, fifth, seventh and tenth. She repeated this a few times.

"To dance, a pupil must first hear this beat before learning the footwork and upper body and hand movements. Although it may seem very free, flamenco is very structured."

"I guess it's like learning how to figure skate, using those inside and outside blades to make figure eights. I learned to ice skate as a child, but I never overcame shakiness and fear of falling. And castanets? Do they take a long time to learn?"

"It's depends on how much you practice. Castanets are fun. I play them all the time, even with Bach. But now we *must* get down to business. I will show you what I would like to sell."

Demetra followed her through the apartment decorated in a mixture of twenties, thirties, and forties style. An *art moderne* bed dominated Conchita's bedroom, its headboard quilted in pale peach satin. The Art Deco dressing table with its large round mirror was massed with crystal perfume bottles hung with tasseled, crochet-covered squeeze and spray bulbs.

"I collect perfume bottles, as you may have noticed." She pulled open a drawer. Inside was a box of vials, long thin glass tubes like thermometers with little bulbous ends. "These were the first. I used to buy them from the little machines in the ladies' rooms. You can see the ends have never been snapped off." She handed the box to Demetra.

"I remember seeing these once or twice when I was a girl. Some of the older girls brought them back to the convent but the nuns took them away from us, saying they were dangerous. She laughed. "Especially the vials labeled 'My Sin.'"

Conchita pulled open more drawers filled with old bottles. Chanel, Lanvin, Guerlain, Caron. "The history of modern perfume is right here," she said. "Beside dance, perfume has been my other passion. I guess you would call it an obsession. I have decided to let go of a few duplicates."

She unfolded a cabinet door and displayed the collection. The entire wall, floor to ceiling, was lined with old perfume bottles from the most famous perfumers in France.

Demetra was astonished. "What an incredible collection! It's like a fragrance museum."

"Look, here is my very favorite—Maja from Spain." She smiled. "And I have even more boxes packed away in the basement storeroom so that I can continue to supply you with after you sell these."

"You have an impressive collection, Miss del Lago, and of course, it's all very saleable."

"Come—please allow me to show you my boxes of laces, quilts, antique fabrics. Maybe you can sell those, too."

"I'll do my best." Demetra whose heart sometimes got in the way of her business dealings added, "And since you have so much to sell, I'll take a lower commission."

"If you will do that for me, then I would also like to do something for you. I insist on giving you dance lessons in exchange."

Demetra laughed. "I'm not sure I'll ever be ready for that! Maybe castanets, though. Now let us have a look at the rest of your things."

Conchita opened an old steamer trunk, each drawer stuffed with large packets wrapped in white paper. "Acid free tissue, the only kind to use when you collect fabric," she said. She unwrapped lustrous brocades from the thirties, a flapper shimmy chemise made from white and silver net beaded crystal fringe, a velvet cloak that seemed to be woven of peacock feathers. There were sequined fans, pleated painted paper fans, pierced ivory fans, exotic, old but still sweet sandalwood fans. She unfurled one and held it flat to Demetra's nose so that she could smell the spicy, faded scent.

"You have enough here to fill my shop twice over."

"I told you about my extensive collection of vintage costume jewelry—but I am not quite ready to sell it."

Demetra heard the urgency in the dancer's voice and realized that she was probably in need of money. "It won't all sell overnight you know, but I'll give you a monthly check for whatever sells in that given month."

"I would prefer it that way."

They shook hands and planned the details of the sale. Conchita would label each item with her desired price. Demetra would then catalogue the separate items, send her a receipt, adjusting the price up or down on each item as she saw fit. The profit would be less, but she had saved hours of searching time, and there was no outlay of cash. A bonanza for *Choses*!

When Conchita walked her to the door, she said, "Here, I want you to have these fandango and *sevillanas* cassettes. I bought them in Spain at the festival of El Rocio. Listen to them again and again. Maybe you will eventually begin to hear the *compas*. And if you feel that you are not yet ready to dance, you might enjoy learning to play the castanets."

"Ma chère, je suis très heureuse de vous voir."

Despite her Scandinavian origin, Sylvie Anderson was all French, a woman who not only cultivated her Frenchness, but embellished it. She lived in Santa Monica in an old bakery she had converted into a workroom and residence. Art reference books in many languages lined the walls. Shallow drawers held her cherished textiles. There were no windows in the room since the strong California light might fade the precious fabrics. Our Lady of the Cloth is what Demetra sometimes called her.

Sylvie had left her native Oslo for Paris where she finished *l'Ecole Superieure,* then went on from there to the Musée des Arts Decoratifs for her training in textiles. Rare textiles were her world. Scraps of woven Coptic fabric, Peruvian shawls, Ming embroideries, Russian *matelassé* gleaming gold and silver threads, Kelmscott fabrics of William Morris, the clothing of the great couturiers: Dior, Balenciaga, Chanel.

"The warp and the woof excite me. I'm nothing more than a rag woman, you see," Sylvie was often quoted as saying. But Sylvie was hardly dressed in rags. She always wore, at least whenever Demetra had seen her, Chanel. Real Chanel from the Fifties and Sixties, clothing designed by the great Gabriele herself. Her suits were exactly as Mademoiselle made them for Sylvie's body that had hardly changed over the years

"You've been very hard to reach, Sylvie. For the past two weeks I've left message after message with your answering service,"

"I've been in Italy—the service never reveals when I'm out of town. I like being elusive, you see." She laughed and patted her grey hair and removed a pearl-centered Chanel earring as though it might make listening easier.

"Now tell me where and how you've been since your divorce?"

Demetra took a deep breath. "My life is very different now but at least when I get out of bed in the morning I can face myself. I don't miss anything about Greenhill House, not even the garden because I never felt that anything there was really mine. Now I have a little shop and I've been taking courses in art history."

"Whatever you have been doing must be right because you have never looked better, *ma chère*. Now let us have a look at what is in that shopping bag. I sense that you are eager to show me your treasure. And before you leave, remind me to show you my new purchase from Switzerland."

Demetra opened the box. Between the tissue paper lay the square of white linen, edged in narrow lace woven from gold thread.

Sylvie stared at the cloth. "Wherever did you find this?" she said, clipping the earring back on her ear.

"A Spanish dance teacher in Hollywood consigned it to me. I'm selling most of her collection of old dresses—Edwardian, Victorian lace—all that sort of thing."

"Why is she selling this piece?"

"She needs money. I knew it was old and important; it reminded me of the rare embroideries I used to see at Spink in London."

"I've only come across one or two in all the years that I have worked with textiles."

"What was it used for?"

"You have brought me a chalice veil, Demetra. It is Elizabethan. You see, the red silk embroidery is so fine it looks as though it's been printed."

Demetra nodded and read the lines *'Omnes sancti martyres ora pro nobis. Santa Maria, mater dei, mater Dei, ora pro nobis.'*

"Look here—you can see the kneeling saints and the Virgin. Because veneration of the Virgin was outlawed, her image was replaced with roses and flowers, so those Anglican chalice veils are quite plentiful. With this piece, though, I am sure I can find a buyer among the museums because that is where it belongs. You can tell your friend that it's worth upwards from $15,000."

Demetra gasped. "I'm so happy for Conchita—she'll be thrilled when she hears this."

"This evening, if I have some success researching my museum and auction catalogues, I shall ring up my curator friend in London. He knows who needs what to fill out a collection. You will know the moment I have a buyer." She stood and offered her hand.

"You told me to remind you to show me your new purchase," Demetra said.

"Ah—thank you!" She opened the large Hermes black manuscript holder and carefully drew out a sturdy manila envelope. "The artistry may not be the same as what you've brought to me but look at this. Do you have any idea what it is?"

Demetra studied the tiny scrap of brownish cloth enclosed in a plastic envelope. "It looks ancient and it appears to be a type of linen. Perhaps a piece of Egyptian mummy wrapping?"

"You're close, Demetra, but it's from a different part of the world. It is from Switzerland, the lake country. This scrap, dug up in the bogs, is some of the oldest fabric on record, probably about four thousand B.C. Neolithic. Lake dwellers' fabric, probably woven from flax in the time of the dawn of agriculture in the West. Amazing, isn't it? It gave me shivers when I saw it. I had to buy these few square millimeters for my collection. That is exactly the way it was sold—by the square millimeter. Every major textile collector had to have a tiny piece. I treasure this fragment of fabric more than anything I own." Tears shimmered in her eyes. "Go ahead, please open it. Touch it gently with your little finger, so you can say you've touched the oldest fibers worked by woman's hand."

"Are you sure it was a woman's hand who wove it?"

"Yes, my dear, you can be sure that it was woven by a woman's hand."

Demetra opened the plastic folder and touched the fabric gently with her fingertip. As she did, she felt a faint tremor within, as though she had hit some archaic nerve, and, at that very instant, been given a clue to her own existence.

Demetra could hardly wait to get back to the shop to call Conchita. How easy it was to make this kind of call, knowing how happy the news would make her. More often she was forced to disappoint hopeful owners who had romanticized about an object or a painting, when she had to gently explain that their treasures were virtually worthless.

Conchita answered the phone on the first ring. "Demetra! I had not expected to hear from you so soon. I thought it might be my agent with some good news about a weekend job in Las Vegas." She laughed. "Dolores keeps reminding me that it has been a bad year for Spanish dancers—and therefore for costume makers."

"I have even better news for you, Conchita." She recounted her meeting with Sylvie.

When she finally spoke, Demetra could hear her fighting her tears. "I don't know how I can ever thank you enough. Now I will not have to worry about my rent for a long time. But I must give something to you, more than just your commission. I insist upon giving you dance lessons."

"That's so generous of you. Even though I love flamenco I could never ever learn to dance. I'm too clumsy—and maybe too old."

"You are *not* clumsy! I can assure you, Demetra. At your age it is not too late to learn flamenco."

Demetra reflected for a moment. "But I *would* like to have some castanet lessons."

"Brava! I shall order a pair for you. We will begin next week."

Demetra and Conchita sat facing each other. Conchita looped the cords that tied the pair of double wood discs around each of Demetra's hands. "Now click the castanets on the right hand and listen to the tone," she said.

Demetra listened hard.

"You see how the castanet in the left hand only marks the rhythm and begins and completes each roll. That's all there is to it! The right hand does all the work. Now—try it—take it very slowly—tap by tap. Be patient. It may take a few months before you can make your fingers strong, but if you practice every day soon your fingers will soon become like steel springs. Then the roll begins to form, each finger sounds distinctly, adding to the sharpness, the smoothness of the trill."

Demetra tried it again.

Tan-tan-car-a-tee-ah—tan

She untied the castanets from her fingers and sighed. "I hope I can find time to practice these."

"You will *make* the time. Always keep them in your purse so that whenever you have a few extra moments in your shop, or when you are waiting in the car, you can pull them out to practice. They might even cure you of biting your nails!"

Summer arrived even before spring with dry desert heat blown in by the Santa Ana winds. Roses shriveled on wilted bushes, tender ivy shoots on the vine were curled and brown as though singed by a flaming blowtorch. Under the sheltering live oaks nights were cooler but Demetra barely slept.

One particularly warm night she had a vivid dream.
Giant sunflowers nodded on tall stalks, their faces rimmed with curly petals, their heads heavy with ripened black seeds. How she longed for some of those seeds! She grasped a drooping flower head, pulled it from its stalk, and tore open its face to claim them. But there were no seeds—only the face of a woman. She knew it was her mother's.

The radio alarm went off at six o'clock. She dragged herself out of bed, still feeling the weight of the flower head in her hands. Another day to deal with and more hours raking over telephone directories for Charles Duval while Farrell minded the shop, still another paper on Venus in Renaissance sculpture to write for Tony Tradland.

The parts of the day she enjoyed most were early morning and late evening when she practiced the castanets. She kept them in a red velvet pouch in her handbag and, whenever she found a spare moment, she would play them. Before long the fingers of her right hand developed what Conchita had described as a 'steel spring.' She was feeling the roll, hearing it chirp like a cricket. She was pleased. So was Conchita. Would she ever have the courage to play the castanets for Thomas?

One morning a few weeks later, she strolled to the mailbox for The Los Angeles Times, scattering stale bread crusts along the way. The sparrows, expecting this daily ritual, fluttered their wings and swooped from the pines to greet her.

She scanned the headlines. Diana Victor stared out from the bottom of the front page. "Social Leader Diana Victor dead at age 75." The obituary recounted Diana's involvement in civic activities, her dedication to Never Too Late to Learn. A memorial service would be held later at the Wilshire Hotel, a fitting venue since the hotel had always been the traditional setting for the organization's events, many of them chaired by Diana.

At first Demetra had no intention of attending the memorial service, but she quickly dismissed the idea as unforgiving—the nuns had taught her to pardon the deceased. She could almost hear Sister Claire's voice urging her on. Go, Demetra, grit your teeth, pull yourself together and go. She knew that she risked confronting Marina and, worse yet, Marshall.

Two weeks after Diana's private funeral, a memorial service was held in the Wilshire Hotel. The Trophy Room was filled with members of Never Too Late dressed in couture, prêt-a-porter, some real, some mock Chanel suits. Heavy metal chains twisted and draped around necks and waists, and fake camellias graced lapels as though they were badges of girlish purity, when, in truth, the flower was Chanel's tongue-in-cheek homage to the tarnished repute of La Dame aux Camellias.

Many of the "name members," those who were publicity conscious, had made themselves up with meticulous care, or better yet, made an appointment to be Hollywood-enhanced for the occasion. Since Diana Victor was such a well-known civic leader, this would no doubt be a photo-op.

Demetra arrived early and found a single seat in the very last row. She was wearing a simple, well-cut navy-blue suit. Black had seemed too somber, too mournful, given that she felt mildly hypocritical for attending. She had convinced herself that she was there because a voice inside told her to be, as though this were a tribal ritual she could not avoid, however painful, however perilous.

She scanned the crowd. Fifteen minutes before the service was to begin, The Agora Room was already filled to standing room. Latecomers were forced to sit in an adjacent room equipped with closed circuit television screens. The members had turned out in full force to honor one of their own.

Marshall had escaped by flying to Tokyo and, as Marina was being ushered to her seat by a young member from the Junior Program, she spotted Demetra in the last row. She had not seen her since her divorce from Marshall. Strange that she should be here today, she thought. Demetra surely must have known how critical Diana was of her.

June Cooper sat resplendent in the first row, fingering the immense Burmese pearls at the white piqué neckline of her obviously couture black Chanel. She was to be the principal speaker. Each side of the stage was decorated with an enormous stone urn massed with tall stems of Casablanca lilies, Diana's favorites.

As a string group played Ravel's sweetly lugubrious Pavanne for a Dead Princess, members searched their Chanel bags for white linen handkerchiefs. When the last notes sounded, June Cooper walked solemnly to the podium and propped her prepared speech against the lectern.

A hush came over the crowd as she stood before them, without applause, the usual Pavlovian response to June Cooper's majestic presence. June cleared her throat and began to speak in her Midwestern accented drawl.

"Diana Victor was a woman of leadership, intelligence and passion. Those of you who worked with her over the years came to respect and admire her. You grew fond of her. Diana's dedication to our organization was complete. We count scientists, artists, writers, and film directors among those women who have been educated from our Never Too Late to Learn Fund.

"When Diana and I set out to organize this charity twenty-five years ago, we had no idea how important the organization would become for women. Women whose high school or college educations were aborted through family disabilities, health, sexual trauma, or lack of funds. These women, through financial and emotional support from our fund raising, could complete their goals of higher education. Diana Victor was always behind the scenes, interviewing candidates, and screening applicants for our scholarships. These are some of the women we have helped." She read the list of well-known women and asked them to stand if they were present. Ironically, only a few were.

June went on for ten minutes intoning the public relations legend of Never Too Late. When she had finished her panegyric, she folded her notes and returned to her seat. A soft murmur swept through the audience.

But everyone knew that June was disappointed by Diana's will. Not a penny had been left to the Never Too Late to Learn Scholarship Fund.

Frederick Marchand, Diana's favorite escort, made his way to the podium. He was tall, ultra slim, and dressed in a natty House of Windsor way, with a puffy black silk handkerchief protruding from his breast pocket. He spoke in a whiny upper-class Old New York-North Shore accent. "Diana Victor had so much pehsonal style. She was, as you know, on the Best Dressed List for many years. I was always proud to be seen with her, whether she wore a vintage Balenciaga or a brand-new Bill Blass. She was always the essence of elegance, whatever the occasion. Diana never followed fads and, believe me, in this city that's not easy."

Marchand continued in this vein for five more minutes. He was followed by a live string ensemble playing the second movement of Schubert's Der Tod und das Mädchen. Hardly a maiden, Diana, but certainly dead.

Marina did not seem in the least nervous about being the next speaker. As she walked to the podium, whispering ceased as all eyes swept over her. Confident in front of an audience as she was at a board meeting, Marina never wanted to become an actress because she had never had the desire to be anyone other than Marina. She obviously enjoyed standing on the stage in her simple, mid-calf dove grey silk jersey dress, gazing out over a rapt audience commanding her admirers to listen. In her left hand she held a small lavender chiffon handkerchief embroidered with her initials and a tiny seashell.

Without notes she began in her measured voice with its precise, almost British diction. Nothing delighted her more than the sound of her own voice: she took pleasure in hearing herself speak her own name. "I am Marina Killingsworth," she said as though they would not have known. "The Never Too Late to Learn Scholarship Fund has become, in its small way, as prestigious as the Rhodes, the Guggenheim or Fulbright scholarships."

Demetra found the comparison hilarious and inappropriate, but Marina knew it would grab the attention of the mourners, who by now would be yearning for a drink.

"When I was invited by June Cooper to join Never Too Late, I was barely out of college myself, and the idea of raising funds for exceptional women to continue higher education intrigued me. It was Diana Victor who introduced me to some of the beneficiaries of the scholarship—in physics, Thelma Bailey, a recipient who has done outstanding research in estrogen therapy, Galina Parnoff, the UCLA scholar of Neolithic migrations.

And, Demetra noted, hadn't Marina become so much more conservative in her dress since she married Marshall? She saw the men staring at her shapely legs, those slender ankles and tiny feet, the wide grey suede belt cinching her narrow waist, her full high breasts, nipples poking discreetly through six-ply silk jersey . Meanwhile, the members must be wondering who designed the dress. Obviously French. What Demetra didn't know was, that at the same time, those in the audience were making mental comparisons comparing Marina, now more blonde than ever, to Demetra, who was dressed discreetly but looking even more beautiful, her now long dark hair tied back with a black velvet ribbon.

Marina held them in thrall, speaking for only three minutes. One minute less than the time allotted. She needed no more time than that because everything to be said about Diana had already been said.

The ceremony over, the mourners rushed off to be first in line for the valet parking, or first to dash into limousines (owned or hired) to head for Chasen's, Jimmy's or The Secret Garden. In all the tributes of the evening, no one had shed a tear for Diana Victor. No one. Not her nephew, a doctor in Indiana who had avoided the ceremony "because of surgery commitments." Not one of the scholarship winners who should have been grateful to her. Not even her closest friend June Cooper. Yes, June had been shaken by Diana's death, made more aware of her own mortality, but her stoic bearing, her regal composure, always belied her emotions. Words had been uttered, tributes made, but not a single tear had slid down a powdered cheek. Now the members would wipe out their grief and the annoying specter of death with food, drink, and gossip about those who had attended the service. But more importantly, those who had not, the predictable subject of discussion.

The moment the ceremony was over Demetra leapt from her seat and exited the side door, avoiding the crush and all that air-kissing and hugging. Walking back to a side street and her parked car, she thought she heard someone calling her name. She turned. It was her landlord, Mr. Skidmore, waving from the corner of Bedford and Wilshire.

She crossed to greet him. "What a lovely surprise!"

"Demetra, I was sure it was you! I have been meaning to drop by or give you a call. Is everything all right with the house?"

"You would have heard from me if it weren't."

"I really appreciate your right-on-time rent checks."

"What are you doing in Beverly Hills?"

"I had a meeting with some musicians earlier this afternoon—a string quartet for the Ojai Festival. I have been helping my sister round up talent. Remember?"

"Of course, I remember."

"They were playing at a memorial service for some society grande dame."

"That's where I was! I thought they played beautifully. Especially the Schubert."

"Come on—I'll buy you a drink and you can tell me all about it. How about Trader Vic's?"

"Not a bad idea. I am feeling a bit shaky. I didn't want to attend but I had a strange, compelling feeling that I should. I still can't figure it out."

He laughed. "Fortuna meant for us to run into each other, that's the way I see it."

***

They sat at a quiet table under the thatched palm roof; Mr. Skidmore ordered Spanish sherry for Demetra and Scotch on the rocks for himself.

He did the talking, mostly about the artists he was helping to bring together for next year's Festival "By the way, one of your neighbors told me he's hearing castanets from your house. No complaints, mind you—just curiosity."

"I've been taking lessons for the past few months." She grinned. "One of my fantasies—I should say goals—is to play the castanet solo in Act II of La Vida Breve." She felt her face color.

"If you practice long and hard enough, I may be able to arrange it. I keep urging them to play more Spanish music down at the Music Center. Have you looked at Los Angeles demographics lately?"

As he described the genius of a young Mexican cellist, thoughts of the Toulouse letter kept looming in her head.

"You seem preoccupied, Demetra. Something the matter?"

"Sorry. There's always something on my mind these days."

"I see from your eyes that whatever is bothering you must be pretty serious stuff. Want to talk about it?" He reached over and clasped her hand.

The words tumbled out as she told him all about Charles Duval and the letter from Toulouse.

"Hey—slow down, slow down. My hearing range is a bit off. Did I hear you say Charles Dutoit? Or did you say Charles Duval?"

She gripped the table with both hands and leaned forward, suddenly feeling the goose flesh on the back of her arms. "D-U-V-A-L. Duval."

"Hell, I used to know the guy. He was a well-known accompanist during the fifties—used to play for the likes of Licia Albanese and

Renata Tebaldi. I haven't seen him in years. Every now and then he's a guest on the Metropolitan Opera Broadcast Quiz."

"What makes you so sure he's the Duval I'm looking for?"

"I have a hunch I'm right and I go by my hunches."

Now her heart thumped so hard it almost took her breath away. "Where do you think I can find him? Do you think he might be dead?"

"I doubt it. I would have read his obituary in one of my music journals. Last I heard he was living somewhere around here. I'll do my best to locate him for you."

"Thank you so much, Mr.Skidmore. I shiver to think of what I might have missed if I hadn't run into you."

"This bit of synchronicity should convince you to trust your instincts. I'll start by making some calls right away, starting with the Opera Lovers Society in Santa Barbara."

Mr. Skidmore called her the next morning. "You're in luck! I found Duval's name listed in the Opera Lovers' Society roster. He is paid up his dues, but the old gal who runs the club says he hasn't attended a meeting in years. In fact, she claims never to have laid eyes on him."

Her heart dropped. "Is that all she had to say?"

"She told me that she'd heard he was gay. Very discreet. He supposedly had a lover, a well-known abstract painter, who died not too long ago. Massive coronary. Duval was so depressed he put their house on the market and moved in with Valli, a famous soprano from the forties."

"Atena Valli? I used to own an old vinyl recording of hers! Old Spanish and Italian songs."

"Valli ended her career in the early fifties. Married twice—second time to a super rich guy who built her a mansion right off Hot

Spring, Nepenthe she called it. Why don't you drive to Santa Barbara to check out the story? In the meantime, I'll make a few more calls for you."

CHAPTER XIII

She had expected the gates to Nepenthe to be closed, but they were wide open. Gardeners were spraying the olive trees with chemicals, no doubt sterilizing them so that their blossoms would not set fruit.

She entered the gate and drove slowly through an allée of tall eucalyptus, then up a road that snaked around the hill to the parking area. A peacock screeched from one of the live oaks surrounding the property. Walking toward the house she passed an outdoor theater set with a backdrop of Ionic columns surrounded by tall cypress hedges. Tiers of semicircular stone benches faced the stage and droll, hook-nosed stone dwarfs flanked the path leading to it

A gardener was clipping the cypress hedges encircling the black reflecting pool. Cemented around the coping were abalone shells, clustered to resemble water lilies, their petals glinting like fiery opals in the sun—a dark pool in a dream.

"Buenos Dias, Senora. La casa es in esta direccion," the gardener said pointing toward the red tile roof half-hidden by a high surrounding wall.

She followed the lane paved with clay tile shards, set in a random pattern. Chunks of sharp slag glass, like huge splintered aquamarines, bordered the footpath to the house. As she approached the gate, she could see that the high wall was edged with jagged, broken bottles. On either side of the wrought iron gate stood tall pillars, each capped by a sandstone image of the writhing Indian goddess, Kali.

The gate was forged like a giant cobweb. Unlatching it, she found herself in an enclosed courtyard. A yellow and black butterfly with one wing torn lay on the stone pavement. She gently lifted it and placed it on a dew-moistened acanthus leaf.

Across the villa's facade, a giant cactus, like an overfed serpent, coiled from the ground and undulated up and over the red tiled roof, partially obscuring the frosted glass windows etched in a Chinese "broken glass" pattern.

Beyond the house, domed cactus cushions bristled with long treacherous needles; cactus like giant phalluses were sheathed in pale grey fuzz and dimpled with pink blossoms. Plants storing moisture for survival, defending themselves from a hostile environment.

Cobwebs, needles, prickles, splinters, shards, smithereens. It occurred to Demetra that everything around this house seemed fractured, menacing, hostile. Although standing in the sun, she felt goosebumps on her arms.

Baskets of pomegranates cast in stone flanked either side of the immense oak door. Above, a plateresque stone cartouche bore the motto *Canto, ergo sum.*

Since there was no doorbell, she lifted the large iron knocker and let it swing hard against the door twice. Sounds of distant jingling bells grew closer and closer. The door opened. The woman who stood there in tight blue jeans was small in stature, so slender, so bone-fragile that she had the look of someone who had shrunk. Her feet were bare and around her ankles were cuffs of tiny metal bells. A parrot perched on one shoulder.

Her eggplant-black hair was drawn back tight in a ponytail. A white stripe marked a path from her forehead. Bare, bony shoulders jutted out above the black and white striped elasticized bandeau that flattened her breasts against her caved-in chest. A bunch of keys hung from a long chain around her neck.

Demetra assumed that the woman was a maid or housekeeper.

"Good morning. I have been trying to reach Charles Duval. I understand he lives here with Miss Valli. Would it be possible to speak to her?"

"You're speaking to what's left of her," the woman answered in an accented, cigarette-husky voice. "And what's your name?"

"My name is Jane Constable. I'm a musicologist." Demetra felt the flush travel up to her forehead. She did not know why, at that instant, she had decided to lie about her name and profession, just as she had when she had visited the clairvoyant.

Miss Valli hesitated, then said. "You may as well come in."

Black marble columns supported the ceiling in the entry hall. Stone-grey walls displayed paintings of Mount Vesuvius; gouaches of the volcano fuming delicate smoke threads, or belching fire in a moonlit sky as fisherman watched from boats on the Bay of Naples. In others small cloaked figures stood at the volcano's edge peering into the fiery crater.

Demetra felt herself grow warmer, as though the volcanoes were radiating heat. As she followed Miss Valli, she had a glimpse of the dining room. The table, set with silver and china, crystal, and tall candelabra, was completely veiled in a dusty plastic film.

Miss Valli pulled a key from the bunch hanging around her neck and unlocked the ornate gilded and carved Venetian doors.

A Steinway grand draped with a Kashmir paisley shawl stood in the corner of the large, dark living room furnished with early Italian antiques. Opposite the piano was a table massed with silver-framed photographs.

Miss Valli drew open the luxurious silk portières, turned on a lamp, but did not invite Demetra to sit. The softened light made the channels on her face less pronounced, the smudged black kohl eyes less haunted. She smiled a tight, strained smile, bright red lips exposing perfectly capped large white teeth, incongruous in her aged face.

"Now tell me, Miss Constable, why have you come here looking for Mr. Duval?" she said, her voice dripping mock sweetness.

Demetra paused for a moment before she surprised herself by saying, "I'm writing an article on early Italian songs. I noticed Mr. Duval's name as accompanist on an old recording of yours, the one that won the *Grand Prix du Disques*. The 17th century Spanish and Italian songs. The songs by…"

"Yes—of course I know them," she said tap-tapping her bare heel, jingling her bells. "However, I must tell you that Maestro Duval is now in my care. He has Alzheimer's disease and is crippled with arthritis. He's confined to a wheelchair and sees very few people, but I will be happy to relay a message to him for you." Again, that tight, dismissive smile.

"Thank you, but I have certain questions to pose and I need his direct answers."

Her eyes passed over Demetra. "You are a beautiful woman, Miss Constable. Are you of European descent?" One hand clutched the bunch of keys. The other hand trembled.

Before Demetra could reply, a rotund Mexican woman rushed in. She was wearing flappy felt slippers over her shoes, most likely to protect and polish the black marble floors.

"Senora, por favor, emergencia en la cocina!"

Atena Valli rushed out of the room, bells a jingle, as the parrot flew from her shoulder to settle on its perch in the corner.

Demetra's trained eyes swept the room. The draperies, the sofas, the over-scaled gilt Neapolitan chairs were all upholstered with the same dark red and silver-gold Fortuny damask in a baroque pattern of stylized, bursting pomegranates.

She scanned the array of signed photographs. There was Toscanini. Churchill, Mussolini. Errol Flynn. One was signed and dated Gabriele d'Annunzio, inscribed *Per Atena, La Divina, 1937.* She looked at another, an unsigned sepia photograph of a tall, bearded man wearing what appeared to be ecclesiastic garb, his long robe girded with heavy cord, sandals on his feet.

Demetra stepped away from the table as soon as she heard jingling bells announce Miss Valli's approach.

"I'm sorry to say that Maestro Duval regrets he cannot see you today. He asks that you write to him. You may state your intentions and ask your questions in the letter. Come, let me show you out." The parrot flew from its perch to her shoulder. She stroked its feathers and kissed its beak.

As she followed Atena Valli out of the room, the parrot still perched on her shoulder, turned, and fixed its sequin-shiny eyes on Demetra who smiled and said "hello."

Then it flapped its wings and shrieked.

Startled, Demetra leaped back.

Atena Valli turned sharply. "Don't you dare frighten my bird! If you want to speak to her you must first say it to me, and I will pass it on to her." There were no handshakes. She opened the door to show Demetra out and she barely uttered goodbye as she slammed it shut.

Demetra had to find the house that Duval had lived in, to see something tangible, something linked to the man who had left her with the nuns.

A real estate agent on Olive Mill Road obligingly gave her the address. "You can certainly drive by to have a look, but we'll need to make an appointment if you want to see the interior."

The stylish contemporary white stucco house in a secluded area near the San Ysidro Ranch was surrounded by a dense grove of old California laurels.

She got out of the car to have a closer look. A wide portico centered by carved double oak doors stretched along the façade, curtains were drawn against the tall windows. She rang the doorbell anyway. She waited and rang again. No response. She had not expected one.

All the way home she thought about the eccentric opera singer. She was obviously in her late seventies or early eighties. She would write to Duval to inquire about the Italian songs without referring to the letter from the convent. And she would sign it "Constable." Something inside her was saying, "Beware of revealing too much information to Miss Valli."

Two weeks passed. Still no reply from the registered letter she had sent to Duval. The time had come to confront Miss Valli.

When she drove again to the gates of Nepenthe, they were closed. She rang the buzzer. The housekeeper's voice boomed out from the loudspeaker.

"*Senora Valli no está en casa hoy.*"

"I've come to leave her an important message."

The gates parted and she drove up to the villa. The housekeeper was waiting at the door. She spoke curtly in Spanish. "Senora went to San Luis Obispo to buy some special plants."

"Is Mr. Duval at home?" Demetra responded in halting Spanish.

"Si, but he cannot be disturbed when he is at the piano." She started to close the door.

"*Por favor*—help me. I think Mr. Duval might be able to give me some information. "

She shook her head. "Senora would be furious if I let you enter without her permission."

"Please—I beg you." She put her hand on the housekeeper's arm.

"You must leave the premises. I must obey orders. "

Demetra's voice cracked. She tried her best to speak Spanish. "What I have to ask him is important. It is my only chance. Please do not deny me that. I beg you."

"If she finds out, I will be in trouble. I should not do this, but come in."

As Demetra followed her through the corridor she could hear the haunting minor chords from *The Maja and the Nightingale*. The *Goyescas* of Granados.

The housekeeper flung open the Venetian doors.

Charles Duval was sitting at the piano. There was no wheelchair in sight.

He glanced up from the keyboard. He stood.

A tall, thin man with a high-bridged, narrow nose and a fringe of white hair, he had the refined look of a Roman patrician. He was wearing a beige raw silk high-necked tunic and loose trousers.

"How may I help you?" he asked in a kind, gentle manner.

"Did you receive the registered letter sent to you by Mrs. Constable?" she blurted out.

He looked puzzled. "No. I've received no registered mail."

"I sent you a registered letter which Miss Valli obviously signed for. My real name is Duval. Demetra Duval."

His hands began to tremble. He grasped the edge of the piano. Demetra leaped forward and led him to the sofa.

He motioned for her to sit next to him. "What do you want to know?"

She stood before him and said, "I will come to the point." She spoke in a measured voice. "The name Charles Duval was on the

document of my entry into an American convent as a foundling."
She tried to read his gaze. "I was told that Charles Duval was
explicitly listed as *not* being my father. The order had no other
information, except that I was an abandoned child, a foundling
Duval had brought to a convent in St. Paul." Her eyes burned into
his. "Are you that Charles Duval?"

He sighed. His pale blue eyes were tear-glazed, his hand shook as
he reached for a handkerchief. "For all these years I have wondered
what I would say when you finally turned up to ask that question. I
was determined to deny that I was that Charles Duval. But you have
finally caught up with me. Now I'm too old and too tired to deny it."
Tears rolled down his cheeks.

She had not expected his answer to be so quick, so direct. She fell
on the sofa. He tried to put his arm around her.

She pulled away and threw her head back against the cushions.
She closed her eyes, suddenly feeling dizzy, as if the world were
blacking out as she approached light at the end of the tunnel.

He buzzed the kitchen. "Inez, bring a glass of water right away,"
he shouted. He put his arm around her.

"Please. Tell me. Tell me from the beginning." She could hardly
form the words. "Who was my mother?"

He blotted his eyes. "I hardly know where to begin. It's such a
long story." He reached for one of the photographs on the table, a
gilt-framed portrait of Atena, radiant, full-fleshed, in a diamond and
emerald tiara. She seemed to be wearing a white Fortuny gown.

She gasped. "My mother?"

He nodded. "Yes, of that I'm sure, Demetra."

"Then who was my father?"

He motioned to the photographs. "Your guess is as good as
mine."

Demetra staggered to the table.

"Get out of my house!" a terrifying voice screamed.

She turned to see Atena, her mother. She wanted to scream out to her, "I'm Demetra—your daughter!" Instead she stood there turned to stone.

"Do you hear me—get out! Or else I will order the gardeners to carry you out. Out!" She stamped her high-heeled boot and began to shriek in a language Demetra did not recognize.

"Please listen, Miss Valli. Mr. Duval just told me that I'm your daughter..."

"You are not my daughter. I have never had a daughter. Never! Get out!" She yanked the bell-pull. "Charles, get her out of my house!"

"You won't have to call anyone to push me out of here. I'll leave on my own." Demetra turned to Duval and began to sob.

His face was ashen. He put his arm around her quaking shoulders and led her away. He could hardly speak. "I'm sorry it turned out this way. It's not how I wanted it to be for you." He opened the door.

Eyes blinded by tears, Demetra stumbled down the path to her car. She fastened her seatbelt and tried to start the motor. The engine stalled. She tried again and again. Finally, the gardener tapped on the car window and motioned for her to leave. She read the distress in his eyes. He was only following *Señora's* orders.

She wiped her eyes and blew her nose. At last she got the engine to turn over, but there was no way she could drive back to Los Angeles in this state.

She booked a room at the Coast Village Inn. In turns she felt nauseated, then hollow, as if something had been ripped from her insides. She felt the emptiness where fear had lodged. Her head throbbed. She could still hear Atena's intense high-pitched voice, that birdy trill, screaming for her to leave. She relived the repugnant scene repeatedly until she began to fear for her sanity.

Yanking the coverlet from the bed, she flopped down on the sheets with her clothes on. Never had she imagined anything as horrible as this encounter. Maybe Duval had lied to her. Maybe she was not Atena's daughter to begin with. Denial became her only solace until, at last, she fell asleep.

During the night she heard dream wails, high-pitched screams.

It was seven o'clock when she woke up. She kicked off her shoes and wrinkled clothes and stood under a warm shower, dousing hotel shampoo over her head, scrubbing her hair, her body until she felt thoroughly cleansed. Then she bent over the bathtub and swatted her hair dry, convent style. When she finished dressing, she walked to the motel office, still dazed.

"Hope you had a pleasant night, Mrs. Duval. I worried about the fire engine sirens waking our guests," said the owner as she paid the bill.

Outside she smelled acrid smoke. She wiped off the thin white ash filming the windshield. When she started the engine, she saw the gas gauge pointing empty. Luckily, there was a service station near the freeway.

She bought a large coffee from the vending machine. "Where was the fire?" she asked the attendant as he filled the tank.

"Down the road. A lot of acreage. Probably started with the eucalyptus trees—they go up in flames like tinder. The house almost burned to the ground. Thank God the firemen got it under control before the Santa Ana winds could spread it through the canyons. Too bad—it was a real nice place."

"What place?"

"Big estate. Belonged to a retired opera singer."

Her knees buckled. She leaned against the car.

"One of the firemen told me about it. There she was, that old dame crazier than a coot, just singin' away. When the fire engines parked up there, they could hear her voice screeching something fierce over the loudspeaker. She'd turned it on full blast and was standing on a stage in a Chinese costume trying to sing along and hit the high notes."

Her hand shook so hard the steaming coffee splashed and scalded her wrist. She dismissed the pain and tossed the cup into the trash bin. "What happened to her?"

"They tried saving her, but it was too late. The old guy who lived with her was in a state of shock."

The coffee cup fell to the ground.

"Hey, what's the matter?" The attendant caught her and led her to a chair in the office.

"Sit tight. I'll be right back with water."

Her eyes were dry as she stared out, seeing nothing.

He put the water to her lips. She felt the water's cool, restoring path down her throat. Finally, she murmured, "Where did they take the man?"

"The paramedics took him to Ventura Hospital. Looked like he had a heart attack."

"Oh no! It can't be—please God—please don't let him die!" She leaned over his desk and wept for Charles Duval and for whatever they might or might not have been to each other.

The gas station owner drove her to the hospital, but they would not allow her to see Duval. He was in a coma the doctor said. The prognosis was not good.

Although she felt her world had come to an end, she had no choice but to collect her car to drive back to Los Angeles. Corey.

Where was she now? And Thomas? Then she prayed that Gail would be home as she drove in a tearless stupor, consoled only by the sounds of *Granados.*

Gail, who had just returned from England a few days before, was putting groceries away when Demetra arrived.

"When I called the shop, Farrell told me you were in Santa Barbara. Any luck? "She stopped. "What's the matter? You don't look right..."

"I found her."

"Found who?"

"My mother," she said calmly, without emotion. "And Charles Duval. It was the beginning and the end all at once."

Gail put her arms around her, but she pulled away, refusing to be solaced. The two women sat at the kitchen table as Demetra recounted the past twenty-four hours in a monotone, without shedding a tear.

"I'd better call Farrell. Tell him I can't meet him at the estate sale.,"

"I wouldn't dream of letting you drive to Los Angeles. You're spending the night right here with us."

"Thanks, Gail—I'll be all right once I get some sleep."

Gail put her arm around her again. "For all you have been through, you haven't shown much emotion, Demetra. What are you really feeling inside?"

"Partly relief. Maybe because I have lived through my greatest fear. That at the end of my search my mother might be dead. Now, at least, I know I am really an orphan. And from what Charles Duval told me, I will probably never know who my father was. I must face up to it.

"As for her love, I don't think I was looking for it. The nuns gave me affection and love. It was all about identity. Now my mother can never give me the identity I've craved all my life."

"Your identity is separate from hers." Gail stroked her hair. "Don't be afraid to cry, Demetra."

"I used to cry a lot, but the well is all dried up. I can't even cry over what might have been between my mother and me."

"Now is the time for you to let go, time to forgive her mistakes. Forgive her without condition. Thank her for your strengths and for the gifts she passed on to you. Thank her for your blessings."

"My blessings—and all my imperfections."

"Even with your so-called imperfections you're perfect just the way you are. Thank your mother for giving birth to you. After all, she was the source of your being. Now come on, please go lie on my bed until dinner's ready. I will give you something for your headache. A miraculous pill made from plants collected along the Amazon."

Demetra dutifully sipped the water and swallowed two moss green pills.

Gail tucked the duvet around her. "Now try to get some sleep." She folded the shutters and left Demetra in the darkened room.

Demetra lay there, staring at the Cuzco Madonna on the opposite wall. She had forgotten how charming she was with her pearl-looped bodice, her rose strewn skirt, her smile so sweet, so serene. Strange that she had not remembered her smile.

The Madonna returned her gaze.

Before long, the burning in her stomach dwindled. The pill had worked exactly as Gail had promised. She lay there for a long time in that half-shadow dream world before she reached for her Walkman and the little red felt bag she was never without.

With her castanets looped around her fingers she began to play a distinct beat, the stately rhythm of the fandango. Her fingers were strong now, and every note cracked clear and true, purring, clicking, roll after roll, hundreds of rolls shaded into myriad sounds. She played *fandangos de Huelva, fandangos de Rocio,* she played *sevillanas* after *sevillanas,* her eyes fixed on the Madonna. Then she fell into distant rain forest sleep until Gail awakened her for dinner.

The next day the obituary notice and photograph appeared on page three of the *Los Angeles Times.* Atena Valli, the Diva in a black lace dress, with a necklace of carved emerald beads. A beautiful woman in her prime. Demetra saw something of herself in that face, the same high, rounded forehead, the intense expression in her gaze.

A few days later she tracked down Valli's recording of the opera *Goyescas* in a used record shop off Pico Boulevard. She played it over and over, reading the libretto. She began to anticipate every note, every melody, as though in understanding the music, feeling the music, she might at last get to know her mother.

On Sunday she felt strong enough to drive back to Santa Barbara to spend the day at Duval's side. Demetra wrote him daily and sat by his bedside on Sundays. After her first visit she wrote:

Dear Charles Duval,

When I visited you today, you seemed so much better. Your face had good color and, when you smiled, your eyes told me that you knew me. I stayed all afternoon telling you stories about growing up in the convent. I was so happy that you knew I was there

Demetra

When she was back home again, she wanted to go straight to bed, but Farrell insisted that she join him for dinner in Chinatown.

Her mind kept wandering as he talked about the upcoming American Decorative Arts Sales in New York.

"You seem so far away, Demetra. I hope I'm not boring you."

"My mind keeps jumping from one thing to another and then it goes right back to Nepenthe. I keep re-living those terrible scenes. It's Charles Duval who keeps me from going crazy."

"You've got to let go—and you need some help. I know you have Gail to talk to, and I'm here whenever you need me."

"I'll never be able to thank you enough, Farrell, for helping me get through this past week. And for something else, as well. I am taking your advice to call Conchita. I'm ready to take her class."

"That's the best thing you can do for yourself. You need to get your body into motion. Dancing will help to clear your mind—and it will surely help mend your heart."

BOOK II

CHAPTER XIV

Marina's life at Greenhill House was the usual round of parties and meetings. On her 1985 calendar: I. Magnin's Fashion Show in the Music Center's Grand Hall, a luncheon in the Directors' Room at Santa Anita, and more important, the Never Too Late meeting at which she would be installed as president.

Marshall was overjoyed. He had reached the zenith of Los Angeles society through his trophy wife and to commemorate Marina's appointment to the Never Too Late presidency, he'd bought her a pin; a diamond-studded scallop shell mounted on carved rock crystal foam.

Marina had discovered Marshall's Achilles' heel. It was not her natural grace, her intelligence, her beauty, but her social standing that had conquered him. As she gained power from this insight, so Marshall began to lose his appeal and Marina began to flirt—but only flirt—-with other men.

She had finally convinced him to strip the Catherine the Great fabric from the walls and auction it off at Christie's. As the bedroom was being dismantled, she discovered the cassette Demetra had left behind, taped to the back of a Spanish still life. "*The Voice of Apollonia Pythias for Mrs. Jane Constable.*"

Who was this Mrs. Constable? Marina wondered. She checked her watch. Time to get ready for the party in Pasadena. She would listen to the tape while she bathed.

No longer did her bathroom walls suggest a Greek colonnade. Now sparkling mirrors of the truest, most faithful quality lined every wall. She sank into steamy, rose-scented water, mirrors before her, mirrors behind her. Marina, reflected to infinity, lay her head back and listened.

At first no sound, finally a crackle.

The voice was compelling. "I see fire, long time ago in opera house. In Europe. She is singing in a long white dress. A fire is breaking out and there is *pandemonium.*"

"Who is *she*?" a woman asks. Marina recognized Demetra's voice.

She listened until the bath water was tepid. Shivering, she stepped from the tub and reaching for the all-enveloping towel embroidered MARINA above a scallop shell, she dried her magnificent body.

Marina, who was rarely given to self-torment, found herself spending far too much time thinking about the tape. She had searched the Los Angeles telephone directories and found Madame Apollonia Pythias listed near West Melrose, not far from a restaurant where she often lunched. Not far from *Choses,* in fact. She thought she might even drive by to have a look. Out of curiosity, of course. Lately she had begun to feel a contrary closeness, a curious compassion, for

Demetra. How, she wondered, had she managed to survive all those years with Marshall?

She made the appointment for eleven o'clock, before her lunch date next Thursday. The clairvoyant told her to bring three hundred dollars in cash for the session. No checks, no credit cards, she emphasized.

She parked the red Ferrari and found the house, one of those major West Hollywood transformations from Craftsman bungalow to grey stucco French Regency. Two Ionic columns supported the front portico, and on each of the black lacquer double doors was a bronze knocker cast as entwined snakes. Poodle-clipped cypresses flanked the brick steps.

The door opened. "Mrs. Carlyle? I am Apollonia. Come in and please sit over here near this table."

Marina sat facing the seer, a lighted chandelier suspended over the marble table between them.

"So why you come to me today?"

"Curiosity, I guess."

"Here—take my brochure. Look at picture. Read underneath," she ordered. It was a tear-out reprint from the Oracles, the psychic magazine.

Apollonia Pythias, born on the island of Crete, 1931. Natural psychic powers since adolescence. Clairvoyant to the most rich and famous of Los Angeles and Hollywood.

"Okay, before we start please pay me three hundred dollars cash."

Marina opened her bag for the money and handed a wad to her.

"Thanks. You never been here before, Miss Carlyle?"

"Never."

Apollonia closed her eyes and put her head back against the chair. "Something about you, some echo I feel, something I smell. Something about a man. You married?"

Why answer her question, why tell her *anything*, Marina thought. After all, she was paying Apollonia to tell *her*.

When Apollonia opened her eyes, Marina's face was without expression. "Yes, you are married but I see from your eyes you don't love him anymore."

Marina, who rarely ever blushed, felt the color rise from bosom to forehead.

"You never loved him. You have control over this husband. Over the last one, too. Why you use your power this way? You do not do good things with your beauty."

"Depends on how you look at it." She laughed a bit nervously.

"It's not a funny situation you are in, Mrs. Carlyle."

"What do you see in my future?"

"Nothing. At least not yet. I will let you know, maybe at end of session-if I see something."

Apollonia's voice seemed less distant, less mystical, less mysterious than the haunting voice on Demetra's tape. This voice was brittle, controlled, knife edged. Now she wished she had not come.

"You use your beauty like a net to catch men. You've got children?"

"My husband doesn't want them. He has a daughter by a previous marriage. Undoubtedly, she will produce grandchildren before long. Besides—I have never seen myself as a mother."

The clairvoyant's eyes swept over her client. "You take good care of yourself. I see you always in front of mirror. You like what you see."

"I've never been dissatisfied with my looks, if that's what you mean,"

"Why does your body need so much love? You want too much. You have too many lovers."

"Not lately, I haven't."

"So far you have never really loved a man. Only yourself. One day you will meet another man you *will* love. He needs you. He is searching for you. You will marry this man, and your husband does not care." She covered her face with her hands, leaned back in her chair and mumbled an incantation. At last she said, "I see this man with you. I see him breaking glass by your feet."

How preposterous! There was no way she would ever walk out on Marshall for another man. And of course, Marshall *would* mind if she did. Marina laughed nervously. And whatever did the psychic mean by the glass broken by his feet? Did Apollonia see a Jewish marriage ceremony in her future?

"You must leave here. I am tired. The tape is yours."

Marina worried all the way home. Could it be that Marshall might already be seeing other women? Perhaps a younger woman now that she had brought him to the pinnacle of social acceptance? She chided herself for taking all this nonsense seriously.

When she arrived home, she went straight to the kitchen. She took the tape from her purse and, with a paring knife, pried out the long brown plastic ribbon, tossed it into the trash compactor and pushed the button. Gratifying tremors ran through her as she imagined it being mangled and squashed against the garbage. So much for Madame Apollonia Pythias and her ridiculous prophecies!

After six weeks of dance classes, Demetra wondered why Conchita kept shouting at her for what seemed like small mistakes. Why was she pushing her so hard? After all, she had never intended to be a professional dancer; yet Conchita was tougher on her than on any of the other students, making her repeat steps over and over until they clicked clear, hard and precise. "I don't want any sloppy, half-hearted foot work from you, Demetra. Give me clear, deliberate steps."

Sometimes she seemed to have mastered a step at home, only to be off beat, or to have forgotten the step while in class. Sometimes she thought she'd done quite well until after class when Conchita would take her aside and say, "Listen to me, Demetra. Unleash that body of yours. Try to break away! Free yourself. *Feel* the music."

But how could she free herself when she had not yet mastered the basic structure, the rigid structure of *flamenco puro?*

Almost every evening, after finishing her studies, she practiced with her hair swept back with a tight sweatband. In the past she'd hated to sweat, but now she looked forward to the damp in the creases of her elbows, sweat trickling down the channel between her breasts. As she danced on the gym-finished hardwood floors, she was relieved that no one would ever hear her. The houses in the compound were far enough away to be spared the relentless *taconeo* she was trying to fit into the rhythm of the twelve-beat flamenco *escobilla.* She fought to make her feet find the pattern, and, when they did, she tried to forget that they had found it.

When she finished practicing *taconeo,* her leotard was soaked, her feet and calves swollen. Then she would stretch her upper body and begin to practice *braceo,* both arms forming wide arcs, her hands pivoting, wrists forming small circles, the thumb and forefinger almost touching. This pattern would gradually evolve into the graceful flamenco hand and arm movements.

Sometimes she would let her mind wander, let it settle on a feeling, usually the feeling of not knowing who she was, the feeling of rootless anonymity. *Transcend the feet, hear the beat.* Maybe someday she might find the dance path to her elusive self.

Dancing was changing her figure. In only a few months, the practice skirt had become too loose in the waist, so she dropped by to ask Dolores, the flamenco costume maker, to take it in. Conchita, who spoke English so eloquently, warned Demetra, "Don't be put off by her coarse manner and her way of speaking. Dolores learned English from migrant farm workers on a ranch in the San Joaquin Valley."

As Dolores was picking out stitches from the waistband, Demetra asked, "Why is Conchita so tough on me? I seem to be the only one she singles out for criticism. The classes have become so painful that I don't know why I keep on with them. I usually go home with a burning stomach."

"She must think you're okay or she wouldn't bother with you. Believe me, I know that one. She wouldn't waste her breath. You must be doing good in her way of thinkin'."

"Sometimes when she yells at me, I feel like walking out—that it's not worth all this agony, aching muscles and bones. Then at night after I've practiced and worked up a real sweat, something happens, and I feel that maybe it *has* been worth it. So I keep on pushing myself."

As Dolores was pinning her skirt, Demetra asked, "Tell me about *duende*. What is it, exactly?"

"That's a tough one. My father was Spanish and he probably could have told you about it better than me. *Duende* is for Spanish people kinda like what soul is to black folks, but it's a gift and don't show up in everybody. Usually it's the singer who's got *duende, but* sometimes the dancer got it —especially in *solea* or *soleares*. You do not have to be the greatest dancer in the world, but if you got *duende* you go way past your limits. You're listenin' to those dark sounds and lettin' out what you got hidden deep inside yourself. It's somethin' comin' to you from way, way back. What *gitanos* call *la pena negra*. Like pluggin' into somethin' far away—connectin' to the memories of all those souls who passed on before you, feelin' their pain like it was your own. *Duende* climbs up from the soles of your feet to grab your heart. Do you see what I'm sayin'?"

Demetra nodded. "I think so."

"When the singer sings *cante jondo*, he's singin' like a bird without eyes—singin' blind, like a bird in a black night that don't know if mornin's ever comin'. His pain shoots an arrow through your heart. And if you're a dancer, you're way into the night, into the earth, deep into the earth even though it feels like you're reachin' up to touch the moon. This kind of dancing is about the earth, Demetra. It ain't about flittin' around the stage like a ballet *maricón.*"

"That's exactly what Conchita told us on the first day of class."

"Want to hear what else she told me? Get ready for this!" she said, "Demetra must be Spanish somewhere. She has the soul of a Spaniard. She *will* have *duende*, I feel it."

"Come on Dolo'—how could I possibly have *duende*? I'm not even Spanish."

"She musta seen somethin'—felt somethin' Spanish about you."

Demetra shook her head. "I really doubt that."

Dolores chortled. "I told Conchita, it sure takes one to know one." She laughed slyly and winked. One a' these days how about us two goin' down to Santee Street. We'll find some gorgeous material for you—somethin' nicer than your cotton work-out skirt. Then we can go over to Olvera Street. I got my special place for enchiladas."

"I'd love to —let's make a date right now."

Two weeks later, as they were driving downtown, Demetra played the tape Dolores found for her, Antonio Franco and Conchita del Lago's famous dance, the Peteneras. After listening intently to the singer Demetra said "What a haunting, passionate song—it's as though his voice is scorched. It makes chills go up my spine. But I only understood those words at the beginning. '*Who named you, Petenera?*' And that incredible footwork! I can just imagine Conchita dancing in black lace ruffles, a mantilla draped high over a comb. But why is this song such a mystery? I wonder why she didn't want me to hear it. "

Dolores turned and looked behind just to make sure that no one was hiding in the back seat. Then she lowered her voice. "Now I'm gonna tell you a little secret, gal. I ain't sure I should be tellin' it to you, but I'm gonna tell you anyway 'cause I trust you. But first I'm gonna ask you what Conchita said that time you asked her to hear the Peteneras record."

"She told me she didn't have one."

"Oh yeah? Is that so? She didn't have one?" She gave Demetra a shrewd little look. "How come? That was her biggest number. Got any idea why she don't wanna play it for you? Come on—take a guess."

Demetra pondered for a moment. "No idea—I give up."

"Don't worry. I know the words. A *cantaor* standin' by a tree blurts out his feeling for La Petenera as she passes by."

Quien te puso Petenera?
No supo ponerte nombre
Este vida han dispuesto
Este vida han dispuesto
La perdicion de los hombres
No supo ponerte nombre

"Okay, Demetra, here goes." *Who named you Petenera, you, the ruin of men. I can't count how many."*

Now here's the part Conchita may not want you to hear." Dolores spoke slowly, translating the lyrics as best she could.

Where do you go, beautiful Jewess, so late, and after hours?
I go in search of a young goat, to offer at the synagogue.
Why do you go so late, looking so enticing?
Whoever named you Petenera should not have done so,
Life has prepared you to be the ruin of men.

Demetra was puzzled. "What do you make of these words, Dolores?"

"The answer is this, Demetra. You gotta understand that people ain't always what they seem to be in this crazy world of ours—sometimes people want to be somethin' else."

"I know that—but what does this have to do with Conchita?"

"I'm the only one in this town who knows the secret. You will be the second. And the only reason I know is that Antonio Franco told me just before he passed, may God rest his soul. Antonio and Conchita—those famous Spanish dancers—well, Demetra, guess what—neither one of them was Spanish. Antonio was born in Italy, in a village way up in the Abruzzi mountains. Both wanted to be Spanish more than anything. Otherwise they thought *afficionados* might not take them seriously —it's this whole *duende* thing—like you can't have *duende* unless you got Spanish blood or gitano blood flowin' through your veins. Conchita don't even know that I know 'cause I been real tight lipped about it. I never told no one else 'cause I know how important it is for her to be Spanish. See, Demetra, being Spanish is her whole life. I ain't ever met anyone in all my life that was more Spanish than her. *Verdad.*"

"What is Conchita then if she isn't Spanish?"

"She's Jewish."

Shaking her head, Demetra laughed. "Come on, so what's so strange about that? You must know that Sephardic Jews came from Spain. After the Inquisition they went into hiding or fled from Spain along with Gypsies and Moors—Hebrew music is part of flamenco along with Arabic and gitano."

"But Conchita ain't Sephardic. Sure—if she was she *could* have *duende*. No problem! But Conchita was born in Brooklyn. Her folks came from Russia. She's Ashkenazi. She ain't got even a drop of Spanish blood in those veins of hers, but believe me, her Spanish is so perfect she dreams in it. So help me, Luis, the *cante jondo* singer ain't got no clue, and 'cause Conchita speaks a little Caló, she even got the Heredias down in San Diego fooled into thinkin' she's a senorita from Granada. During his last days Antonio told me that he wanted to push this *decepción* out of her mind forever, and on his deathbed that's just what he did. But don't you worry, I'm not gonna bust her bubble. No way. I'll tell you why—'cause Conchita is the best friend I ever had. She's havin' a tough enough time makin' a livin.' This has been a bad year for Spanish dancers. She don't need no more headaches."

A few months later after dance class, as Demetra and Rafael, the gifted young guitarist, walked to the parking lot, they had their first real conversation. She had never had a chance to speak with him before. Conchita always spoke to him in Spanish, so Demetra assumed it was his native language.

"What part of Spain do you come from?" she asked.

"I was born in Sevilla, but I grew up in Provence—in a small town near Arles."

"Parlons français, alors?"

"Bien sur, Demetra. .Je serai content."

When did you arrive in Los Angeles, Rafael?"

"About a year ago—with a group called Los Reyes Ombra y Sol. We're looking for a recording company to sponsor our group. But I'm homesick for my brothers, my cousins. I miss our *juerga* weekends, when we play what we call *'nouveau flamenco.'"*

"Tell me what it sounds like."

"Classic flamenco blended with modern, simpler Latin rhythms. We've given it a whole new sound, a new beat."

"Can you play it here, this *nouveau flamenco?*"

"Of course. When would you like to hear it?"

" How about tomorrow night at my house? "

"Seven o'clock?"

"I'll cook something for you."

"Please don't bother. I'll be there with my guitar and some of our tapes."

The next day she asked Farrell to keep an eye on *Choses* so that she could leave early. By five o'clock the soup was simmering. The doorbell rang promptly at seven.

"Nice place you have, Demetra," He produced a flask from his black leather jacket. "Special olive oil from Mouriès. Last year we performed at the oil pressing festival," he said with pride.

She thanked him. "We can pour a few drops into the pistou I just made and then it will really taste of Provence."

"Last May we played at Les Saintes Maries de la Mer. For the Feast of Saint Sara, our patron. I always carry her photograph for good luck." He pulled it out from his shirt pocket.

Curious. The image of Saint Sara, draped in pink lace, reminded her of Dolores. Was the statue carved from ebony or had it darkened from centuries of candle smoke, she wondered.

He laughed self-consciously. "I suppose you people don't believe in this sort of thing."

She shook her head. "I wish I had your kind of devotion. I seem to have lost my mine over the years." She sliced through a baguette. "Getting hungry?"

"No. I ate dinner at my aunt's house."

"I am starving. Why don't you at least have a taste?" She ladled the soup into two earthenware bowls, and dolloped each with a spoonful of garlic, Parmesan and basil mixed with the olive oil.

He looked down into the bowl but did not pick up the spoon. "I must tell you, Demetra. This would be the first time I'd eat in a *gadjo* house. Do you know what *gadjo* means?"

She had a sudden recall of a similar word that she had learned from reading a novel about Gypsies years ago. "Does it mean the same as *gorgio?* Someone who isn't a Gypsy?" Two words had stuck in her mind all these years, *gorgio* and *patteran*, the title of Thomas' first novel, which meant a directional sign made of sticks, leaves and stones left by Gypsies at crossroads.

"Is it a Gypsy custom, never to eat in a non-Gypsy home?"

He nodded. "More than a custom. It's what we call, *marime*. Forbidden, impure. I do not know how else to explain that word to you. Some of our people observe rigid rituals—my father's people. He comes from a Romanian tribe. My mother is Spanish *calò*. She is not strict. And speaking of strict, I want to tell you that you take your class too seriously. You don't seem to get any joy from it."

"I am getting tired of hearing Conchita yell at me."

"*Compas, compas!* She keeps telling you to hear the music and free yourself. "

"Conchita's tougher on me than on anyone else."

"She told me that she was going to make a dancer out of you yet. But unless you begin when you are young, that might never happen. Flamenco is so structured. It can take a long time to learn the basics unless you practice for many hours every day."

She laughed. "I'm not sure I'd be a dancer even if I did."

"Our group wanted to break those old boundaries—that's why we mix the old flamenco with the newer Latin rhythms, Cuban rumba, bossa nova, the samba. Andean sounds, too. Even Russian Gypsy. As you dance to our music, you can still use your traditional Spanish arm and hand movements. *Liber tad* is what we're all about."

He slipped a tape into the stereo cassette. "This should make you feel like dancing. The last time we played this in a theater in Nimes, the audience jumped up and danced in the aisles. Listen."

Ciento, ciento tus pasos
Ciento la sensa di abandon.
Listen; listen to your own steps
Feel the sense of abandon.

He was right. The beat was seductive, the melody contagious. She couldn't help tapping her feet to the rhythm, but she squelched the urge to leap up and dance. She did not intend to make a fool of herself in front of Rafael.

By the end of the evening she had listened to and copied all the *Los Reyes Ombra y Sol* tapes.

"It makes me happy that you like our music but maybe you shouldn't tell Conchita about it. Not just yet, anyway. She has not heard me play anything but *flamenco puro.* I don't want her to think that I'm undermining her."

"I promise that I won't tell Conchita or anyone else. Who knows—one of these days I might try dancing to your music."

"If you do, you might loosen up, so one day it might even become easier for you to master the classic *taconeo.* You know how Conchita keeps saying how you fight her, fight the music. First you got to empty your mind—you got to hear the stillness inside of you—that is when you let the beat take hold. Do not worry Demetra, there is no right way to dance. Only *your* way."

After Rafael went home, Demetra re-played the tape. Whirling like a maenad, she abandoned herself to its beat, its pulses, carving out space with her body. By the time the tape played out, she was completely breathless.

She fell into bed exhausted. That night she woke up with a dream.

She sits in the first row of a theatre in Madrid. A woman stands on the stage. A woman with a face the color of gleaming mahogany, like the face of the gypsy Saint Sara. She sees the strange, sweet smile on the woman's face. She hears the thrumming of an unseen guitar, the palma sorda of the sequiriya.

The woman begins to dance in her bare feet. Her eyes are closed as she dances like one possessed, as though she, too, were in a dream. Her body quivers and she kicks her billowing flounces behind her, ending her dance. Demetra applauds and cries out, "I want to dance like you. Just like you!"

The dark woman responds, "Then you must dance like you, you fool!"

CHAPTER XV

Conchita had arranged a birthday dinner for Dolores at Sevilla de Oro. When the cake was wheeled out it was ablaze with 72 candles.

Conchita rose from the head of the table and turned to Dolores.

"We all wish you a happy birthday, dear Dolores, with many more to come. When we are all together, and I look at your happy faces, I think how fortunate we are to have chosen to live in this city of the Angels.

'Here we are living our dreams with music and dance. '*La vida e sueno, e los suenos, suenos son*'—those wise words of Calderon de la Barca. "There was a burst of applause sending a rhythmic message to Dolores who jumped up from the table applauding Conchita. The other women joined in and with an enthusiastic *palmas along with the staff and some diners.*

"Come on "Dolo', baila*!* "They shouted.

Dolores did not need to be coaxed She stood center spotlight on the stage. For a long moment she held the shawl stretched high over her head. The smile left her face. Her eyes stared past the audience. Lights dimmed. Dolores began her *solea,* the most inward, most sacred of all flamenco dances. With a haughty, yet graceful_motion, she tossed her shawl to the floor. She stood in place marking the *compas* with her heels, expressing her feelings with only her upper body, shoulders proud, hands like swallows, darting, swooping. She was dancing with her shadow as partner. When she had danced her way off the stage, the audience shouted and clapped as Dolores made her return to the table.

The guitarist struck up another *bulerias.* Everyone at the table joined in with *palmas.* Conchita called out for the other women to take their turns. Except for Demetra. Demetra knew and Conchita knew that she was not ready to dance the *bulerias.* She heard the *compas,* she knew how to respond to the guitarist's command, the *llamada,* with her heels, and she could join in with her *palmas.* Still she was far from ready for a solo.

"Come on, Demetra—now it's your turn! Get up on that stage, gal. *Baila!*" Dolores stood up and pulled her from her chair and pushed her up the stairs to the stage. Conchita pleaded, "No, Dolò, please not yet! She is not ready. Please don't force her!" But it was too late. There she was. Center stage. Just as in the dream. She could run from the stage. Or she could dance.

"Nouveau flamenco?" Rafael whispered.

She nodded. "*Siento tus pasos.*"

"*Que la Sainte Sara te bénisse,*" she heard him say as he struck the first chords.

She saw the dark-faced woman's smile. She remembered her words. "*Then you must dance like you, you fool! Do not be afraid. Hear the music —dance what you are.*"

Demetra moved with the music, arms spiraling, hands darting, head snapping right to left, left to right, body spinning, her heart's chambers pulsing, flooding with joy.

Now the music moves with her. The *jaleo* begins

"*Mira, mira,*" the women cheered as they clapped in syncopated *palmas.*

After she made her last turn, she bowed and, breathless, stepped down from the stage toward the table. Sweat trickled from her forehead, her chest gleamed.

Dolores leaped up to hug and kiss her. "Hey gal, you did it! You did it! Now you're one of us!"

Conchita threw her arms around her. "Your free steps were marvelous! I have never heard that music before. I must ask Rafael to play it for my class."

The margarita had melted into a lukewarm pink puddle. She gulped it down in one swallow. Behind her she heard a familiar voice say "*Olé.*" She turned. It was Thomas. He gripped her shoulders and kissed her. "I flew in from London. Just in time for your performance! You were wonderful!"

She felt the flush from bosom to forehead. "Thomas, please let me introduce you to my good friends.

"Demetra, why didn't you return my phone calls?"

She told him what had happened with the answering machine.

"You could have written or called."

"I tried to reach Gail in England for your number, but she wasn't home."

"That's no excuse. I really want to know what's going on."

"I don't know what kept me from calling you back. Maybe it wasn't the right time."

He took her hand and put it to his lips. "It is now. Tomorrow night we are being honored with an award for *Morris Dance*. Best collaboration between writer and director. I shall be accepting for Simon, as well. Will you come with me? The event is at the University Club. And it's black tie."

"I would love to." Dolores' doorbell chimed away in her head. *Amapola, my pretty little poppy.* Farrell's red chiffon dress with the ring of poppies around the neck. She would wear it to the dinner.

***

After the party Demetra drove Dolores home.

"I like your boyfriend, Demè," Dolores said. "Smart guy, all right. Very polite. You gone out with him a lot?"

"Only twice."

"He speaks real good Spanish. I like hearin' him talk. He sounds somethin' like that actor, you know, the guy who gave the humungous diamond rock to Liz Taylor."

"Now that you mention it, his voice is a lot like Richard Burton's. I will be sure to pass on the compliment. He will be flattered."

"You should have seen the way he kept looking at you, all goo-goo eyes."

"Come on, Dolores! He spent most of the time chatting about Spain with Conchita."

"From those eyes of his I could tell he musta had lots of pain in his life."

"I seem to attract that kind of man. The last one I dated still was not over losing his wife. Although he was searching for a woman, I soon found out that I did not fit the picture he had in mind. Just as well. I'm not ready to commit."

"Hey—what's the matter with you?"

"Part of me may want a steady relationship, but most of me doesn't."

"Tomorrow I'm gonna go straight to the *santeria* to buy you a love potion, the kind you use to catch yourself an hombre." Somethin' to 'light your fire' like in the song."

"Last year I might have thought that a good idea, but since I've been dancing, I don't think I'll need tricks and treats from your *santeria*."

"Now you listen to your old pal Dolores. I got this feeling that Thomas won't make one move unless you give him the go-ahead signal. He don't want any more women saying bye-bye to him neither."

***

That night Demetra dreamed that she was back at Greenhill House. Bulls were running among the ficus trees, trampling the lawn's tender grass, grass that had once known no foot.

BOOK III

London, March, 1947

Opening Night. The impresario has assured her that every seat, every inch of standing room space has been sold.

The diva hums a few bars to test The Voice. Turning her head from side to side, she studies her face in the triple mirror. Yes. Just enough makeup for a Druid princess, she muses, staring into her eyes, green eyes that she knows are her best feature. But tonight, her brain burns behind them. She finds two aspirin and swallows them with water instead of the tall glass of lukewarm black coffee she usually drinks before a performance.

She trills The Voice once more, then shrugs the black satin wrapper from her shoulders. The wardrobe mistress slips the white Fortuny gown over her head and fastens the tiny glass beads along the shoulders.

She turns to study herself in profile. No hint of a stomach. Not yet. She is anxious to share her secret with him and hopes that he might surprise her with his presence.

She lights a black Sobrani and fills her lungs with smoke. To relax The Voice. She lays the cigarette in the ashtray on her dressing table next to the pile of fresh linen towels she uses for removing her makeup.

When she stands back from the mirror, she takes another long, admiring gaze. Her dark hair hangs halfway down her back: with both hands she sweeps it up from the nape so the wardrobe mistress can encircle her neck with the golden torque. Then she thrusts out her arms for the wide gold cuffs at each wrist.

Now she *is* Norma.

The Diva hears her cue. She leaves the dressing room and, lifting her gown, climbs up to the stage floor, the wardrobe mistress following behind.

The House is filled, standing room crammed. In her long white pleated gown, the Diva makes her entrance to a burst of wild applause.

The orchestra plays the stirring march, the chorus hails Norma, their priestess.

Norma silences them. She moves to the altar in the center of an oak grove to perform the Druid ritual. After she places a sprig of mistletoe on a salver, an acolyte offers her a torch to light the sacred fire. Smoke spirals from the offering.

Norma raises her arms to the moon goddess.

The Voice begins.

Casta Diva, che inargenti
queste sacre antiche piante....

Chaste goddess, whose ancient trees bathe us in your silver light,
Turn your fair face upon us.
Calm the burning hearts the brave passions of my people.

The Voice has never been stronger, more resolute, its phrasing more eloquent, its tone more burnished.

In the Diva's dressing room fire tongues leap up, devouring the white linen towels, melting the black silk filaments of her robe.

The Voice rises as the Diva sings with every fiber of her double being.

Dal Druidico delubro
From the Druidic temple.
La mia voce tuonerà.
My voice will thunder
Cadrà; punirlo io posso
He will fail, I can punish him
Ma, punirlo, il cor non sa.
But my heart does not know how…....

Shouts and screams as smoke billows from the pit.
The music stops abruptly.
The audience rushes to the exits.
The Diva sings on. And on. Until stagehands drag her away.

CHAPTER XVI

Marina left her Never Too Late office early that afternoon. She wanted plenty of time to dress for the literary awards dinner at the University.

She drove the red Ferrari through Greenhill House's gates, admiring her landscaping. Because she loved its scent, she' had myrtle hedges planted along the drive. From now on all flowers at the front entrance were to be white, so much better with rich green Marathon grass. Marshall always heeded her suggestions. After all, he knew she came from a background long familiar with formal gardens and stately houses.

She smiled at the ultimate comment made by a member at yesterday's board meeting. "What you've done to those front gardens! It's like driving up to a house in Kent or Surrey."

And Marina had laughed. "Marshall will be so pleased to hear that. He loves anything to do with England. For him, anything English cried out good taste. Even Bovril, Marmite, and Typhoo Tea. And bangers, too!"

She had become tired of his pretensions. Although he acted grand, collected grand, he was so uninformed about history, art and literature. He had never ever set foot in a museum in Paris or London. Politics interested him only so far as it was expedient to business. She had never seen him read a book. Any kind of book. He was not interested in theater, dance or music, just the occasional macho movie or porno video. He liked to travel only when he worked on deals; travel to Marshall meant flying from Ritz to Ritz. He and Marina had little in common, except for one thing. But even for Marina, sex soon palled without tenderness.

Marshall was in England again, a perfect night for her to stay home and crawl between her rose scented satin sheets by nine o'clock. She was overdue on beauty sleep, but this was an invitation she felt she ought to accept. Thomas Pierson was being honored for *Morris Dance;* his novel turned into a film. Marshall had often reminded her that her presence bestowed glamour, added prestige and tone to an event. *Noblesse obliges.* In contrast to the gilded cage restrictions he had imposed on Demetra, he had encouraged Marina to accept invitations on her own, so she felt no qualms about attending without an escort.

Late as usual. Marina, wrapped in a pale silver charmeuse one-shouldered dress, made her entrance with singular and conscious dignity into the Library Rotunda where the Nine Muses frolicked among clouds painted on the domed ceiling. As the respectful crowd parted to let Marina pass, soaring voices hushed to a collective murmur. The Dean of the Library welcomed her.

Marina scanned the room for familiar faces. Was that Demetra in the red halter dress, her hair long and swept up? How lovely she looks. Quite a metamorphosis! And she was with Thomas Pierson, of all people! The guest of honor.

After cocktails, as she made her way to her place at the Dean's table, she discovered, to her distress, that Demetra was seated close to

Thomas Pierson and was whispering into Pierson's ear. Who, Marina wondered, had botched up the seating this time?

Throughout dinner, the women took great pains to avoid each other's glances.

The Dean introduced Thomas Pierson and presented him with the prized award. Thomas gave a short speech about keeping the integrity of the novel by close writer-director collaboration, something exceedingly rare indeed in Hollywood.

Marina applauded with gusto. Without doubt Pierson was the most attractive, sexiest man she had set eyes on in a long time. And fascinating. And cultivated. Although he had attended the awards dinner with Demetra, it made no difference to her. A man, whoever, wherever, was fair game, except, of course, those men, those *very* exceptional rare men, who were, or at the very least who *seemed,* happily married.

When Thomas returned to his place at table, Demetra put her hand over his. "Well done! Your speech was perfect—and how right you were about the integrity of being faithful to the writer's vision. "

"Thanks, but I'll be relieved when the evening's over. For your sake. You've managed the situation very gracefully, Demetra." He glanced across at Marina who was busy beguiling the Dean. "Marina's a woman who demands to be noticed."

"And discussed. Farrell Minton told me that Marshall has supposedly given her *carte blanche* to sell whatever furniture she wants from Greenhill House. He's spending much more time in England these days. Buying more companies, I guess."

He gave her an odd, sideways glance. "I've heard that, too."

Excusing herself, Demetra made her way to the ladies' room. As she passed the stacks, she noticed the shelves lined with those familiar bindings. Loeb Classics. Sister Claire used to keep them in her office. Her eyes were drawn to Lucretius, De *Rerum Natura. On the Nature of Things.* She smiled inwardly. Although the theory of Lucretius was about the repose of the mind and the pursuit of virtue, her mind flew to the nature of "*things.*" "*Choses*", Farrell's Theory.

When she returned from the ladies' room there was Marina sitting in *her* chair at *her* place, her wide apart forget–me-not blue eyes fixed on Thomas who seemed spellbound. "*Steady, Demetra, calm down, keep your cool, don't let her get the better of you,*" she urged herself as she made her way to the table.

He leaped up from his seat almost guiltily, Demetra thought, but Marina stayed put in Demetra's chair.

"Come on, Marina, *pousse ta viande,*" Demetra laughed, surprising herself.

Marina rose from her chair with a smile on her face.

Thomas, who never lacked for words, seemed sheepish and a bit flustered. He blurted out. "I suppose there's no need to introduce you two. Or perhaps you should be re-introduced."

He laughed a bit too self-consciously, Demetra thought, but maybe it was only her imagination.

Marina kept passing her hand over her hair, a nervous habit she probably picked up from Marshall. She smiled sweetly, seemingly sincerely. "I think of you often, Demetra, more than you'll ever know."

"I'm not sure I *want* to know, Marina. Ever!" Demetra retorted as though ice encased every word. "I've been far too busy to relive scenes past."

Marina blushed, knowing exactly what scenes Demetra had in mind.

Then Demetra surprised herself. She smiled and let go. "But somehow things *do* have a way of working out. In fact, you may have done me an enormous favor, Marina. So thank you!

Marina stood, smoothing the satin clinging to her buttocks and thighs. She grinned, "He's all yours, Demetra, you two make a great looking couple." she said, giving Thomas one long, intense gaze before gliding away.

Demetra heaved a sigh. "That confrontation was much easier than I imagined it would be."

"You were so poised and self-assured! I liked the way you told her to get herself out of your chair—you made a joke out of it. And then how you reached out to her."

She laughed. "Sometimes I resort to my first language in difficult situations."

He checked his watch. "Come on. Let us say our goodbyes and be off."

Neither of them did much talking as he drove her home.

She turned on the lights. "Would you like to come in for a drink?" she asked as though she was not sure she meant it.

"You don't seem yourself," he replied." What's wrong?"

"I'm just fine."

"You're *not* fine. What are you feeling?"

"Always straight to the point, aren't you?"

"Try to express yourself. You're an articulate woman."

"Not always about my feelings."

"Was it my conversation with Marina that bothered you?"

"Like Aphrodite, she was trying her best to lure you into her golden net."

He laughed. "But her best wasn't good enough. I'm not the least bit interested in or attracted to her."

"Then why were *you* so silent driving home?"

His voice turned serious. "Because I have to tell you that I'll be leaving Los Angeles. My publisher called me this morning. Now that *Morris Dance* is ready for release, he is pressing hard for the Ruskin book and I've got to go back to work in the British Library. After a few weeks I shall find myself a little flat in Venice so that I can soak up some mood and texture for the novel, as well as find the peace I need to finish. I have to be near the sea when I write."

"Tomorrow morning, I fly to New York."

Her voice broke. "*Now* shall I tell you how I feel?"

He put his arms around her. "I want you to come with me, Demetra. I've been quiet because I was afraid if I asked, you'd say no."

"If it weren't for Charles Duval, I would have said yes but I have to see him through and be patient."

He frowned. "Patience has never been one of my strengths." He drew her closer.

She lay her head on his shoulder. "Thomas, do you remember when you once asked me about my fantasies?"

He nodded. "You told me you rarely had any."

"Since I've been dancing, I've had lots."

"I hope some are about me."

She smiled. "They're *all* about you. But I keep pushing them away."

"Not any more you won't." He kissed her, and, rubbing a silken poppy petal between his fingers, he said, "I wonder what *you're* like inside, Demetra." Then he spread the petals and pressed his lips against the poppy's black velvet depths.

When he had unhooked her dress, his sinewy, tender hands caressed her back, her breasts, her thighs, her own dark center. She quivered with pleasures she had never felt before. Then he pulled her to him and kissed her as though he were making up for his lifetime without her.

***

The next morning, as Demetra drove to Santa Barbara for her weekly visit to Charles Duval, she relived the evening over and over again—his every word, every gesture up to the moment they walked in the door. But she could not remember how they found their way to the bedroom and onto the bed. She remembered only her body's tremors, the earth's tremors, as she surrendered to sounds of distant, galloping horses.

The next day when Marshall called to tell Marina that he had decided not to fly home from London for another week, she was delighted. Katie, her old Pasadena friend, was giving a dinner party. Thomas Pierson had accepted, and Marina was sure he would be seated at her side tonight. She left the office early to allow lots of time to get ready.

Marina walked into Greenhill House's rotunda, pausing as she invariably did, to admire the ballet dancer. She had always given Demetra credit for the Degas. Such a sound investment! Marshall had expected her to make similar decisions, but no, she would never take on such responsibilities. Instead, she had found him a New York art consultant to help her make her selections.

She went straight to the bedroom, peeled off her dress and wrapped herself in flesh-pink satin so that she would feel sensual while she planned her conquest of Thomas Pierson. She was not yet ready to give up.

***

Her driver turned off the freeway at Orange Grove, toward the hills of San Rafael. Carole Nelson's house was at the top of a circular drive planted in the spiral of tall cypresses. Marina loathed cypresses. They reminded her of cemeteries in Italy and Greece.

After greeting Carole, Marina's eyes swept the room. No Thomas Pierson. Not yet, anyway. She asked Carole, "Isn't Thomas Pierson coming tonight?"

"He flew back to England this afternoon."

Marina tried to keep her face from collapsing.

A tall, handsome man stepped forward. "I'm Tony Tradland—and I know you're Marina."

Aha—maybe the evening's not a waste of time after all, she thought. "Anthony Tradland, the art historian?" she asked. "You're a professor at…"

As a guest moved forward toward Marina, he knocked the wine goblet from Tradland's hand, shattering the glass on the marble floor.

"I'm sorry! What a way to meet! Please forgive me." He stooped to gather up the broken pieces and, with trembling hands, wrapped up the shards in his pocket-handkerchief.

Marina looked down at her legs. Pale stockings and ivory satin shoes wine splotched. Apollonia's words. *A glass broken at her feet!* What a joke! Not Tony Tradland. No. That could never happen. A professor? What could this man ever mean to her?

She smiled sweetly, as though the glass had never been broken. "No harm done. Please excuse me while I wash up. I don't want to smell as though I just hopped out from a wine barrel."

They laughed together, but Tradland's face was red.

Ignoring the guests who greeted her, she pushed her way through the living room with one purpose in mind, to cleanse herself of Tradland's wine.

***

When she returned, Tony and Gail Claiborne were chatting. Gail was dressed in yet another outlandish outfit Marina couldn't understand.

Marina scanned the room for Clem. The actor had always fascinated her, but he was supposedly still in love with his wife. Abiding by her own set of rules, Marina did not consider him fair game. She looked over the *placement* chart. *No*! How could it be that she was seated next to Professor Tradland? At least she should have been seated next to Clem, but Carole had placed herself next to the actor, and her mother, the guest of honor, sat at his right. For an instant she had an urge to exchange place cards, but her breeding and good manners prevailed.

Tradland approached and pulled out her chair. "My lucky evening, Marina."

She responded with a wan smile

During the first course, salad with goat cheese, she made no effort at conversation with Tony, practicing her every charm on the man seated to her left, a boring broker from Hancock Park.

As they waited for dessert, Tradland finally forced her to listen, and, to her surprise, she found him riveting.

"Do you still spend a lot of time in Italy?" she asked.

"Yes, summers mostly, and sabbaticals. I may not go this summer because I'm working on a book and I have a fall deadline."

"On what subject?"

"Aphrodite, her Neolithic origins in the Eastern Mediterranean, and her reappearance in the *poesia* paintings of Giorgione and Titian, Bellini. Aphrodite or Venus in her Roman guise had been forgotten in the art of the Middle Ages."

"I've always been fascinated by the myth of the birth of Aphrodite."

"You know it, then?"

"Oh, yes—," she smiled, her wide-open, forget-me-not blue eyes quite serious, "But I'd like to learn more." Marina was convinced that she was keeping the conversation on a purely intellectual level.

They stayed on the topic of Aphrodite until Carole announced that demitasse would be served in the living room.

As they waited for the coffee, Katie and Marina had a chance to talk.

"Tony seems infatuated with you, but I noticed that dinner was almost over by the time you spoke to him," Carole said.

"I purposely avoided him."

"Were you annoyed by the spilled wine?"

"Certainly not by the stains or the discomfort. Under ordinary circumstances, it would not have mattered. It was just that it *happened*, in the first place, that he broke a glass by my foot. That little scene was supposed to be fraught with meaning."

"What do you mean?"

She told Carole about the tape she discovered at Greenhill House and her visit to Apollonia.

"How can you believe such utter nonsense? I am surprised at you. Get it out of your gorgeous head! Besides, one of the guests told me that Tony has been escorting Marshall's first wife. He's supposed to be crazy about her."

"Strange. I saw Demetra just last night with Thomas Pierson."

"That may be. Tonight, she'd been planning to attend with Tradland but she changed her mind when she learned that you were coming. So forget that ludicrous prediction."

I could never be the wife of a college professor, no matter how enthralling he might be, Marina thought, making a silent vow that such a preposterous thing would never happen.

Madness, sheer madness Marina thought as she drove to Hollywood in the old Mustang Corey had left behind. Better not to have to worry about the Rolls parked in front of those fusty musty apartments on a side street in the Los Feliz hills.

Marina, who had always loved color and texture and *luxe,* wondered what Tony's digs would be like. No doubt bland, academic, anemic. It was usually that way with art curators or art professors, as though they were fearful should something less than museum quality hang on their walls. She was sure that once having set eyes on his place her wild attraction would be over. She would probably spend the evening doing a mental makeover, the way she did whenever an ambience jarred her. And she hoped he would not order Chinese take-out. Or God forbid, pizza or deli! None of those foods agreed with her.

She peered through the grillwork portal. What a pretty garden! She rang the highly polished doorbell. The electric gate door popped open.

Tony was there in an instant. "I've been waiting for you," he said, taking her hand to lead her through the courtyard.

She paused. "That statue—how lovely. She reminds me of someone,"

"She reminds me of you, Marina."

She studied the statue, her lips turning up in its corners, as she mimicked the goddess's mysterious, archaic smile. "Well, now that you mention it, I can see the resemblance." So far so good, she thought.

When she walked in the door, she took a deep breath of a scent she adored, one so hard to find these days. Guerlain's *Extracte des Plantes Marines.* Hand in hand Tony led her through each room then back to the living room, her ears never missing a rippling cadence of Debussy's *L'apres-midi d'un faune* emanating from everywhere. When she'd sunk deep into the down cushions, her eyes scanned the walls. "What an amazing collection. I never would have believed it."

"How do you mean?"

"Your place. Everything about it. These rooms—the art, the gardens. Even the fragrance, the music. I feel so at home here. All my life I have wanted to live in a place like this. An earthly paradise."

He put his arms around her and shyly kissed her full lips.

She felt her knees go weak, heard her heart beat like an anvil striking iron.

"My darling Marina, I've been searching for you—hoping one day to find you." He poured champagne into crystal flutes. They raised their glasses, their eyes meeting in a salute to their good fortune. "We can have dinner before or after I show you my slides,"

She gazed at him worshipfully. "Let's see your slides first. We can have dinner later. I'll help you."

"It's all ready. I have made my special pasta. *Lo scrigno di Venere.*"

It's a good thing I drove here in the old Mustang, she thought. No need to worry about leaving it on the street overnight.

Whenever Demetra came home from work, she found that an hour of dancing gave her the added energy she needed to study or read. On Fridays or Saturday nights she saw an occasional movie or went to a concert or opera with Farrell. Sundays were for visiting Charles Duval. Her days were full, and she prayed things would stay that way because it helped to keep the pain at bay. And it helped her to miss Thomas less. Early in October Conchita asked her to stay after class. "Demetra, I have decided to sell the remainder of my perfume bottle collection and all of my costume jewelry, too. I have bought far too many things in my lifetime, and I am tired of roaming from rental to rental. If you can sell it for me, I shall be able to buy myself a condo, thanks to you."

"No, Conchita, thanks to *you*. You are the one who had the good sense to collect. You might even find that you have made a terrific investment. Better than the stock market. Certainly, better than the bank."

"I never thought I was making an investment. I was only buying things I liked. I always tried to stop myself from collecting. I regarded it as a sickness. Sometimes I bought *things* instead of food, instead of paying my debts." She laughed. "Please you must take it all away before I change my mind.

Word got around fast that *Choses* had the best and most comprehensive costume jewelry collection ever amassed by a private collector. Trifari pins like baskets of faux cabochon rubies and sapphires, Coro duet-clips *en tremblant* with rhinestone blossoms, enameled flower brooches, pansies, roses, potted daisies, jeweled butterflies, dragonflies, silver and amethyst jewelry from Mexico, Art Deco jade, copies of Cartier "fruit salad" bracelets. It took Demetra two weeks to inventory the collection of more than a thousand pieces.

An Italian dealer flew to Los Angeles to buy fantasies collected by the famous flamenco dancer, Conchita del Lago. A New York dealer opened his shop with stock almost completely furnished by jewelry from *Choses*. Many pieces would be on display at the upcoming Victoria and Albert Museum's exhibit on costume jewelry, eventually to be shown at the Los Angeles Museum of Art.

Some of Conchita's perfume bottles Demetra sold to a museum in Grasse, some to a writer who was compiling an art book on perfume bottles, some to a museum in London. Before long there was no doubt that Conchita would have enough money to buy her condo—with cash.

Business was so good that Demetra hired a full time assistant, her days so busy that she made no attempt to decorate the house for the Christmas holidays. Thomas, who had found himself a flat in Venice, kept urging her to come for Christmas, but she planned to spend that time at Charles Duval's bedside. Holidays with Thomas would have to come later.

On the twenty-third of December, she received a letter from Corey.

***

Christmas Eve. She closed the shop at three o'clock and drove straight to the nursing home. She set a little tree by Duval's bed, hoping that the scent of pine might reach his consciousness.

"I think he's made real progress this week," the nurse told her. "More than once I saw his lips trying to form words. Wouldn't it be a miracle if he spoke for Christmas?"

When the nurse left the room, Demetra sat close to him. "Charles, I had a letter from Corey yesterday. I was so happy and so relieved to hear from her. Let me read it to you."

Dear Mother,

Australia has been an experience. Michael and I have been so happy in our work. After a few weeks in Alice Springs, we went to Adelaide for the festival, then on to Melbourne, finally to Sydney where we have rented a house near The Rocks, the oldest part of the city. Michael has had terrific reviews on his sets, and my reviews haven't been too bad either.

We will be leaving for California in April. In May I have a part in Ring Around the Moon, *by Jean Anouilh. I will write later with the exact dates. Michael and I wish you a Merry Christmas and a Happy New Year.*

Maman, je t'embrasse,
Corey XXXOOO

At seven o'clock the nurse brought her a tray of soup and a sandwich. By eleven-thirty she had told Charles all about Conchita's collections, about her dance class, her assignments from Tony Tradland. She also told him about Thomas who was calling her daily from Venice.

"Even though we have been together only a few times, I think I've already fallen in love with him. I hope he feels the same about me. "

Absentmindedly she snapped off a small piece of pine branch and rubbed it between her palms. Whenever she smelled fresh pine, it seemed to lift her spirits. As she put the handful of crushed needles to Duval's nose, she thought she saw his eyelids flutter, his nostrils flare slightly.

"Merry Christmas, Charles," she whispered. "I'll be back tomorrow morning. I am off to midnight mass at the church at Our Lady of Mount Carmel down on East Valley road. Maybe next year we can attend together."

CHAPTER XVII

Around seven o'clock in the evening on the first of February, she had a call from a doctor at the nursing home.

"You'll be happy to hear that Mr. Duval has had a real breakthrough this past week. He's gained lucidity and insists upon going home. "

Demetra's heart jumped. "Oh, what wonderful news! When can I see him?"

"If he continues this way, he could be allowed home by the end of next week. But he should not have too much excitement until then. He is still a bit fragile, so call the nurse and make an appointment—better that way. You don't want to walk in and surprise him."

As soon as she hung up, she started to dial Thomas. She counted forward eight hours. Only three in the morning in England, so she ran next door to share the good news with Farrell. She would call Thomas after she had seen Charles.

***

Her appointment at Duval's home was set for four o'clock. A nurse opened the door before Demetra reached the portico. "Please come in. Mr. Duval has been waiting for you. I'll go get him."

The living room was neo-classic in inspiration, sparsely furnished with two large ivory linen covered sofas and deep armchairs, and a pair of Regency lyre-back parcel gilt chairs. A shaded blue Rothko shimmered on one wall, shelves of gold-tooled leather-bound books and scores on the opposite wall. On the square stone cocktail table, a Greek marble head of Apollo sat next to a Kang H'si blanc de chine beaker filled with laurel branches.

A black Steinway concert grand stood in the far corner.

The nurse wheeled in Charles Duval. When Demetra leaned over and gently embraced him, she caught the faint scent of fresh bay.

"Thank you, my dear Demetra, for all you've done for me. My spirit must have known you were at my side." Tears glistened on his pale cheeks. The doctor credits my recovery to you. How moved I was to find your stack of cards and letters—what joy I had from reading them again and again." He sighed deeply then signaled the nurse to leave the room.

"Please sit down. I'll tell you everything."

She pulled up a chair close by his side and commented on the beauty of the house and grounds.

"This was my home until I moved in with Atena after my painter friend died. I had put it on the market, but it never sold. Someday I hope you will accept it as yours." He reached for her hand and held it tight. "I have always wondered if it would ever come to this. When you were a little girl, and when I was much younger, I used to dream about reuniting you with your mother, but as the years went by I knew that this dream would never come true. She had no desire to see you, or even hear about you, so I stopped informing her of your whereabouts. I can assure you that I followed you during those years." He smiled. "I do have my little network of spies, you know. I knew all about your divorce from Marshall Killingsworth. I even know about your little shop on Melrose. My friend used to know all the antique dealers on La Cienega, including your friend and neighbor, Farrell Minton. Although I may not be your father, I've always felt as though you were my daughter."

She smiled wide as she tried to blink away the tears.

"Tell me, my dear, have you ever tried to sing? You know I have often wondered if you had a voice."

She shook her head. "Once someone else asked me the same question."

"Who before me?"

"A psychic. A Greek woman in West Hollywood. But that is another story. Please tell me yours."

"You must know, Demetra that Atena was never meant to be a mother. Some women just are not. The problem was that she just could not let go of the idea. She may have felt, when she was young, that she was missing something. She had everything else. Besides having a superb voice, she was a gifted actress. She had the adulation of an adoring public, countless lovers. Her voice was beginning to fade so she sought out an old sorceress in Lucania who told her that giving birth to a child might restore it. Toward the end, so that her fans would never learn anything about the pregnancy, I took her to a midwife in Montreal to give birth. A week later we drove to St. Paul. My family had moved there from Quebec when I was a child. My second cousin was Mother Superior at the Convent of the Divine Transfiguration. You must remember Sister Anne Francesca."

"Yes, I loved her."

"She took you in and I gave you my name, Duval. You had to have a name and so I thought it should be mine. I know that Sister Anne Francesca wanted to believe you were my daughter. Maybe I did, as well. She loved you as though you were mine. I was honored to give my name to Atena's child. I was always in love with her."

"I wondered if *you* were ever her lover."

"Not her real lover. My love for Atena had turned into an obsession. I am a musician, after all. That voice, that electrifying voice. I have played for many singers before I retired from the concert stage, but none was ever as talented as Atena, who was an astonishing actress as well as a brilliant soprano. And the taste she had in those days—what style she had developed! When I first played for her, she was living with her friend in Venice—a woman was her real lover, you see. Yet it was when we were still living in Italy that you were conceived. She was almost forty years old." Demetra felt her stomach twist. She got up to pour herself a glass of water from the drinks tray.

"To understand what she was like is to try to fathom a deep, dark, ice-covered pond. Atena's mother was Greek, not by the way of Athens, but by Alexandria, and then Tangier. You must have some idea of what Tangier was all about in the thirties—luxury and decadence. Unspeakable poverty. In a weak moment she told me all about her childhood. Her mother kept a brothel in Tangier. She had grown up with sex and lust all around her. Atena never knew her Spanish father who came from somewhere in Andalusia, Malaga, I seem to recall.

"One day, as she was imitating the sounds of a soprano voice on the gramophone, a rich cotton broker from Barcelona heard her. Her mother struck a bargain with him—he would give her daughter lessons in exchange for her favors. She was only sixteen when he took her from the brothel. By the time she was eighteen, she was already in Madrid, singing in the Palm Court of the Ritz. One day, an impresario from Paris was dining there. He was struck by the quality of her voice and by her beauty, so he took her back to Paris to study. Then, after a few years of singing lessons, she got herself a contract in London. All the rest is public record. That voice of hers was God-given, but I knew a streak of madness ran through her, a wildness that terrified me. That winter, Italy in early 1947, when she found out she was pregnant, she almost went to a well-known abortionist in Eboli."

"Who was my father, Charles?'

"Do you remember the photos at Nepenthe?"

 "I'm haunted by them."

"I believe her lover's picture was among them. Your father, whose name she never revealed to me, convinced her not to have an abortion, for his sake as well as the child's. Although he had had a long and happy marriage, he'd never had any children."

"She agreed to have the baby and so we returned to St. Paul. When I left you with my cousin, I gave you my name, Duval."

"Soon her guilt soon got the better of her. So that she could forget her mother she went to a plastic surgeon in Switzerland and had her own navel removed. One evening, after an opera gala, where she had drunk far too much champagne, she pulled down the waistband from her skirt and showed me her stomach. I saw with my own eyes that it was hard, flat and smooth and without any trace of a navel." 'You see, Charles,' she said proudly, 'now the cord has truly been cut, and no trace remains-not even a trace of a mother, as though I were really Atena born from the head of Zeus.' I knew then that she was crazed, and I was glad that I had left you with Sister Anne Francesca.

"Soon after, in London, during a performance of *Norma*, fire broke out in the dressing room beneath the stage. The musicians rushed out from the pit, the audience fled, but Atena stood there, singing. The stagehands finally dragged her off the stage. She was in a mental institution in Turin for a while. I always wondered if the nervous breakdown was partly due to the guilt of abandoning you so completely.

"Her American lover Marjorie Stromberg nursed her back to health after her final performance in Munich, a total disaster. By then her anger began to erupt. It took its toll on her voice. She began to screech; her high notes were appalling.

"A few years later, Atena met Carleton Stanley, the industrialist, at a party in Milan. She saw him as the ultimate patron-protector. He was rich enough to buy all that land and build Nepenthe, fill it with beautiful objects, clothe her in couture and jewels. About fourteen years ago, after Stanley died, she urged me to leave New York and live in Montecito where we could continue to work together. So many musicians and singers lived there, she told me. Ganna Walska, Galli-Curci.

"I urged her to teach master classes, as Lotte Lehman was doing, but that was expecting too much from a woman who was not used to giving. When she built the theater at Nepenthe, she would play old records and tapes, put on her costumes, and lip-sync the words. I could not bear to watch. Her body gestures had become so stiff, her acting so mannered. It broke my heart watching her trying to relive her past.

"And then, when she could no longer sing, she tried to design gardens, but the gardens she created were like her mind, filled with curious oddities. The gardens help to normalize her for a while, but her mind was atrophying. She hardly ate, she was almost crippled by arthritis, but she would not take any medication. A few years ago, she was horrified when the doctor ordered estrogen for her brittle bones. She was repelled by the idea of taking female hormones.

"She was riddled with eccentricities. She insisted that I was never to throw out the cardboard toilet paper rolls. Just before she died, she proudly showed me drawers and drawers filled with them. Imagine—almost twenty years' worth! As time passed, she began to control everything at Nepenthe, the world she had created and would share with only me, and for a while, my friend. Nothing could be done without her permission. Nothing. Not a plant moved in the garden, not a piece of string thrown out. The day you came there, do you remember how the maid called her to the kitchen?"

"There was an emergency, I remember."

"That day she had ordered the maid to defrost the large storage freezer, but she had not told her to place a water pan beneath, so as the freezer thawed the pantry floor was inundated. The maid was afraid to use a water pan because Atena had not *told* her to!

"And then, that day you first appeared, she sensed that you *were not* a musicologist turning up for an interview. She knew instinctively that you were the child I had taken from the hospital, and that is why she told you that ridiculous lie, that I was crippled and had Alzheimer's. She should have known that someday you would discover the truth. That same night she turned on me. When she faced you on your second visit, she was confronting the ultimate denial of her life." He wiped his eyes. "It was too much for her. The next day she began to play her old *Turandot* recordings over and over. I went into my room, clamped earphones over my ears and listened to Mozart. Then around midnight, I must have fallen asleep in my armchair."

"Do you think she intentionally set fire to Nepenthe?"

"I don't think so. She was careless, always leaving candles or smoldering incense pots around the house, or the cigarettes she chain-smoked. The night of the fire, Juanita the maid told me that Atena ordered her to put paper bag *luminarias* all along the path to the theater. What a dangerous thing to do! With all those pines and eucalyptus! That night there was a Santa Ana blowing—you know the rest…"

She listened to Duval with the same rapt fascination as a child listens to a frightening fairy tale, no longer overwhelmed with longing for connection to her mother. She was emerging from Atena's shadow.

Tears ran down her face unchecked, tears not for herself, but for this gentle, kindly man.

Duval reached out for her. "You see, my dear, she was so lacking in love in her own childhood, so crippled emotionally, that she was comfortable with me because I have a clipped wing. She was terrified of being controlled by a man. Never again, she admitted to me when her husband died. I often wondered why she had so many flings, so I asked her. She told me that except for me and your father, her lovers were merely revenge. There was a streak of self-hate in her that even her charming friend Margery Stromberg couldn't assuage." He reached for her hand and kissed it. "I've said more than enough. Now it's your turn."

"When I think back on my own childhood," Demetra began," I realize the nuns must have given me all the love and affection I needed. I never really missed having parents as I was growing up. And then, I remember giving birth to my own daughter, the closeness I felt. It was not until my marriage became so unhappy that I became obsessed with finding my parents. Today I have learned it simply does not matter anymore. *I am.*"

"You are also her rightful heir, but you should know that she has willed the bulk of her estate to a local college. She left me an annuity in trust, and a few pieces of her magnificent jewelry, yours if you would like to have them."

"I left Greenhill House without my jewelry, with hardly any money, and I don't want or need any of hers."

He pulled a handkerchief from his pocket and blotted his eyes. "My dearest Demetra, I don't know about you, but I need a good stiff drink. Would you pour me a vodka? Is there anything else I can tell you about Atena?" he said.

She nodded. "In one of those photographs, she was wearing a white Fortuny gown."

"Yes, I know the portrait and I certainly remember the dress. It was one of my favorites. Strange that you should ask about it. She was wearing the white Fortuny during that ill-fated performance of *Norma*. London, it was. It came from Mariano Fortuny's shop in Venice"

"In Venice?"

"Yes. Do you know Venice? "

"I've been there only once but I've always longed to return."

"I was with Margery and Atena the very day Mariano Fortuny gave it to Atena her as a gift. I remember it as though it were yesterday. We had been to tea at Palazzo Barbaro. It was a warm, sunny day and Atena was wearing a leghorn straw cartwheel hat. She had lost a lot of weight. Earlier in her career, she had a weight problem but under the guidance of her friend, Margery, she had become quite slender. After tea we strolled over to San Beneto, to Fortuny's palazzo."

She felt frissons spiraling up her back. "What happened to the dress?"

"I never saw it after London. She never wore it at Nepenthe."

"Charles- the white Fortuny came from a little shop on the Dorsoduro, not far from San Vio. I was told that Fortuny hoped she would wear it on the stage when she sang the title role in Norma."

He smiled and shook his head. "There must be hundreds of those white Fortuny gowns all over Venice and London. Not too long ago I saw one for sale at Spink. But I must admit it is a real coincidence that you bought one for yourself. And in Venice!"

"Can you recall the date of the fire? The last time you said she wore it?"

"I can check the exact date." He pointed to the bookcase. "My old diaries are lined up on the second shelf from the top. Look for 1946. I recall that she sang Norma that winter."

She found the diary and handed it to him.

He turned the pages." Here it is. Norma, March 12, 1947, London."

"What was my date of birth?

"You were born at 10:14 in the evening on the 12th of November, 1947."

The green satin bag was safe in a locked metal chest. *Venezia, 3 gennaio 1947.*

She counted back on her fingers. Was she making a giant leap when she should not? There was only one way to be sure. She picked up the phone and called Thomas in Venice.

"Christ, Claudia," he said groggily, "Where the hell are you?"

Her first impulse was to hang up. Instead, in an even, unapologetic voice she said, "Thomas, this is Demetra. I wouldn't have called you at this time but it's important."

"Darling! Please forgive me for barking. Ever since Claudia's husband Rupert died, she rings me up from everywhere at any hour to ask my advice about her countless boyfriends." He laughed. "But then she never heeds it. I hope you called to tell me you're coming to Venice."

She heard the formality in her response. "I didn't know that Claudia's husband died. I haven't heard from her in months."

"I don't suppose you would have."

What was he implying? she wondered.

"Now—you told me you were calling about something important."

"Many years ago, I bought something in a shop near the Accademia. I would like you to find out if the shop is still there. It was on a little *campo* near the Guggenheim, to the side of a small canal."

"The shop *is* still there. I just passed it yesterday. Signora Morelli was re-stocking the window. I waved to her."

"I wonder if she's the same woman who owned it about ten years ago."

"It's been her shop for years. My mother used to buy Christmas gifts there. Why do you want to know?"

"It's too long a story for the telephone. I'll be coming to Venice, probably tomorrow if I can get a flight."

"Get here as fast as you can! Be sure to bring a warm coat though because it's freezing cold and very damp. Just let me know your flight number as soon as you book. I will be at the airport waiting for you with a motorboat. And don't forget to bring your red dress with the poppies!"

**

Thomas lived in a narrow *calle* near Santa Maria della Salute in a building converted from humble gondoliers' dwellings into small flats; until the 19th century, gondolas were still made in this quarter of Dorsoduro.

They walked up three short flights to the little apartment. He unfastened her long black fleece wool cape and tossed it over a chair. Then he took her in his arms and kissed her again and again before pointing out the vista beyond the red tiled roofs. "*Ecco!* The Lagoon and San Giorgio." He grinned. "Not exactly Ruskin's favorite view!"

"I've never understood why he so despised Palladio's monuments."

He laughed. "Let us talk about the vagaries of taste over dinner, and speaking of dinner, I've made a reservation for us at eight-o'clock. At the Riviera—over on the *Zattere*, a new place owned by a former waiter at Harry's Bar. I hope you won't be too tired."

"Never in my life have I felt less tired."

"While you have your appointment with Signora Morelli, I will stop by the English bookstore, then I'll be waiting for you by the Accademia Bridge. After dinner we shall walk to the Piazza. It's Shrove Tuesday. *Carnevale.* People turn up in the most fantastic costumes."

She took in the living room at a glance, a cozy, antique-filled room with one large modern painting over the sofa, a curious picture of Venice and its palaces, painted as though the waters of the Grand Canal had been drained away. Supporting the palaces was a forest of woodpiles sunk deep into the black silt.

When she commented on the painter's intent, Thomas said, "I call it 'Venice Exposed.' See how much lies below the surface. The painter may be saying that "Venice, like life itself, was born of the marshes." He paused. "I see it as a union of earth and sea."

"Come on, let me show you the rest." He grasped her hand and led her to the small bedroom. The walls above and opposite the bed were covered with old Redouté rose prints.

"When the estate agent showed me the flat, she offered to exchange the prints for something a little more *maschile*, but I told her to leave them. I knew you would look lovely lying in a bower of roses. Shall we prove that I was right?"

Demetra felt her legs giving way under her.

"Now?"

"Darling, right now."

They finally fell asleep in each other's arms. At six-thirty the bells of the *Salute* pealed so loud they almost knocked Demetra out of bed. He laughed when she leaped up in a daze, not knowing where she was. He kissed her again. "You'll soon become so used to the clanging you won't even hear it."

By seven o'clock she was standing outside the shop. The window display was still a jumble of Venetiana—just as she had remembered it. She drew a deep breath and went inside.

Signora Morelli greeted her warmly. "Of course, I remember you! You bought the white Fortuny! It has been some time now. When Mr. Pierson told me that you wanted to come by I wasn't sure I could place you without knowing what it was you'd bought. What can I tell you about the dress?"

"When did you buy it, Signora?"

"Not too long before you bought it from me in the mid-seventies. I remember it because up until that time I had had many tinted dresses, but only one white dress. After the war, the vogue for Fortuny_dresses_was over—they had been around a long time, you see. Famous women like Lillian Gish, the actress, wore them in the twenties. But during the early fifties, Fortuny only produced white dresses. Those were rarely bought by Venetians, so very few have remained in Venice."

"Do you remember from whom you bought the dress?"

"I bought it from an American woman's estate. She had a most important collection of Fortuny gowns—in a great range of colors and styles, but all those were given to an American museum. The signora kept the white dress for sentimental reasons"

Her heart raced. "What was her name?"

"Margery Stromberg. She lived in a deconsecrated church near San Trovaso. She had transformed it into a charming house and was well-known for the salon she kept. Mostly people in the arts."

"Music? Opera?"

"Especially opera. Her best friends were opera singers. in fact, the great collection was amassed by one of them."

"Did she know Atena Valli, the soprano?"

"The dress I sold you was hers."

"Hers! My dress was hers? Atena Valli's?

Demetra clutched a chair to steady herself. She could hardly get the words out of her mouth. "But how can you be so sure? I know from my own experience that people often romanticize their possessions," she stammered"I was there the day she was given the dress, right after the war, so it might have been the end of '45 or '46. What is the matter Signora? Are you all right? *La faccia e così pallida!"* She put her arm around Demetra and sat her down in the chair. "I'll be right back with some water."

Demetra blinked away the tears. Maybe there was something to *Farrell's* theory *that seemingly inanimate objects might be connected to people. And people to objects. She had found the dress, her mother's dress. Or maybe the dress had found her.*

The Signora returned with the water. Demetra thanked her and gulped down half the glass. Shaking her head, she asked, "Why, *why* didn't you tell me its provenance when I bought the dress? I remember that I asked you about it."

"Because the lawyers had warned me against revealing the provenance, something about a claim on her estate. But so many years have elapsed, there is no reason why I cannot speak freely, so now I will tell you the rest of the story.

"I was about eighteen years old. It was summertime. My mother had a fitting at Palazzo Pesaro degli Orfei, Mariano Fortuny's studio. I remember Atena Valli arriving in a big cartwheel straw hat. I had once heard her sing in *La Traviata* at La Fenice. Valli was with her friend, Margery Stromberg. I used to hear my mother whispering about Signora Stromberg, so I was aware of her relationship with Valli."

"Were the two women by themselves?"

"There was a man with them. A very tall, handsome man. He reminded me of a film star, so I remember being surprised when I learned that he was Valli's accompanist. I am sorry I cannot remember his name. When they asked to look at the dresses, the Contessa opened the *cassone* and out they came like mammoth white cocoons, until they were unknotted, and the pleats shaken out. Miss Valli was enchanted. She thought the dress would be perfect for her role as Norma, so she asked to see Mariano Fortuny, already known for his set of La Scala's production of *Tristan and Isolde*. Fortuny was in Rome, but he had left instructions that Atena Valli Should receive the delphos as a gift from an admirer.

"Was Fortuny born in Venice?"

"He wasn't Italian at all, Signora. He was a Spaniard, Mariano Fortuny y Madrazo, born in Granada. An old Spanish family. His father was a well-known painter."

"How old a man was he by then?"

"In his early seventies, but he was still vigorous, tall, strong and very handsome with his piercing blue eyes. He cut quite a figure around Venice—especially when wearing his long robes and sandals."

She threw her arms around Signora Morelli and thanked her. She could hardly wait to tell Thomas.

CHAPTER XVIII

He was waiting for her by the foot of the bridge, surrounded by a group of rowdy *Pulcinelli*, black masked clowns, dressed in white with ruffled collars and tall, pointed caps, looking as though they'd stepped from a Tiepolo drawing. "A group from Naples," he said. "They told me that they came up on the train just for tonight." When Thomas kissed her, the *Pulcinelli* made a ring around them, prancing, squealing, tooting horns.

"Was the Signora able to answer your questions?" he asked.

Demetra nodded. "She told me exactly what I wanted to know. I'll tell you all about it during dinner."

"Yes, so we can savor it." He drew her hand through his arm, holding her fingers close to his as he led her up the steps to the San Marco side of the Grand Canal.

"I thought we were going to stay here on Dorsoduro, Thomas."

"We have just enough time to stop at Campo San Maurizio."

"What for?"

"You'll see. Have you ever worn costume and mask before?"

"Only as a child for Halloween. The nuns seemed to enjoy planning our masks and disguises." She smiled, heart-warmed by the tender memory. "Maybe they were projecting their own fantasies on us. They always wanted to dress me up as a ballerina in pink tights and a tutu even though I'd never taken any ballet lessons."

"When we wear a mask, we expose our true natures. We show what we really are by hiding behind one," he replied.

They strolled arm in arm through Campo Santo Stefano. "What do you know about the origins of *Carnevale*?" she asked.

"Long before Christian Lent, they were all about fertility and nature rites. The *Rites of Spring*." He squeezed her hand then put it to his lips. "Or as Dylan Thomas so aptly put it, 'the force that through the green fuse drives the flower'."

Demetra's thoughts flew to the blue Himalayan poppy seeds she tried to germinate at Greenhill House. She wondered what had become of the delicate seedlings.

By this time, the crowds were so thick they had to push their way through the narrow *calle*. When they reached illuminated Campo San Maurizio, he led her toward the costume stalls where vendors were selling doublets, tabards, capes, and crinolines in rich brocades and velvets. Others sold all manner of fantastic masks.

They stopped to admire a stall piled with hats—ostrich-plumed, be-ribboned bonnets, Sicilian paladin helmets, Venetian Doges' hats, gem-studded crowns, jingling jesters' caps.

"During Carnevale week it's the custom for Venetian ladies to wear the black tricorne. This one seems right for you. Try it on."

She adjusted the hat while he spread the net veil over her face and tied it behind her head. He handed her a mirror. "Have a look at how beautiful you are, Demetra."

She smiled. "Now I know why women wear veils." Her eyes, through the black net seemed more smoldering, her lips redder, more sensuous, her features somehow more defined.

He chose a simple black mask for her to wear with the tricorne. "These are a present from me."

She thanked him. "But if I wear a mask then so should you!"

"Not only do I have one, I have *two*." He pulled them from his coat pockets passing each mask across his face with a flourish "Take your pick. Comedy? Or Tragedy!"

She touched the Comedy mask. "So, you *really* want to be an actor! With your love of the sea I've always thought of you as Poseidon."

He grinned. "I think of myself as Poseidon but lurking within me is also the spirit of Dionysus."

She kissed his cheek. "Gail once told me that I needed Dionysus in my life."

"Sounds just like her. She sees everyone in archetypal terms of gods and goddesses."

They laughed and walked off arm in arm, pressing through the *calle* crowded with masquers and tourists. A Doge strode by in full regalia followed by his entourage of turbaned Turks and Saracens straight out of *Orlando Furioso*.

When they passed the Campo of Santa Maria del Giglio, a shabbily dressed little girl was standing by the portal of the church. In her arms she held a bunch of long-stemmed red roses. She pulled one from the bunch and offered it to Demetra. *"Una rosa per la bellissima signora."*

Demetra smiled as she accepted the rose.

Thomas pulled out his wallet.

"Please, let me," she said, as she gave the child some lire.

She offered the rose to Thomas. "And now my present to you."

He kissed her veiled lips. "With your black cape and your tricorne, you look as though you've just stepped out of *Der Rosenkavalier.*"

"My favorite Strauss opera."

"Mine, too." He checked his watch. "We still have some time. Instead of taking the number five boat to the Zattere. I'll try to find us a gondola. It's such a beautiful night and the sea is calm. There's a *traghetto* stand by the Gritti

The gondolier stroked them away from the mooring. She sank back against the black leather cushions, Thomas pressed against her side, his arm around her. They floated by flocks of gondolas filled with Japanese tourists, past palaces, some dark, some flashing brilliant light from chandeliers. As they glided toward the Lagoon masked merry-makers leaned over banner-draped balconies and waved.

Santa Maria della Salute, bathed in light, sat enthroned at the entrance of the Grand Canal.

"Too bad Ruskin could never see the *Salute* looking like this," Thomas said, "With all those spotlights making the marble dome look so white against the dark sky."

"To me the buttresses seem like gigantic seashells," she replied. "And when I squint my eyes and look up at the dome, I see naiads and sprites and sea gods instead of saints and prophets." She laughed and kissed his cheek. "A fitting palazzo for Poseidon."

He smiled. "I can imagine my horses galloping down those marble steps."

The gondolier was making an easy passage around Punta della Dogana into the waves of the lagoon. Across the shimmering water, the Giudecca seemed a strip of firefly lights. She could hear sounds from along the Zattere, plinking mandolins, a soprano practicing scales. A mist like silver tulle had fallen, creating a scrim for the stars. A Greek liner glided by stealthily.

When the gondolier edged toward the *fondamenta* by the restaurant she asked, "What's that deserted building across on the Guidecca? Its windows are all boarded up and the place is all overgrown with weeds."

"It's the old Stuckey Flour Mill, hasn't been used for decades. Occasionally, a plan surfaces to do something about the eyesore, but so far, nothing."

He ordered a celebratory bottle of prosecco the instant they were seated at the most private corner table of the crowded restaurant. She slipped the

fleece-lined cape from her shoulders. The room was warm and cozy enough for her to be comfortable in her poppy-red dress.

The waiter returned with the *prosecco* and took their order for *tagliarini* with *scampi* and *rucola* followed by grilled sole.

"You already know that patience isn't one of my virtues," he said, filling their wine glasses. Now—tell me about your visit to Signora Morelli from the beginning."

She lifted her veil and took a long sip. "Before I begin, I want to say something about the 'nature of… things.'"

He knit his brows. "The theory of Lucretius?"

She laughed and shook her head. "No. The Theory of Farrell. He believes that not only human beings are connected, but also *things* can be connected to human beings, human beings to things. Matter attracting matter. He told me that when he feels a call it's as though something is shouting at him to stop and look, something that's crying out, yearning to be found."

"Sounds like Lovelock's Gaia Principle—the earth being viewed as a single organism, matter attracting matter in one live, seething cosmos."

"Farrell claims that all of his best finds were made that way. I know that finding my dress was."

He leaned forward, his chin on his hand, eyes fixed upon her, ready to be held in thrall by her story.

She began. "Once upon a time, as I was climbing the Accademia Bridge to Dorsoduro, there was a sudden cloudburst. By the time I left the Galleries, the rain had stopped, the sun was shining, and a rainbow arched the sky over Dorsoduro. I decided to follow it toward Santa Maria della Salute, the church I'd been admiring from the Hotel Gritti."

When she had finished, she wiped her eyes and took another swallow of wine. He put her hand to his lips. "You must call your story *A Gift from Fortuny*. It is the stuff novels are made of. Another proof that truth is often stranger than fiction."

The waiter appeared with dessert, squares of flaky multi-layered pastry dusted with powdered sugar and toasted pine nuts.

"*Millefoglia*, the house specialty," Thomas said. "When I made the reservation, I asked Franco to put aside two for us."

At ten o'clock, when they left the restaurant, sea breezes had blown away the mist. The sky was clear, diamond strewn, a full moon silver-shimmered the lagoon. They walked back briskly, arm in arm, taking the shortcut through Dorsoduro and crossing the Accademia Bridge to San Marco.

In the brightly lit Piazza the Basilica gleamed in its golden glass robe. The square was packed with costumed revelers and masses of gawking tourists. Photographers huddled around the Campanile, immortalizing all entries and exits from Café Florian, the unofficial gathering place for masquers. Inside its mirrored salons, Commedia dell'Arte Harlequins, Columbinas, and gallant *cicisbei* posed and preened. Under the arcades, masked courtesans fluttered fans and flirted with Spanish grandees. A group of French masquers, each swathed in yards of dark blue tulle dotted with silver stars, struck poses for photographers. A golden-framed Mona Lisa strolled by, followed by a man and a woman locked together, dressed as though they were Klimt's painting, *The Kiss*.

"Let us walk across the Piazza to Quadri. I hear cymbals clashing over there," he said, grasping her hand to lead her across the Square toward the Piazza's other famous café.

A large crowd had gathered around the beautiful woman with long red hair seated in a chariot being drawn by four men dressed as lions. The woman, dressed in white satin, wore a golden cap with a curved peak. Handmaidens, girls in sapphire blue robes printed with gold bees, clustered around her. Behind the chariot, stood a group of white-robed men with rouged lips and cheeks.

"She must be a goddess," Demetra said. "But which one?"

"With her Phrygian cap and lions, she could only be Cybele, the Great Goddess of the Mediterranean. The men in white are dressed as the castrated priests of Attis, who was Cybele's lover. They're enacting the Rites of Spring."

The "priests" began to shake their tambourines and clash their cymbals. Flute players piped a haunting, high-pitched melody in a strange minor key. Two "priestesses" beat a stately rhythm with finger clappers.

Demetra delved into her bag for the red flannel pouch. She deftly tied the castanets to her fingers and without skipping a beat, began to play, slowly, solemnly, in perfect time, every click, every roll crisp and confident. When she ended the last roll with a flourish, what pleased her most was not the *bravas* or the blessing bestowed on her by Cybele; it was the look of wonder on Thomas' face.

He hugged her. "You've been hiding your talents from me! I think you enjoy being a performer."

Before she could say a word, Khachaturian's insistent *Sabre Dance* blasted out from the loudspeakers. A Harlequin, all bright, diamond-shaped colors, approached Demetra, rocking from side to side, spinning his club, beckoning her to dance. When she laughed and shook her head, he grabbed her rose, stuck it into his cockaded hat, then whisked her away, spiraling her round and around the piazza until, panting for breath, she fell into Thomas' arms. As he whirled her away to the broad, sweeping waltz from *The Masquerade Suite*, she tossed her cape back over her shoulders, red chiffon billowing around her.

They danced and danced among the frenzied merrymakers until the Moor's hammer struck fifteen minutes before midnight. Shrove Tuesday would soon be over. Racing from the Piazza to catch the next boat, they arrived at the landing just as the *vaporetto* sidled to the *pontile* where they could hop on to cross the Canal back to Dorsoduro, to the bed in the bower of roses.

They did not make it as far as the bedroom. She tossed her cape and tricorne over a chair. He tossed his coat on the floor then reached out to help her out of her dress. Locked in each other's arms, they fell on the sofa and made love while above them, in the moonlit painting, the palaces seemed to sway as the sea rolled in.

At last she fell asleep listening to the soft tide slapping against the *fondamenta*.

Demetra's Dream

Beyond the courtyard she can see his palazzo with the tall pointed gothic windows. She climbs the well-worn steps to the piano nobile. Now is the hour of the siesta. He is sure to be home.

She opens the oak portal. Paintings of full-fleshed odalisques and senoritas in ruffled dresses and black lace mantillas adorn the crimson damask walls. Silk lanterns like inverted coolie hats hang from the ceiling.

She sees the writer Gabriele d' Annunzio embracing Eleanora Duse the famous Italian actress. Gabriele says in a seductive voice "Mariano is not here, but you are most welcome to stay."

Eleanora looks like Irene Pappas, the Greek actress—or is it Apollonia the psychic with her dark-circled eyes?

"Where can I find him?" Demetra asks.

"You will find him at the factory. To get there you must take the Number Five boat from the Zattere," Duse responds.

She climbs the wooden steps of the Accademia Bridge. The bells of Santa Maria della Salute are tolling. She descends to Dorsoduro, walks past the Accademia to the Zattere. The sky above is like a Baci candy wrapper, midnight blue studded with tiny silver stars. The ticket seller at the kiosk tells her that she has just missed the last Number Five boat. How should she cross the lagoon? It seems so wide and the waters are dark and deep.

A Greek liner passes. A dolphin, swimming along its side, snaps its tail hard, inviting her to ride across to the Giudecca. She mounts the dolphin, grasping its sleek, slippery sides. The water is warm as it laps and splashes around her. The dolphin swims so swiftly that soon she is standing on the quay of the Giudecca.

Warm amber light shines from the windows of the Stuckey Flour Mill, no longer a dark, somber, deserted pile of red brick with boarded-up windows, overgrown with dank weeds and choked by vines. Smoke rises from the chimneys.

She sees Mariano Fortuny waiting for her. He stands tall above all the others. He has a beard and wears a fine blue wool cape, that he has tossed over one shoulder. On his bare feet are leather sandals. He extends his hand to her and speaks.

"Demetra, my dearest daughter. I have been waiting a long time. Come with me."

They enter a workroom. Women are everywhere. Some are dipping lengths of white silk into huge, steaming dye vats. Children fan the flames with bellows. Bobbins spin rainbows of silk filaments. Women, squinting as they thread golden needles in the candlelight, sit cross-legged on carpets.

An immense basket is filled to overflowing with glimmering, carded silk skeins. One basket seems empty. Demetra looks inside. She sees only one white pleated dress. Like hers.

She knows that she stands on the brink of discovery. She asks Mariano Fortuny, "You who created the bright sky, who turned day into night and night into day on the stages of the world—for whom did you design this dress? What woman inspired you?"

Mariano smiles at her. "Many years ago, long before I met your mother, I had become bored with my sky machine, my stage sets and my oil paints. One night I dreamed that I saw a beautiful naked woman standing before me. She told me that she lived in the flour mill next door. I had never been inside that flour mill. It did not interest me or pertain to me in any way. You see, my child, I had been so busy looking towards the sky that I had ignored the earth.

"One day, the miller came to visit me. Slung over his shoulder was a sack. He placed it at my feet, then, with his scimitar he slashed it open. Ears of barley and wheat like golden tassels spilled upon the ground. And when I looked again, I saw a goddess standing before me, her white flesh unmarked by corset bruises or welted by whalebone stays. She glowed like a pearl from the flour dust. 'This is how the flesh of women should look,' the goddess told me.

'Go, Mariano Fortuny, and find the purest silk that has been spun by the worms of my earth—those fat worms who feed on the leaves of the mulberry tree. Take the cloth,' she said, 'and treat it as though it were my bread. Knead the silk, roll it with long porcelain tubes, not unlike those wood cylinders the baker uses to roll his dough. Heat those glass rollers until the silk crimps into itself and forms narrow pleats, like these exquisite millefoglia that Venetians love to eat. Then you will have a delicious confection. The rest of the secret I shall whisper in your ear.'

Demetra asks, "The idea came from her? The Lady of the Mill?"

"Yes. As for Atena, I mistook her for a goddess. When I heard the

angelic sounds she made, I became possessed by her voice, then her body, but soon I learned that her spirit was blighted by darkness."

I hear the Redentore's bells tolling. "I must not miss the Number 5 boat this time. Please tell me the rest of the secret before I must cross the lagoon."

"Demetra, mi corazon, mi querida—you must find the secret in your Self."

She throws her arms around her father.

She wakes from her dream, embracing her pillow damp from her tears. Then she reaches over to touch Thomas, still sleeping by her side.

They planned to stay in the little flat until the week after Easter. Deadlines were over; the novel was at Thomas' publisher in London. Now they had the time to spend part of each day looking at and admiring Renaissance paintings.

A few days before she was to return to Los Angeles, Thomas learned that his novel was accepted with a generous advance.

"We've been so happy here,' he said, "I decided this little place should be ours. And so now it is."

"You've taken a long lease? "He smiled. "No—it will be a present for the both of us. It's ours."

CHAPTER XIX
April

Demetra drove to the Ojai Valley for the first time. Shadows made the purplish-brown mountains look like gigantic heaps of dried lavender. Gorse was in full bloom, a fringe of gold along the roadside. The air was fresh and sweet, the town deserted, so quiet that she could hear bees buzzing, birds chirping. She had arrived too early for her meeting with Corey. Slinging her raffia bag over her shoulder, she clasped it to her body and walked to the theatre.

The Playhouse, Spanish in style, was built of adobe and brick. A framed poster of a silver moon ringed in gold against a dark blue starry sky announced the new production. "The Ojai Players present *Ring around the Moon* by Jean Anouilh and Christopher Fry, starring Corey Killingsworth as Isabel."

The auditorium was locked so she walked around to the stage door.

"Good morning. I am Demetra Duval, Corey Killingsworth's mother. She's expecting me."

"Sure. Go right in," the guard said, handing her a cast list.

The stage was set as a rococo winter garden in an English country house, not unlike Greenhill House's *jardin d'hiver*, all lush potted palms, orchids, and ferns. The backdrop was painted as a vast park with blossoming fruit trees. Corey was already on stage.

How strongly her voice projected, Demetra thought, each line was enunciated with perfect diction and just enough of a British accent to be convincing for the role.

Corey was dressed as Isabel, the Edwardian ingénue, in lace-collared white batiste. She had lost weight. Her figure was perfect, with just the right curves.

The grey-haired woman playing the role of Isabel's mother, was raving on and on about this stately home where her daughter was a guest, obviously impressed by the way the house was run with butlers and footmen following three steps behind.

Reminded of her former life at Greenhill House, Demetra smiled inwardly at the irony of the dialogue.

When Act I was over and the house lights brightened, Demetra clapped along with the cast and crew, then moved forward so that her daughter could see her.

The cast filed out for a lunch break.

Eyes fixed on her mother, Corey spoke. "I'll be right with you, Mom. I want to change into something cooler."

In a few minutes she returned wearing a simple green sleeveless shift. Demetra reached out to embrace her. Even though she hugged her daughter close, she could still feel the distance between them.

"I'm surprised you got here so early."

"There was hardly any traffic today. Such an easy drive—pretty, too —everything so green from the spring rains. Chaparral and lupines in bloom." Demetra heard herself rushing through her words. "And the yucca! I have *never* seen such yucca—like giant white torches all along the hillsides. And blankets of poppies. Do you remember the California poppy seeds we used to toss around the back yard?"

"Of course, I remember."

Demetra fidgeted with the raffia bag. "Do you have any plans for lunch? I'd like to take you to some nice place where we can talk."

"I'd love to talk to you, but I've got lines to memorize."

"How I wish I knew what you're feeling at this moment."

"You walked out on us, Mom. It's as simple as that and I just can't seem to let go of it."

"You've taken your father's side without listening to mine. Do you think that's fair?" She reached out to touch her daughter. "We used to be so close. What happened to our relationship?"

"I've always thought I was closer to Dad than to you."

"Things started changing between us when you turned twelve. You stopped wanting to be around me. You began to find fault with me. But don't you remember how it was when you were a little girl when we lived in Seattle?"

"Yes, I do have happy memories of Seattle, but when we moved to California you usually sat around reading art books or listening to music. You always seemed remote, in another world that wasn't mine, a world I thought would never be mine. Somehow, I felt as though you were always unconsciously undermining me, making me feel like a slob whenever you walked into my room. Even when I moved into the loft with Michael, I could tell that you were itching to change things."

Demetra shook her head. "If I did, it was only because I wanted you to have lovely surroundings. Growing up in a convent I never had a room of my own. And I admit that I've have always had an urge to transform. I guess I was just born that way."

"I thought I could never be like you, beautiful *and* organized. I wanted to be more like Dad. He has rough edges, I know, but you'd never accept that."

"For a long time, I did." She sighed. "Maybe I'll never be able to make you understand. Yes, I may have had all the material rewards—especially during those last ten years of our marriage, but then your father began to demand perfection in everything. Nothing I did was ever good enough. Nothing was ever quite right. He cut me down, belittled me, criticized me, blamed me, sometimes in front of friends. He gave me all sorts of mixed messages. I began to feel like his property, eventually a piece of damaged property. And then there were the…" She paused, the image of Marina astride Marshall flashing across her mind.

"Dad told me you neglected him. You know how macho he is so what did you expect of a man such an energetic man? And you were strict with me. All those rules you set. No phone calls from boys during the week. You made me feel that there was something wrong in talking to them."

"I didn't mean it the way you think. I guess I was too old-fashioned. But your father was often away. I was doing double duty."

"You wanted to fit me in a mold of the daughter you wanted me to be—a little clone of you. And you didn't want me to act. You never encouraged me."

"But neither did I discourage you. I had seen so many disappointed girls, daughters of friends, who had tried to go on the stage or find work in Hollywood. I heard about their bitter disappointments; all the studio horror stories. I wanted more than that for you. I wanted…"

"Forget what *you* wanted," Corey said cynically.

Demetra glossed over the hurt. "Today when I heard you speak your lines, I knew I'd made a big mistake. You are a talented actress. For a long time, I've wondered whether it was nature or nurture that formed a person's talents. You are living proof that nature will have her way. I am sorry you thought my mind was closed. I may have been projecting my own set of inhibitions on you. Since then I've learned there were many. Please forgive me, Corey." She put her hand on her daughter's arm. "Please."

Corey checked her watch. "I'd better leave. I told you I have lines to memorize. Besides, I think we have said all we could possibly say for today.

"By the way, when I called Greenhill House, Marina told me that Dad is still in England and should be home in two weeks. I'm sure he won't be happy about my marrying Michael. How do you feel about it, Mom?"

"I'm happy for you, Corey." Demetra reached for the raffia bag. "Here's a present for you—something I bought a long time ago. Do you remember the trip we took to Venice?"

"How could I forget? You spent your days in the museums and churches while Dad and I had a wonderful time swimming on the Lido."

"I bought this dress on that trip. Do you remember the Fortuny gown? I want you to have it."

Corey accepted the green satin bag but left it unopened. "You want me to have this?"

Demetra nodded, her eyes brimming with tears.

"I can remember Dad hating that dress when you tried it on for him at the Gritti but I thought you looked beautiful. He told me you wore it to the Feast of the Gods benefit to spite him. Why are you giving it to me?"

"I want you to have it because it changed my life. I'm giving it to you because..." This was hardly the time to tell her daughter about her conversation with Signora Morelli.

"I'm not sure what I'm supposed to do with this dress."

"Someday you might need it. You'll know when."

Demetra threw her arms around her daughter and clung to her. Corey pulled away and turned to leave. Demetra struggled to keep her voice clear, unwavering, although her heart felt as knotted as the dress in the satin bag. "Call me whenever you need me, Corey. Remember that I'm less than an hour away."

Demetra hurried along the path toward the car. The sunlight hurt her eyes. Her tears refracted in the light, making it seem stronger as she imagined Corey opening the satin bag, unknotting the crimped pleats of gleaming pearl white silk.

The drive home had seemed endless. Elysian Park. Almost there. No stopping at the mailbox tonight. As she drove up the lane, she noticed a blue blur on the door stoop, the same intense blue that unmistakable blue of the Himalayan poppies she had once admired in English gardens and had never succeeded in growing. These poppies were thriving in clay pots set into a wood flat, the kind the gardeners used at Greenhill House.

She was sure she had never mentioned the Tibetan meconopsis to Thomas. Or to Gail. Not even to Farrell.

There was a note tucked beneath. Thick cream- colored writing paper with *Marina* engraved above a seashell.

For Demetra.

These blue poppies have finally come into bloom. Kevin said the gardener told him it took forever to get them to blossom. Kevin thought— and I agreed with him—that you should be the one to enjoy them.
Marina

In mid-April, two weeks after she had the poppies delivered to Demetra, Marina told Marshall, who had just flown in from London that afternoon, that she had some business to discuss with him over their evening cocktails. She had made up her mind to marry Tony Tradland. Wouldn't Marshall be furious! Who knows what rage he might fly into? Oh well, all men cannot be blessed with the finesse, the breeding of Harcourt McFarland.

Marshall and Marina sat in the far corner of the *jardin d'hiver* behind the dense stand of potted palms. After pouring her husband a flute of his favorite Cristal and an uncharacteristic double vodka on the rocks for herself, she sank down into the sofa and braced herself

Marshall sat opposite in his favorite straight-backed wrought iron chair.

They talked about his new firearms company in Birmingham, about the coming tennis matches at Wimbledon, about the Royal Enclosure at Ascot, about everything English including the rotten weather.

Neither of them heard Corey driving through Greenhill House's gates.

Neither of them heard her soft-soled steps in the Long Gallery.

Marshall cleared his throat. "I have something to tell you before we start on *your* business." He snickered. "I'm sure yours is about something else you want to get rid of or sell around here. Let me put it to you very simply, Marina. I want a divorce."

She felt her heart dance a little jig. "You want a divorce? To marry someone else?"

"Yes. I hope you won't stop me." He stared at her with unresponsive honed-steeled eyes.

Yippee! He beat her to it! Now she would have the upper hand in the settlement. Laughter bubbled up inside, Marina tried to force some tears. *Come on, Marina. Think of something sad, something really sad.* But the best she could do was wring her hands and, lacking her usual chiffon square, blot her dry eyes with a linen cocktail napkin.

Corey paused at the entrance of the *jardin d'hiver.* She heard voices behind the potted palms. Marina and her father.

"Will you give me the divorce, Marina, or will I have to fight you every step of the way?" her father asked in a harsh, unfeeling tone.

She heard Marina stifle a sob. "*Why* Marshall? Why so suddenly? I'm not prepared for this kind of treatment."

"Don't worry, Marina," he said impatiently. "I'll make sure that your pre-nuptial contract is honored. And you can have all the jewelry."

"I don't want those jewels. Most of them were Demetra's. One day Corey should have them." Marina raised her voice. "Who is this woman, Marshall? Tell me!"

"I'll be honest with you, Marina. I'm going to marry Lady Claudia, Countess of Cherwell."

Marina's voice was tremulous. "So that's why you've been spending so much time at the Manchester factory!"

"*And* because I'm negotiating for another factory in Bradford."

"Always business in the picture," she said, her voice oozing sarcasm.

"I've already seen my lawyer. I advise you to find one for yourself. I'll take care of the billings."

"How *generous* of you!" Marina sneered. Suddenly she began to laugh. She could hardly get the words out she was laughing so hard. "I know the title impresses you but remember, Marshall, Milady won't be Countess This or Lady That after she marries you." More laughter.

"She's the daughter of a lord, so she'll still be an Honorable," Corey heard her father snap back defensively.

"When do you plan marry Her Ladyship?"

"By early September. The Prince and Princess von Hallstattstaufen are planning our wedding reception at their villa in Biarritz, "he said as though he were awed by the mere idea of it.

"And to think I left Harcourt McFarland, a *real* prince of a man, to marry you, you, a boring, social climbing, snob."

Corey heard a slap against skin. She heard her father growl. "Hey, what about my letting Demetra walk out on me. For *you*? You—with your reputation as a high- class fucking whore!"

Corey rushed in.

Marina, crying, ran out.

Marshall's face had turned pewter grey beneath his bronzer brush-on tan. "Corey! Where the hell did you come from?"

"Michael and I got back from Australia two weeks ago," she said casually, as though she had not overheard the conversation.

His eyes darted around the room. "Where is he now?"

"With his parents in Malibu."

"For Chrissake—make sure he stays there! I don't want that wop roaming around Greenhill House."

"Why not, Dad? Isn't this really *my* house, after all?"

Later that week, Demetra sat in the back room at *Choses*, mending a linen tablecloth, her mind raking over the reunion with Corey. She was wearing jeans,

a crisp white shirt and a red sweater knotted over her shoulders.

She heard the doorbell. Through the glass she could see that it was Corey; she was dressed in jeans, a crisp white shirt, a red cardigan knotted over her shoulders.

"Hi Mom—I wanted to surprise you."

Demetra unlocked the door and threw her arms around her daughter. "You see, we're both thinking alike—about clothes, anyway." They laughed together.

Corey unknotted her cardigan and placed it over the arm of an old Morris chair. "I was curious about your shop—it's very different from the way I imagined it," she said, reaching for one of Dolores's pomegranates, now dried to dark red, piled in a terracotta bowl.

"How do you mean?"

"There's none of that major stuff around here, and certainly none of that perfection we used to have at home." She passed her hand across the seat of an antique Venetian chair before she sat on it. "See how the paint's worn away. It looks as though people loved this piece, as though it was sat on more than once. There was never anything as genuine as this chair at Greenhill House."

"At Greenhill House every piece of furniture had to be flawless. That's what your father liked. In the trade it's called 'Mallet condition'. You must remember that London shop." She paused, remembering how repellently pretentious Marshall could be and with what superciliousness he had treated the expert at Mallet's.

Corey smiled. She had been trotted around those London citadels of fine furniture. "Mallet's—isn't that where you paid $150,000 for Dad's desk? Mom, did you know that when I couldn't get a job, I tried being a junk dealer for a while?"

"I learned that by coincidence. If there *is* such a thing as coincidence." She smiled.

"Two days ago I went to see Charles Duval."

Demetra held her breath wondering how much Charles had told her about Atena. "How did you find his address?"

"Farrell gave it to me. You were not in the shop when he answered the phone. Now I know everything. "

"Did he tell you about the Fortuny gown?"

She nodded. "Like you, I'm beginning to believe there's no such thing as coincidence. He also told me even more. About Atena, my grandmother. He said that she was a wonderful actress. When I heard the whole sad story, I realized how lucky I have been to have you for a mother. I guess I am more like you than I thought. When I was growing up, the words I used to hate hearing most were 'Corey, you're just like your mother!' I do not feel that way anymore. I came here to tell you that now I understand what happened the night you left home. What *really* happened? At first, I wouldn't let myself believe that Dad was capable of abusing you or betraying you."

Demetra held her breath. "Why have you changed your mind?"

"I went to Greenhill House last week. I saw a side of Dad I'd never wanted to admit to." Her eyes welled up.

Demetra put her arm around Corey. "I'm sorry. I know how painful that must be."

"You've heard that Dad and Marina are getting a divorce?"

Demetra shook her head, then, remembering the blue poppies on the doorstep, said, "But I'm not at all surprised."

"Please forgive me, Mom. For the selfish way I acted, for the things I've said."

"Of course, I forgive you. And please forgive my mistakes, Corey." Demetra did not try to check the tears.

Corey's voice caught. She wrapped her arms around her mother and held her close. "No one could have been a better mother than you. As soon as the play is over, I would like to stay with you for a few weeks to help me plan the wedding. We have set the date for November 28. And if it's all right, I'd like to be married in the Fortuny gown."

Demetra wiped her eyes.

"Then Michael and I will be leaving for Milan. He has been asked to design the sets for another George Strehler Shakespeare project. And I've signed a contract to do another Christopher Fry play next year. In London. I've got the role of Alizon in a revival of *The Lady's Not for Burning.*"

"*The Lady's Not for Burning?* Sister Claire loved that play. She took me to see it at the Playhouse in Saint Paul. After, she read it aloud so often that I'd memorized some of Alizon's lines."

"Come on, Mom—let's hear you recite them."

Closing her eyes, Demetra drew a deep breath then let it out.

In a few moments she opened her eyes and looked into Corey's.

Coming in from the light, I am all out at the eyes,
Such white doves were paddling in the sunshine
And the trees were as bright as a shower of broken glass.

Corey was more moved than she could show. "*Ne quitte pas, Maman.* Out there…."

Demetra closed her eyes and took another deep breath.

Out there— in the sparkling air, the sun and the rain
clash together like the cymbals clashing when David
did his dance.
I've an April blindness.
You're hidden in a cloud of crimson Catherine wheels\........

Corey could not hold back the tears.

Demetra shook her head in disbelief. "How could I have pulled up those lines from memory?"

"You remember them because you see the world the way Alizon does." Corey threw her arms around her mother. "Mom—I love you! Come on, let's go somewhere for lunch."

"No need to go anywhere. I'm about to make us some grilled cheese sandwiches. Right here."

"Can you help me memorize some lines for tomorrow's rehearsal?"

"I'd love to."

"I'd better move my car before I get a ticket." Corey kissed her mother and ran out.

Demetra smiled to herself. She reached for the phone to call Thomas in Venice. How happy he would be to hear about her reunion with Corey. He planned to be back in Los Angeles by June. Then Corey and Michael could get to know him before their wedding. She thought about the meeting with her daughter with a certain joyous inner clarity—how bright and promising everything now seemed! She realized, at that moment, how much the four of them would have to talk about.

FINIS

Terry Stanfill, born in West Haven, Connecticut, is a first generation American of Italian descent. She received a degree in English Literature and Medieval Studies from the University of Connecticut.

For her efforts in raising funds for the restoration of San Pietro di Castello, the ancient cathedral of Venice, the President of Italy honored her with the Ordine al Merito, Cavaliere della Repubblica Italiana, and Commendatore. She is Vice President Emerita of Save Venice, Inc, and was founder of The California Chapter of Save Venice, Inc.

Terry Stanfill is a founding director and Life Trustee of Los Angeles Opera. She s a Governor Emerita of the board of The Huntington Library, Art Museum and Botanical Gardens in San Marino, California as well as a Reader, her subject of research, the Normans in Southern Italy and Sicily in the 11th, 12th and 13th centuries inspired her to write her first novel, *The Blood Remembers*.